T0195011

Something about *Kate*

Also by this author:

Holocaust's Child
The Dead Side

Something about Kate

W. R. BLOCHER

SOMETHING ABOUT KATE

iUniverse books may be ordered through booksellers or by contacting:

iUniverse
1663 Liberty Drive
Bloomington, IN 47403
www.iuniverse.com
844-349-9409

ISBN: 978-1-6632-3725-5 (sc)
ISBN: 978-1-6632-3724-8 (e)

Library of Congress Control Number: 2022904869

Print information available on the last page.

iUniverse rev. date: 03/21/2022

To Amy Q., who brought peace and happiness into my life.

CHAPTER 1

Jake wasn't drunk enough. He fell asleep. He didn't pass out. The Dream came. Unbidden. Unwanted. It's the same dream, a nightmare really, that comes every night when he isn't dead drunk.

The Dream opens with him and Charlotte in bed. They have just made love. His six-foot naked body is wrapped around her equally naked petite frame. His right arm is wrapped around her stomach, his left under the pillow her head is on. Her right arm is around his arm, her hand on top of his, tiny in comparison. She snuggles up against him, their bodies coming as close to being one as it is possible to get. They both drift off into a contented sleep.

They wake up together as the first light of the new day filters through the blinds. Same position as when they fell asleep. Charley stretches her legs and swivels around to face him. She wakes up faster than Jake, so she kisses him back into consciousness.

"Good morning, sailor," she whispers to him as he blinks his eyes open in The Dream that is so vivid it seems real, throwing Jake back into an earlier time.

"You realize I am no longer actually in the Navy," he says, playing into what has become a morning routine for them.

"You've found your port?"

"Damn straight I have," he says, smiling. "And I'll never ship out again."

"Better not," she replies, pushing him onto his back as she rolls on top on him. They begin to kiss deeply, their hands running over each other's bodies.

The alarm goes off.

Charlotte freezes. She glances over at the clock. "Crap. I have to get moving."

"What?" Jake protests. "You're going to leave me like this?"

Charley rolls off, laughing, eyes sparkling, "You'll get over it, darling."

"Not until tonight," he shoots back.

"You should be so lucky!" Charley says over her shoulder as her naked body heads for the bathroom.

He lies in bed, staring at the ceiling, waiting for his erection to subside. He hears the shower come on.

"Hey! You coming?" she calls, her head sticking out of the bathroom door.

"Yeah, yeah, I'll be right there." He throws off the covers, rolls to a sitting position on the side of the bed, then pushes himself erect and heads to the shower. She is already lathering herself up as he opens the shower curtain at the back of the tub and climbs in, the steam pouring over the top of the curtain.

"Damn! You have this really fucking hot!" he protests.

"Steam clean!" she replies happily.

"Yeah, but I'm no fucking lobster!" he protests. "You promised not to make it this hot anymore. And you'll set the damn smoke alarm off again with all this steam!"

"You're a real wimp, you know that?"

"Why? Because I don't want to be boiled alive?"

"Shit," she says as she turns down the hot water to a more moderate temperature. "Happy?" The sarcasm pours out of her.

"Ecstatic," he says, turning her around so he can kiss her. The kiss starts to turn into something else. Until she pushes herself away. "Not now. I can't be late. Wash my back." She turns around, holding her long hair out of the way, as he soaps up a washcloth to do as she asks. Then she returns the favor. She gets out of the shower and starts to dry herself as he finishes washing.

When he starts to dry himself, she has already been to the kitchen, put on the coffee, and started dressing. He joins her, both putting on shorts and light shirts as the late-spring weather has taken hold.

He finishes first, heads into the kitchen. He pours coffee into two travel mugs and pops an English muffin into the toaster. Combing his hair and beard, he waits impatiently for the muffin to pop up. When it does, he pulls the hot muffin halves from the two slots and butters both as Charley comes walking in. She has her backpack on and is carrying his.

"Here," she says, handing him his backpack. "We have to get out of here."

"Why? I'm done with finals!"

The withering look he gets in response is enough to make him laugh.

"Yes, my lady!" he barks out, slinging the backpack on. Ignoring her look, he hands her a mug and her half of the muffin. As they head for the door, he grabs a couple of apples, sticking them into his pockets.

"Whose turn to drive?" she asks as they head for the curb where the old car they bought together is sitting.

"Yours," he replies.

"Bullshit! I drove yesterday. You're not pulling that on me!"

"Then why ask? Besides, you have the keys," he says, trying his best to keep laughter out of his voice.

"Here, jackass," she says, throwing him the keys.

He snatches them out of the air as they sail past. "Your aim stinks."

"Get in and let's go. I'm going to be late."

"Yes, ma'am," he says in his best mock military style. He throws his backpack in the back seat, gets in the driver's seat, and starts the car. The engine pauses a moment before catching and roaring to life; they need a new muffler. They need the car. It may only be a small town dominated by the university, but they live three miles from campus in a tiny old house they rent. So they'll get the muffler fixed before the next state vehicle inspection, which isn't for five months.

"You know," he tells her as she slides into the front passenger seat and buckles the seat belt, "you could let up a bit. You're 4.0, scored in the top 98 percentile on the MCAT, and have all those screwy community involvements med schools love to see. Besides, you've already been admitted."

"No way, freshman," she says matter-of-factly as they pull away from the curb. "I've worked too hard and too long to let up now. You're just starting out in this academic rat race. I've been at it for four years."

"When will you let up?" he asks as they head down the street toward campus, although he knows the answer since this is not a new conversation.

"Never!" she says emphatically.

"Ever!" he adds cheerily.

"Besides," she says, "I'm not going to let you win. No way."

"No way you win," he shoots back happily. They have a bet: The one with the lower GPA when he gets his bachelor's and she finishes med school will have to do the laundry for a year. That's four years away for her, a long haul, and both are determined to win. Right now, they're tied with 4.0s.

They ride silently for a moment as they reach what passes for a downtown in this small town. "Have you decided on a major yet?" she asks.

"Probably history. The only problem is I don't know if I can make a living doing that."

She swivels in the seat so she is facing him. "But if you love it—"

The impact smashes into the front passenger door, propelling the car across the intersection and into a panel truck sitting at the red light on the other side. The force of the impact leaves Jake stunned. The pain comes a bit later and grows as the shock wears off. His head whipsawed around, broken glass cut his face, and his side of the car collapsed when his vehicle hit the truck, trapping his legs up to his pelvis and knocking him unconscious. When he comes to, he looks over at Charley. Blood covers her face; her hair is all disheveled. Her breathing is shallow and irregular.

"Charley? Charley? *Charley!*" he screams as he fights through his own pain, a pain that is nearly physical in the dream. He reaches out for her, touching her face. "Charley?" he says weakly. "Please Charlotte," he begs her, leaving the plea hanging in the air.

"Hey, mister," a voice comes from outside the car. Jake turns to look at the firefighter reaching in through the window after the panel truck has been pulled back. "We'll have you out of there as fast as we can."

"Take care of Charley," Jake pleads. "Please take care of her."

"We'll get to her as fast as we can," comes the reply. "We have to get the pickup pulled back first," the firefighter says, gesturing to the other side of the car. Jake looks over, past Charley. The grill of the pickup is protruding a foot into the car, shoving Charlotte into the console. He looks back at the firefighter, tears rolling down his cheeks. "Please save her." The words come out weakly, pleadingly.

"We'll do our best," the firefighter says as reassuring as possible. "When we get you out, the EMTs can start working on her."

"What are you waiting for? Get me the fuck out of here!" Jake demands, energy and determination returning to his voice.

"Will do," comes the reply.

Another firefighter comes up with the Jaws of Life, pries Jake's door open, and rips off the portion of the roof over him. A third firefighter jumps in and cuts off Jake's seat belt and dismantles the steering wheel, pulling it out. Then the first firefighter uses the Jaws to free his legs. As soon as that's done, two EMTs push in, give Jake a quick check, put a neck collar on him, and with the help of two firefighters, ease him out of the car and onto a backboard. The whole thing takes perhaps ten minutes, but it seems like an eternity to Jake. He keeps trying to look over at Charley and what's happening on the other side of the car. He keeps pleading with the EMTs to help her, asking why they aren't helping her. They keep assuring him they are. He tries to get up, but he's strapped onto the stretcher.

"Take it easy, brother," one of the EMTs tells him, putting a reassuring hand on his shoulder. "You can't do anything to help your friend. And we're doing everything we can to get to her. Let us do our work and get you to the hospital so we can keep you alive."

Jake gives him a withering look. "If she dies, I want to, too."

"Well, let's keep both of you alive. Starting with you right now," the EMT says as the stretcher is loaded into the ambulance.

Jake gets a last look at the car before the ambulance doors are closed. An EMT has crawled in through the left side and is working on Charley. The pickup has been pulled away from the car, allowing the firefighters to rip that side open as they did his.

"It's my fault, all my fault," Jake says to no one in particular after the doors close, reliving the pain in The Dream as if it just happened. "I should have been more careful. I should have been watching the intersection. I should have protected her." Tears roll down his face as the pain wells up. He welcomes the pain as punishment for what he has done to the love of his life.

"Hey, brother," the EMT in the back of the ambulance says soothingly as she puts an IV in Jake's arm, "the cops say it was the other guy's fault. He blew the red light, didn't even slow down. And he was going real fast. You didn't stand a chance." The EMT puts some morphine into the IV to cut the pain. "Now just lay back. We'll take care of you."

"You don't understand," Jake says, the pain and regret rising in his voice, "I am supposed to take care of her. I am supposed to protect her. I …" The words fail him as he puts his head back. "It's all my fault. My fucking fault."

The EMT is silent as she goes about her work, doing her best to avoid losing her patient.

In The Dream, the rest of the ambulance ride is a blur to Jake. He passes in and out of consciousness. The opening of the ambulance doors snaps him back into wakefulness. He feels the stretcher being taken out of the vehicle. The next thing he remembers is a bright light in his eyes as someone asks him his name and some other personal information. He mumbles in reply. He feels himself being lifted up and put down on a hard surface. He vaguely hears a click-clack sound. He doesn't know what it is. And doesn't really care. He is lifted again and put on a softer surface. He feels movement. He is being wheeled somewhere. He senses no urgency in the movement. His world goes dark.

He opens his eyes, regaining consciousness. He is looking up at a pale ceiling. It takes a moment for him to figure out where he is. Then the memory comes flooding back. He starts to get out of the bed he is in, but he has two IVs and some wires in the way. He yanks the IVs out and sheds the wires. As a loud beeper starts going off, he gets his feet on the floor. He pushes himself upright, immediately falling against the wall.

"Hey, you can't do that," says a nurse who grabs him before he collapses.

"I have to …"

"You have to get back in bed," the nurse says. "I could use some help in here," he calls out as he struggles with Jake, who is trying to get to the door and is slightly bigger and much stronger than the nurse.

"Charlotte. I have to find Charlotte. How is she? Where is she? What room is she in?" The words come pouring out, the scene still vivid in his dream.

"I don't know," the nurse says. "What I do know is that you have to get back in bed!" Two other nurses arrive, and the trio manhandles Jake back into bed.

"Stay there," the first nurse orders as Jake tries to get back up, "or we'll have to put you in restraints."

Jake settles back into the bed, realizing he is fighting a losing battle. "I need to find Charley," he pleads with all three nurses.

"We'll see what we can find out for you," one of the other nurses tells him as they reinsert the IVs and hook him back up to the vital signs monitor.

"Thanks. When can you do that?"

"As soon as we can," that nurse says.

"The doctor will be in to talk to you soon," the first nurse says as the other two head for the door. "Are you going to stay in bed?"

Jake nods weakly, staring down at his feet. The nurse looks hard at him for moment and then leaves the room.

In The Dream, Jake wakes up with a start. He must have fallen asleep. The sunlight is coming in at a sharp slant through the window. He sees a woman in a white coat scrolling through a computer monitor on a portable stand.

She looks over at him. "You're awake. Good."

"Where's Charley? Where's my girlfriend?" Jake asks pleadingly.

"First things first," the doctor says. "You are banged up but have not suffered any serious injury. No broken bones, no internal damage. You have a concussion and are badly bruised over most of your body. You are going to be in pain for a while but nothing that won't heal. We are going to keep you in the hospital overnight to make sure you get over the concussion."

"OK," Jake says impatiently. "What about Charley? Where is she? How is she doing?"

The doctor gives him a sorrowful look. "I'm afraid she didn't make it."

Jake stares at her, his face as blank as his mind.

"What?" he finally manages to get out, the pain and disbelief evident in his voice.

"I'm sorry," the doctor says, coming over to the side of the bed. "We did everything we could, but her injuries were just too severe."

"Did you try? Really try? She has to live! We have a bet!"

The doctor looks down at Jake. "We did everything we could. She had massive internal bleeding and injuries, eight broken ribs and a crushed pelvis. I'm sorry, we did all we could. Her injuries were too severe. I'm sorry."

Jake lies back in the bed, staring at the ceiling.

"I'm Dr. Sandaval. I'll be taking care of you," she says, patting his forearm. "I'll be back to check on you later this evening. The nurses will be checking on you frequently to make sure you don't fall asleep again." Sandaval starts to leave, and then turns around. "I am truly sorry for your loss."

Jake doesn't respond, his eyes fixed on the ceiling. He drifts into the space between consciousness and oblivion.

The Dream takes him back to the day he met Charley right after the start of the fall semester. The cafeteria in the Student Commons was full. He was sitting at a table by himself, his long legs stretched out, a pile of books in front of him as he studied Spanish I, wondering how he would get through it. He's never been good with foreign languages. But a foreign language is a graduation requirement, and he figures Spanish is the most useful he can take. He's been out of school for four years and is determined he will be a better student than he was in high school.

"Hey! I'm talking to you!" The woman's voice cuts through his concentration and the noise of the room.

He looks up to see a wisp of a woman more beautiful than he has ever seen before. She has long, lush hair, but what really captivates him is the fire in her eyes. She is holding a tray with food and a drink on it. A backpack is slung over her shoulder.

He's speechless.

She's not.

"Well, glad to see you're not a statue," she says sarcastically, which is another trait that appeals to him. "May if I sit down? This place is packed."

He nods and gestures at the chair across from him. He moves his books from the table to a chair next to him to make room for her.

"Thanks," she says, putting her tray down and dropping her backpack on the other open chair.

Jake nods and goes back to his Spanish, trying to study again but his concentration is shot. He keeps looking over the top of the book as surreptitiously as he can.

The woman settles herself and picks up her sandwich. Pausing in midbite, she looks hard at him.

"What?" she demands.

"What?" he responds sharply, jolted back into his normal verbally aggressive self.

"I asked first!" she shoots back.

"So you did."

Silence hangs between them.

"Well?" she finally asks.

"My name's Jake."

"Congratulations."

"And yours?"

"None of your business."

Their eyes lock for a long moment. "Suit yourself, None of Your Business," he finally says with a shrug, closing the Spanish book and picking up one for the history class he's enrolled in, figuring he will find an easier time studying something he is really interested in.

The woman finishes eating and gets up to put the tray in the return area. He notices that she leaves her drink and backpack. He gives a little nod and a small smile as he reads, yellow highlighter in his hand. He studiously ignores her when she returns, the chair scraping on the floor. He hears her opening her backpack and pulling out a book. His mind concentrating on her, but his eyes locked on the book in front of him.

After what seems like forever, the woman speaks. "Hey, you, Jake."

He looks up at her, the question on his face, his eyebrows raised.

"I'm Charlotte. My friends call me Charley. Your full name Jacob?"

"Something like that."

After a moment of just looking at each other, they both go back to their books. He wonders who names their daughter Charlotte but decides not to ask. He will later find out that it's a family name; one of her great-grandmothers had it.

"Want to have dinner with me?" Jake asks without looking up, instead of asking about her name.

Silence.

He looks up to see Charlotte studying him.

"What's your major?"

"I haven't decided yet."

"What?" she says, confused.

"This is my first semester."

"You're a freshman?" she asks incredulously.

"Yep."

"I don't date teenagers."

"I'm twenty-two."

She digests that for a moment. "What have you been doing?"

"I was in the Navy. I didn't have money for college, and, to tell the truth, I wasn't mature enough. I would have made a mess of it and flunked out."

"You mature enough now?"

"I think so."

Charley considers this for a moment. He can feel her eyes boring into him.

"Want to have dinner?" he asks again.

"I have to do my laundry tonight."

"OK," Jake says, knowing when he is being blown off, leaving him feeling disappointed.

A moment of silence.

"That's it?" Charley asks.

"That's what?"

"You're just going to give up?"

"Well, when a girl says she has to do laundry or wash her hair, that's a good signal she's not interested. And I'm not the kind of guy who's going to push it. You are either interested or you're not."

"Tomorrow night," Charlotte says after a pause. "Give me your phone."

Sliding his phone across the table, Jake asks, almost humorously, "You actually have to do laundry tonight?"

"Yep. What you see are the last clean clothes I've got," she says, putting her name and number in his phone directory and checking to see how many girls are in there. She doesn't find many.

"You go to a laundromat?" he asks.

"Yeah, the one on Fifth Street."

"Want some company?"

"Sure. Why not?"

The two repack their backpacks and push away from the table. They walk to Charley's apartment where Jake meets her roommate, and then he helps her lug her laundry the three blocks to the laundromat.

The Dream kicks into fast forward. That evening is spent in conversation—and a lot of laughter—leading to dinner the next night. That leads to meeting in the Student Commons every day before, between and after classes. To studying together in the evenings, going to the movies and concerts together, and nights in each other's apartment.

At the end of the winter semester, Jake's roommate moves out because he graduated. And Charley moves in. Now they have the place to themselves.

Life's good. Better than Jake has ever had it before.

And it all comes to a sudden, brutal end. The pain wells up, sweeping away the good feelings that had infiltrated his sleeping mind.

Locked in The Dream, Jake's memory keeps wandering, jumping to different times. He leaves the hospital and goes home to the small wood-frame house where he can still smell her, see her in bed, getting dressed, taking a shower, cooking with him, studying, laughing …

He goes through her clothing, her jewelry, her books, trying to bring her back.

The Dream shifts to the morgue, where they won't let him see her because he's not family. The Dream then takes him to the police station, where the cops tell him the driver who killed her blew a 0.27 blood alcohol—and blew the red light at 70 mph. He was being charged with vehicular homicide, DUI causing death, DUI causing injury, reckless driving, speeding, and running a red light. The cops also tell Jake the driver walked away with a bump on his head. A cop starts to tell Jake the driver's name, but Jake stops him. The way he feels right now, he would probably hunt the bastard down and kill him, slowly.

Charley wouldn't want that.

The Dream then jumps to the funeral. Charlotte is in a casket. The top half is open. Jake starts to walk toward her down the church aisle. Her mother intercepts him, demanding to know what he's doing there.

Before his confused, pain-infused mind can answer, she slaps him as hard as she can. "You did this to my little girl!"

Her mother chases him away at the graveside service later. He watches from a distance. When everyone leaves, he goes to the grave. Staring down at the coffin he tries to see through the top. His reverie is broken by the earth hitting the coffin. He looks at the workers across from him. One of them pauses. "Sorry, bud, but we're on a schedule."

Jake nods and walks away. No tears now. He's cried himself out.

The Dream jumps several days. He's in their—his—home trying to study for a course he will be taking in the fall when a knock comes on the door. He tries to ignore it, but the knocking becomes persistent. Finally, he gets up and answers the door, if for no other reason than to stop the noise. When he opens it, Charley's mother is standing on the porch, a large suitcase in her hand. Two cops are behind her.

Jake surveys the scene. "What do you want?" he says harshly.

"I've come for my daughter's property," she announces, disdain in her voice.

Jake stares at her, incredulous. "It's not yours," he finally says.

"I'm her mother! You have no right to it!"

"And you brought cops. Why?"

"I know you military types! You're all violent, and I'm not taking any chances!"

"Really."

"Let me in!"

Jake looks at her. Looks at the police officers. They both look back, the professional expressions locked on their faces. He steps aside, allowing Charley's mother to enter.

"You better come along," he tells the two cops as he turns to follow her. Margaret has the suitcase open on the bed and is filling it with Charley's clothes from the closet by the time Jake enters the bedroom. He goes to the dresser and pulls out Charley's favorite sweater. The sound of the drawer opening gets Margaret's attention.

"What are you doing?" she demands.

"I'm keeping this sweater," Jake says quietly.

"*No, you are not!*" Margaret nearly screams as she starts to cross the room.

One of the officers moves between them, facing the angry woman. "Ma'am, you need to stop."

"He can't keep that!"

"Ma'am, stop. He's letting you take everything else," the officer says. Turning to Jake, she says, "Sir, is that all you want to keep?"

Jake nods.

"Then why don't you wait out in the living room."

"OK," Jake nods, walking out clutching the sweater tightly to his chest.

A short time later, Margaret and the officers come out of the bedroom. She heads straight for the kitchen.

"What in here belongs to my daughter?" she demands.

"Excuse me?" Jake says, getting out of the chair he's sitting in and going to the kitchen door.

"I want everything that belongs to her!"

"Well," Jake says after a pause, "most of this stuff is mine. She moved in with me. The other stuff we bought together." He looks around the kitchen. "That blender, you can have half. But you have to leave the other half."

"You think this is funny, don't you!" Margaret accuses him. "I lost my daughter! What did you lose? Your *meal ticket*, that's all! You'll find another one, I'm sure of that. History major! Charlotte told me! She told me all about you! She wouldn't admit it, but I know you abused her! That's the only reason she'd stay with you! And you, you just wanted someone you could leach off of! If she hadn't made this mistake," Margaret says, jabbing a finger at him, "she'd be alive today!" In her anger, she slaps him hard across the face. In The Dream, he can feel the slap as if it just happened.

Jake's face goes red with rage, and he takes a step toward her. The strong hand on his shoulder stops him. "Let it go," the male officer tells him. Jake looks over his shoulder, nods, and retreats into the living room.

"Ma'am, I think it's time for you to go," the male cop tells Margaret.

Margaret, fusing and fuming the whole time, is ushered out by the female cop, with her partner coming behind. The male cop nods to Jake as he walks out.

The door closes behind them.

And Jake wakes from The Dream. A wave of self-loathing washes over him, followed immediately by a painful hangover. The hangover he can recover from. The self-loathing stays.

CHAPTER 2

arl stands near the entrance of the Student Commons, watching his friend across the large, brightly lit rectangular room. It is three days after Jake's last encounter with The Dream. Two and a half years after Charley died.

There is not much for Karl to see.

As usual.

Just Jake sitting immobile at a small, round table about two-thirds of the way back on the right, on the side of the room opposite the cafeteria line. His hands wrapped around the cup of coffee he's staring down into. His elbows are resting on the small, round table, supporting his hunched-over body. A bottle of aspirin sits next to his left hand, the cap off.

As usual.

Karl sighs and walks over to the table with four chairs, one of about seventy-five in the room, which at this early hour of the morning is nearly deserted.

As usual.

The emptiness of the room makes finding Jake easy. Especially since he sits at the same table all the time.

Karl stands on the opposite side of the table from Jake, waiting patiently to be noticed.

Jake leans forward a bit, lifting the cup a couple of inches in his cupped hands. He slurps a bit of the black, unsweetened coffee, then puts it down.

He never looks up.

Karl waits a few seconds more and then clears his throat.

No response.

Karl waits another few seconds, then clears his throat again.

No response.

'This is worse than usual,' Karl thinks.

He pulls out a chair and sits down, his six-foot-two large frame filling the chair. He locks his eyes on his friend across the table.

No recognition.

"Did y'all make it to class this morning?" Karl finally asks after waiting nearly a minute to be noticed.

Jake looks up with his red, blurry eyes, his head still hovering over the coffee. He takes another slurp.

"Well, did you?" Karl persists, leaning forward, his body coming halfway across the table.

"Asshole," comes the mumbled reply. "You know I did. I always do."

"If you say so," comes the dubious response. "Do you remember anything that was said?"

"I took notes, lots of notes," Jake answers, mumbling the words into his coffee. He takes another slurp.

"How's the head?" Karl says, leaning back into his chair, staring at the mask that doubles as Jake's face.

"It hurts." The reply is said in a matter-of-fact way.

Karl nods as he looks around the room for the girl Jake has been dating for about three months. "Where's Jen?"

Jake shrugs.

"She's not here?"

"Nope," he says, never looking up from the coffee cup.

"When's she coming?"

The answer comes after a long pause. "She's not."

"She out of town?"

Another shrug.

Karl looks long and hard across the table at the top of his friend's head. "Did she dump you?"

"Yep."

Karl nods knowingly. "It was the drinking, wasn't it?"

"That," Jake says, pausing, "and she said I wasn't there for her. Ever. I was fixated on the past."

"I warned you about losing her," Karl says accusingly. "I told you to quit drinking and pay attention to her. What did it take? Three months?"

"Yeah, yeah. You were right. Make you feel better, does it?"

"Fuck, you know better than that," Karl says to the top of Jake's head. "I'm worried about you. You have to get your head out of the past and into the here and now. You lost Charley. She's not coming back," he says, repeating what has become a kind of mantra. "It wasn't your fault, so stop blaming yourself. Jennifer was your chance at a new beginning, a new start in life. And you fucking blew it."

The last gets Jake's attention. He lifts his head, glaring across the table at his fellow veteran and student. "I have to go to class." He spits out the words like he has a bad taste in his mouth. He takes some more aspirin, washing the tablets down with the last of the warm coffee, grabs his backpack, and stalks off toward the door, crossing the courtyard to the classroom building on the other side of the courtyard, about one hundred feet away.

Karl watches him go. He shakes his head, gets up, and heads toward the cafeteria, which is off on one of the room's long sides, to get some breakfast. While standing in line with a tray and tableware, waiting for his pancakes, bacon, and coffee, he tries to decide whether he should try to talk Jennifer into giving his broken friend another chance.

As he eats, he decides it's a bad idea. The woman has put up with enough. She deserves to find happiness with someone who will value her.

'Maybe I should call her?' he thinks, briefly considering dating her himself–she's smart, beautiful, has a quick mind, beautiful, and has a wonderful sense of humor, and she's beautiful——before dismissing that as a bad idea on so many different levels. *'Too bad. In another life, we could have been great together.'*

CHAPTER 3

Jake stumbles out of the American lit class, the last one to leave. As usual.

He sits in the back of the fifty-seat room, so his bleary eyes won't be as obvious to the professor, although he suspects she notices anyway. At least she notices he doesn't say much when she gets a discussion going. The current novel is a Fitzgerald work. Jake hates F. Scott Fitzgerald, finding his writing boring. He has never been able to grasp why Fitzgerald is considered one of America's great writers. Oh, well. He has decided he can fake it. He can play the game to keep his 4.0. The goal is to get his bachelor's degree, and he has a year and a half to go, and then … what? He decides to worry about that later.

The blast of cold in the early December weather helps jolt him awake. The bright sunlight hurts his eyes. He flips down his sunglasses and pulls his jacket closer around him. He has to be on his toes for his next class, Spanish III, which is in another classroom building near the Commons. He's not good with foreign languages, but all he has to do is survive a couple of more weeks, and he's done with that degree requirement. He has always arranged his class schedule so Spanish is no earlier than midmorning. Enough time for him to come fully awake and for his hangover to dissipate.

As he heads toward McGinty Hall, he freezes. She's across the courtyard, walking away from him. Jen. Like everyone else, she is bundled up against the cold. But he recognizes her coat. Her hat. The way she walks. He can see the shape of her body in his mind. He swallows hard, stifling a rising desire to call out her name.

'Damn,' he thinks, 'Karl was right. I fuckin' blew it. She was my chance. My last chance.' A student roughly bumps into him as he pushes past with his girlfriend, shaking Jake out of his reverie.

"Sorry, man," the kid says, glancing at him.

"Yeah, no prob," Jake replies, looking at him and then down at the couple's two gloved hands holding each other. When he looks back across the Quad, Jen is gone. 'Good,' he thinks, happy to be able to push those thoughts of loss out of his mind. Shaking his head—a head now mostly free of hangover—he heads for his thrice-weekly language torture. 'Two more weeks,' he reassures himself as he resumes his walk to class.

The mid-December sun is beginning to set as Jake leaves the classroom building after his foray into the Spanish language lab, his head now clear. Entering the Student Commons, he's relieved to see that his favorite table is free. After getting some coffee from the cafeteria, he crosses the room and plants himself in a chair facing the main entrance. He surveys the room, happy to see no one he knows is there. He sighs in relief. Then he breaks out Fitzgerald's _The Beautiful and Damned._ And grunts in resignation. On the good side, he's only about twenty pages from the end, from relief. He settles into the hard cafeteria chair, holds the paperback in his left hand while he sips coffee from the cup in his right.

He is nearly at the end of the novel when the chair on the opposite side of the table scrapes back across the dark linoleum floor. Jake glances up without raising his head. He sees the tall frame, dark hands, and quick movements of his friend Samee. He feels relief. Samee won't bother him; besides, he likes the Syrian kid, even if his accent can make it hard to understand him at times. But in the nearly four years he's been in the U.S., his English is noticeably improving.

"What's happening?" Samee asks from across the table.

"Nothing," Jake replies. "I'm trying to finish this idiotic novel."

"Sounds good," Samee replies, "I have work to do too." He pulls a tablet out of his backpack, logs on, and starts to read. The two sit in silence, ignoring each other as they work.

"Hey, guys, how's it hanging?" a cheerful voice booms out as a big body plants itself in the chair between them.

"Shit, Karl!" Jake blurts out in frustration. "I've got two fucking pages of this crap left. Let me finish in peace!"

"Oh, OK," comes the reply, in about as sarcastic a voice as Karl can manage, which isn't much. "I'm going to get some coffee. Anyone want anything?" He looks back and forth at the two others.

"No!" Jake snaps. "Let me the fuck alone!"

"No thanks," Samee says, almost as a question, looking first at Jake and then up at Karl, his face wearing a quizzical expression.

Karl motions with his head for Samee to come with him. Samee quietly gets up and walks to the cafeteria line with Karl.

As they stand in line, Karl, speaking in a low voice, tells Samee about Jen dumping Jake.

"I heard," he replies. "And it doesn't surprise me."

"Me either," Karl says. "We all warned him, but what are you going to do? Yes, he can be an asshole but he's still hurting. And deep down, he has a good heart."

"I just wish it wasn't so deep down," Samee says in exasperation. "Sometimes I just avoid him because he is too unpleasant to be around."

"Well," Karl says as he pays for his meal, "let's just be supportive. Maybe he will come back to his old self."

"One can only hope," Samee says as they head back to the table.

As his friends head off, Jake gives a disgusted grunt and settles down to finish the novel, which he thinks of as his torture for the sins he's committed. He finally finishes the last page and throws the book onto the table in disgust. "I could really not care less about café society in New York a hundred years ago, or even today," he says, quietly, almost to himself. He scoops the book up, shoves it into his backpack, and rummages around for Umberto Eco's _The Name of the Rose_. The mystery novel by an Italian writer and professor is on the reading list for his history class. His professor wants his students to read it because it is supposed to give a good idea of the culture and politics of that time in the Middle Ages. At least in Italy and the Roman Catholic Church. That all may be true, but it's also a fun book to read, well written, and an interesting murder mystery. A relief after F. Scott. Sort of like the sundaes his mother would buy him after a trip to the dentist or when he had to get shots as a kid. He opens the book to where his bookmark is and is about to start reading when the other two come back.

He looks up to see Samee with a cup of coffee, and Karl with, well, a lot more. He has the coffee he said he was going for, plus two hamburgers and fries.

Karl looks at the food on his tray and then down at Jake. "You said you didn't want _nothing_," he says, with the emphasis on the final word, as he sets down his tray.

"And this is good English spoken by an educated American?" Samee asks Karl as he sits down.

Karl grins at him as he plants himself in his chair. "Done for emphasis, my dear sir, done for emphasis," he says cheerily in his most authentic, fake British aristocratic accent.

"You have to work on that accent," Samee observes as Jake just sits silently, watching his two friends, hoping the conversation doesn't go in the direction he fears.

Samee takes a sip of his coffee and then looks across the table at Jake, a serious expression on his face. "Karl tells me—"

"What do you think of William Marshal?" Jake quickly asks, cutting Samee off as he desperately tries to change the subject.

"Who? What?" Samee asks, confused by the question and by being so abruptly cut off, something out of character for Jake, who always lets you finish a question before launching into an explanation of why you are either wrong or right, or maybe a bit of both.

"William Marshal," Jake repeats.

"Who in the hell is William Marshal?" Karl asks, as confused as Samee.

Jake feels triumphant as he looks at the other two across the small table. He won't have to talk about … her.

"William Marshal," Jake says in his most authoritative voice, "was a small-time English-Norman knight in the late eleventh and early twelfth centuries who ended up as an earl with large landholdings in western England, Wales, and eastern Ireland."

"And I, we," Karl says, indicating himself and Samee, who is just sitting there looking confused, "should care why? By the way, you are not—"

Jake quickly goes on, cutting Karl off. "He's a fascinating guy. I mean, here you have this second son of minor nobility who was almost killed as a kid and ended up one of the most powerful men in England, an earl. He served three kings, four if you want to count Young King Henry who never actually ruled anything—"

"Wait a minute!" Samee interrupts. "How can you be king and never rule?"

"Hmmm," Jake says, taking his turn to look momentarily distracted as his monologue is interrupted. "Oh, that," he says, regaining his composure. "Well, it seems his father, Henry II, wanted to make sure everyone knew who the next king would be, so he had his oldest son, Henry, crowned. The problem was old Henry wouldn't let young Henry have any real power and kept him on a short leash, creating—"

"Hi," Setareh's voice cuts in.

All three heads turn to look at the wisp of a woman with an oversized personality, one of those people who can take command of a room just by walking in.

Jake swallows hard, knowing what is coming.

Samee glows as he looks up at his Iranian girlfriend. They exchange a quick kiss as she sits down in the table's fourth chair, scooting it over a bit to be closer to Samee.

'They are almost the odd couple,' Jake can't help thinking—an impression that crosses his mind almost every time he sees them together. 'They are a beautiful couple,' he thinks, 'but Samee's six, one, solidly built, and has to weigh 180 pounds if an ounce. Setareh's maybe five, three and pushing 105, when she's soaking wet. The physical sizes might be out of whack, but their personalities are completely in sync.'

Jake looks across the table at the two dark, piercing eyes which seem as if they are drilling through him. He swallows hard, tries to get back on track, away from the subject he's doing his best to avoid.

"Anyway," he says tentatively, "the old king kept the young Henry on such a tight leash that it drove his son into rebellion, and William Marshal supported the young king so—"

"What are you talking about?" Setareh says, cutting him off.

"William Marshal," Jake says defensively. "You must know about him. After all, you're the history scholar, even if it isn't the Mideast," he says, desperate to keep her off the subject he knows she wants to talk about.

"Yes, I know about Marshal," she says curtly, her eyes boring through him.

"Well, then, what do you think motivated him?"

"No!" she says emphatically, a tone of voice which accepts no contradiction.

"No what?" Jake asks meekly after a brief pause.

"We are not going to talk about some twelfth-century dead guy," Setareh declares, waving a finger at Jake.

"We're not?" Jake asks, swallowing hard. Karl and Samee are just sitting back in their chairs, watching the exchange. Karl is almost enjoying it; Samee feels sorry for Jake. Both know what's coming, and Jake is not going to be able to distract his way out of it.

"No! We are not!" Setareh says.

A brief silence descends on the quartet as the sounds in the quickly filling room swirl around them.

"What happened?" she asks, much as a prosecutor would ask a hostile witness, speaking in clipped English, tinged by the British accent she acquired from her teen years in England.

"What happened about what?" Jake responds meekly, not able to look at her anymore, his eyes fixed on the tabletop.

"You know what I'm talking about," Setareh says, her tone hard and pressing.

"No, I don't know," Jake says, his voice quiet.

"Bullshit!" she snaps, before launching into a tirade, her hands as animated as her mouth.

"What's she saying?" Karl asks Samee.

"Umm, I'm not sure," he says as he listens intently. "My Farsi isn't that good, and she's going really fast. I think she's cussing him out. Something about being a fool, a stupid ass. Stuff like that."

Oblivious to Samee and Karl's conversation, Jake sits silently, shrinking in his chair as the words pour over and around him. He has no idea what she's saying, but her tone of voice makes her meaning perfectly clear.

Setareh finally runs out of breath. She sits there just glaring at him, her body stiff and leaning slightly forward. Jake glances up at her and then quickly back at the table.

"Well?" she finally says.

"Look, I ..."

"How could you do that to Jennifer?" she challenges him. "How could you do that to yourself?" she goes on quickly, not giving Jake a chance to respond.

"At least she's back to English," Karl says in a quiet aside to Samee as he leans closer to the other man.

"Shut up!" Setareh orders Karl, giving him a hard, quick glance.

He just raises his hands in mock surrender, sitting back in his chair, a small smile flickering across his face.

"You know what you lost? Don't you? How much you hurt her?" The accusations come pouring out of Setareh.

"How much I—"

"Don't you dare play dumb with me!"

"Look, I …"

"Look nothing!" Setareh snaps. "All you had to do was stay sober! And I don't want to hear how you have to drink to sleep," she says, cutting Jake off as he opens his mouth to begin defending himself. "You need help! Jennifer told you that! I told you that! We all told you that!" she says, motioning to the others at the table. "But would you get it? *No!* You just retreat into a bottle of booze! Now look what happened! You drove Jennifer away! She's all torn up about it! And you, you sit here talking about a dead guy from the Middle Ages!"

"What the hell do you want me to do about it?" Jake shoots back, glaring in his turn at her, but immediately regretting saying that. He knew the answer.

"I just told you," Setareh says.

"Yeah, you did," Jake responds weakly, his eyes fixed on the table again. "Well," he says, pausing, "I've got to get some dinner." He grabs his backpack and his stuff on the table, stands abruptly, pushing the chair well back from the table, and flees across the room toward the doors.

"That went well," Karl says as the trio watches him go.

"He will stay a mess until he gets his head straight," Samee observes.

"He needs help. Badly," Setareh comments, sadness in her voice.

"That won't happen until he's ready to let it happen. And he probably won't be ready until he hits rock bottom," Karl says as they watch Jake push through the doors into the frigid night outside.

"Unless he gets a miracle," Setareh adds.

"Yeah, that too," Karl says.

CHAPTER 4

Jake pauses outside the Student Commons, taking in a deep draught of the cold air. The chill inside his lungs and on his face feels good. He shakes his head to clear it and then heads toward the apartment he moved to after Charley's death. It's off campus, about a mile away. He enjoys the walk.

He keeps a fast pace. As he walks, he stuffs what he picked up off the table into the backpack he then slings over his shoulders. The fast pace helps to keep him from thinking too much. What thoughts he does have he forces onto his schoolwork: the paper he needs to finish for poly sci and the analysis of *The Beautiful and Damned* he has to write. "Fucking Scott couldn't even get his book titles right. It should be *The Beautiful and The Damned*," he grouses out loud to himself.

While he walks, he watches the people he passes, all of them wrapped tightly in their coats, hats, scarves, some with gloves, others with their hands pushed into their pockets. The guys look at him as they pass; the women glance away. Not many women are like Setareh, who never shrinks from exchanging glances, which Jake finds odd, given how girls in that part of the world are usually raised. "God help the guy who misinterprets that look,' Jake thinks, amused by the memory of what that double black belt did to a fool who decided to see what he could get away with. Not only did he end up in the emergency room, but he also ended up in jail. 'Served the asshole right.'

Lost in thought, Jake nearly walks past his apartment house, a large three-story redbrick building most of the way down on the left of the block, lined by oak trees. He has always thought this neighborhood is fitting for a small city dominated by a university and its students. He pivots a bit more than ninety degrees to his left and heads up the walkway, through the door into the warmth, and bounds up the stairs to the second floor, apartment 2B.

Inside, he drops his backpack on the dining table, the only one in the two-bedroom apartment. Looking in the fridge, he decides he's not really hungry. Sitting down at the table, he pulls out his laptop and opens the file for his F. Scott analysis. *'Might as well get this bullshit out of the way,'* he thinks.

Before he starts writing, he decides coffee will help. He makes a pot, watching as the coffee flows into the carafe in the small kitchen off of what passes as a dining room. Then he pours a cup, taking a sip as he sits down at the table. He makes a face and looks at the hot black liquid. *'This needs something.'* He goes to the fridge and starts to open the door before abruptly closing it.

Instead, he goes to the kitchen counter. He stares at the bottle for a moment. He reaches out for it, pauses, pulls the top off and pours whiskey into the coffee. A good, stiff pour. He takes a sip as he heads back to the table. *'That's better,'* he thinks approvingly.

He sits down, staring at the screen and the partially completed paper. He takes another sip. He sits back for a moment, happy in the thought that this paper is all personal thoughts—no research required. The only problem is the professor loves F. Scott, so he can't write what he really thinks. His 4.0 is at stake.

"Bullshit it is," he announces to the empty room. "Bullshit I must, so bullshit I will," he says as his fingers move across the keyboard.

Six hours later, he pushes back from the table, looking at the clock as it clicks over to 1:04 a.m. on the red digital display. The paper is done, title page and all, spellchecked and ready for the printer. He pushes the print button triumphantly. The fifteen pages of what Jake considers incredibly beautiful bullshit come flowing out. He doesn't have to turn it in for two days, but it's done. He feels like a stick has just been pulled out of his butt.

Getting up from the table, he goes over to the cabinets to get a tumbler. He pours a big drink into the glass from the new bottle, his last. He suspects he will have less than half of it left after tonight. *'I'll get some more tomorrow,'* he assures himself as he takes a big swig, the amber liquid burning as it goes down. He quickly finishes that drink and pours himself another, sitting down into an easy chair in the living room, the bottle on the table next to him. He finishes the second drink and quickly pours a third.

"No dreams tonight," he says looking at the booze-filled glass. "This boy will get some sleep."

CHAPTER 5

*M*orning. Jake knows that because the alarm on his smartphone is going off. So are the alarms on his two clocks.

He closes his eyes against the unwanted thoughts trying to push their way into his head. He knows the others are probably right. *'No,'* he admits to himself, *'they are right.'* But no amount of talking is going to make that dream go away. OK, The Dream. The one he fears to confront. So, he drinks. And he'll keep on doing that to keep it at bay. So he can sleep at night. And get through the day.

He will get through today like he got through yesterday, only today, Thursday, he has just two classes, poly sci and psych—and another date with the language lab. He'll get through the day and tomorrow and the day after that and the day after that.

Friday arrives, the first of two days he both looks forward to and dreads. He looks forward to Friday because he doesn't have to wake up Saturday morning; he can sleep until his hangover is gone. He dreads Saturday because he doesn't have classes to occupy his mind, to keep his thoughts occupied.

He crawls out of bed and stumbles off into the kitchen, puts on coffee, and then stumbles into the bathroom. He takes the aspirin bottle out of the cabinet, pries the top off, and takes half a dozen of the extra-strength tablets, washing them down with water. He turns on the shower, and as the water warms, he brushes his teeth. He gets into the shower, letting the hot water wash over him.

Half an hour later, he's dressed and out the door, travel mug in hand. Coat on, backpack slung around his shoulders, he stumbles outside into the cold, which makes his first breath hurt deep down in his lungs. The frigid air might burn his lungs, but it also helps clear his head. He sips the hot coffee to both wake up and to warm his insides. It's well below freezing. How much, he doesn't know—and doesn't want to know, thank you very much, Weather Person.

He has a banana and an apple he grabbed as he left to eat on his way to campus, along with sips from the travel cup. The coffee will stay hot if he drinks it quickly enough during the less than one-mile walk to campus.

Heading down the street in the twilight of dawn, Jake holds the cup in the angle created by his bent left elbow pushed against his body as he pulls the banana out of his right coat pocket. With the help of his teeth, he strips the skin down and begins to eat it. He has the routine down to a science–he finishes the coffee and the apple as he reaches campus and heads into his first class of the day, Modern European History. It's the same routine every Monday, Wednesday, and Friday: 7:40 a.m. for history. At least he finds this class enjoyable. When he can remember it. That doesn't happen all that often.

But this is Friday, which means he has the weekend to get through. He will survive it the way he survives every weekend, with booze and studying. He has to keep that 4.0; he can't let Charlotte win. Jake shakes his head to rid himself of that intrusive thought which will bring him nothing but pain. He reminds himself he has to keep the 4.0 because that is what she would expect him to do—and he can't let her down. Not now. Not ever. Not after what he did.

At the end of the day, Friday, he heads for The Garage, a student gathering place where the beer is cheap and the peanuts free, and it's on the way to his apartment. He has taken to spending every Friday night there, swilling beer, filling up on peanuts, and watching the crowd of students, of boys and girls, hitting on each other, sometimes hooking up and sometimes getting shot down. Sometimes Jake is the target. Fortunately, the music is so loud it is impossible to have a conversation unless you are just about yelling into each other's ear.

A shake of the head usually is enough to discourage someone, but occasionally he will dance with some girl. But since conversation is impossible, Jake is able to avoid exchanging numbers and walk away after they have both had enough of dancing.

He likes it that way. He intends to keep it that way. Watching others is enough for him, until the memories start edging in, and the pain of seeing happy couples gets to be too much. At that point, he heads out.

When he gets to his apartment, he throws his backpack in a corner by the door, sheds his coat, and heads for the kitchen and his booze.

"Shit!" Jake is looking at the bottle–his last–that is only about a quarter full. He drank a lot more than he planned to last night, and on top of that, forgot to stop at a liquor store for resupply. He pulls out his phone to check the time—11 p.m. The liquor stores are all closed, and the bars charge more than he can afford for a bottle. But he needs it. He considers going back to The Garage. He'll have to pay $80 for a pint. After thinking about it for a bit, even starting to head for the door, he rejects the plan. He would need at least two pints. Too expensive.

'If I drink it fast enough, I can get drunk enough,' he assures himself. After all, he's already had half a dozen beers.

He pulls off the top and upends the bottle, pouring the whiskey down as fast as he is able. He gags on the liquid as it burns down his throat but forces himself to keep swallowing until he has drained the bottle.

As he puts the bottle on the counter, he shakes his head. The burning in his throat subsides, and he has to steady himself with a hand on a chair and the other on the counter.

"Yep," he says to the universe, "that should do it."

He heads for the bedroom, wondering how long it will take for the booze to hit full blast. He strips off his clothes. Sitting on the bed, he plugs in his phone and scrolls down the music list until he finds Jimbo Mathus's solo blues guitar album. He pushes "shuffle" and the first song comes—"Gary's Got a Boner." Jake crawls into bed, burrowing between the sheets. *'I wonder how he comes up with those names? It's not like the songs have words. Who's Gary? And why does he have a boner? Well, I know the answer to that last one. One of these days I am going to have to find out how he came up with that name,'* Jake thinks as he drifts off to sleep, knowing full well he never will. He'll forget about it in the morning.

CHAPTER 6

$\mathcal{S}$till in bed, Jake is staring at the ceiling. His body is shaking. He can feel that slap on his left cheek as if it just happened. It is burned into him. That is how The Dream always ends. The bourbon—or was it scotch? He can't remember now, although it really doesn't matter—wasn't enough to knock him out.

He finally gets control of his emotions, but he can't stop his mind going back to Charley's death. He had spent the summer recovering. Although his physical injuries weren't severe, his muscle and skeletal pain took time to subside.

His emotional pain was debilitating. He agreed with Charley's mother–he was responsible for her death. It might not make sense, but it was there all the same. Karl talked him into going to counseling to help him deal with his loss and self-loathing. He went to two sessions and stopped. Talking was just making things worse.

Instead, Jake turned to work and drinking. He withdrew from school for a year and buried himself in working, turning a part-time job he'd landed at an independent grocery store into a full-time gig for a year and drinking, heavily. Getting drunk was the only way he had to stop The Dream. He found an apartment in a different area of town, unable to bear returning to the house he shared with Charley or walking the same streets and going to the same restaurants and stores. He sold or gave away everything he had shared with her, including their bed. He had to skimp on food for a time while he replaced furniture and other stuff, but it was worthwhile. He didn't have the constant reminders of Charley around him. For a year, he isolated himself, staying away from people, especially women, even his friends and his family, ignoring repeated calls from his sister and grandparents.

Finally, he was able to face walking onto campus again. He reenrolled at the university, throwing himself into his studies as a way to dull the pain he still felt. He reconnected with his friends who chided him about his absence and pushed him to call his family. They also worried about his heavy drinking, trying unsuccessfully to get him to stop, or at least ease up.

He finally reconnected, after a fashion, with his grandparents and his sister. But he didn't stop drinking. And he kept a wall up between himself and the world.

Then he met Jennifer. They were in a lit class together—the only two who seemed to appreciate Kurt Vonnegut's play "*Happy Birthday Wanda June*". They started talking about the play after class. That grew into meeting in the Student Commons every day, talking about just about everything and anything—except the darkness inside Jake. He wouldn't, couldn't really, talk about Charlotte and what happened, how he felt.

And he couldn't, wouldn't, stop drinking. He had to keep The Dream at bay.

It took less than a semester for him to drive Jennifer away. The wall he had put up and the drinking were too much for her.

'Oh, well,' Jake thinks, still staring at the ceiling. '*Life sucks.*'

He looks over at the clock on the stand beside his bed. Just shy of 10 a.m. "Oh, shit!" He starts to spring out of bed before he catches himself–it's Saturday. He has no classes.

He is, however, hungry. And it's the day he goes to the corner café for breakfast. They don't switch to lunch until 11 a.m., so he has time.

He gets up, heads for the bathroom and the aspirin bottle on the counter. He wasn't drunk enough to avoid The Dream but was drunk enough to have a hangover. That he finds very irritating. His head still pounding, he throws on clothes, grabs his coat, and heads out to the café at the top of the street.

The Delightful Chew's door faces the corner, so when you walk in you have to turn slightly to the left. The room is long with tables lining both sides. Bench-style seating is along the walls, with chairs in the middle. A long aisle goes between the chairs on either side. Large windows dominate the street side, while a brightly painted mural stretches down the opposite wall. The kitchen is at the far end.

The café is nearly empty; the breakfast rush is over, and it is a bit early for lunch.

Jake slides into a seat against the wall about a third of the way down. He's facing the window so he can watch what and who goes past.

Not that he's looking. He's staring down at the table in front of him, fighting down the pounding in his head, wondering how long it will take the aspirin to kick in.

He jumps back a bit when the coffee mug comes sliding across the table at him, barely stopping at the edge. He looks up to see the server glaring at him.

"What?" he asks.

"Your usual?" Vivian spits out.

"Yeah," he says as he looks down at the mug, cupping his hands around it, not caring why Vivian is being hostile.

She glares at him a moment more and stalks off toward the kitchen to put in the order. Jake ignores her departure, sipping at the hot coffee, thinking about how much it would have hurt if the cup had gone over the edge, spilling onto his lap. He winces at the thought.

He's just about finished the coffee when the plate with his breakfast comes sliding across the table at him. This time it would not have stopped if he hadn't put up a hand to act as a barrier.

"I don't look good in over-easy eggs," he tells Vivian, looking up at her. "More coffee, please."

Vivian is just standing there, glaring at him.

"What!" he finally says.

The heavyset, middle-aged woman stares at him a moment longer. "You are an asshole," she pronounces, emphasizing each word.

"Tell me something I don't know," he mumbles back.

"How could you treat that sweet girl that way?" Vivian demands.

"What? Who?" Jakes asks, looking up at her, confused.

"Who? *Who!* You know damned good and well who!"

"What am I? The subject of a university-wide conspiracy to grind my faults into my open wounds?"

"She was the best thing that ever happened to you!" Vivian spits out.

"That's debatable," Jake says, his irritation rising, "but I certainly wasn't the best thing that ever happened to her."

"You're damned right about that! That girl cared about you."

"Oh, how do you know?" he fires back.

"I could tell by the way she looked at you when you two were in here."

"Very observant of you," comes Jake's sarcastic reply.

Vivian glares at him to the point of making him look away. "It took a lot for you to drive her away!" she tells him, her arms crossed in front of her as she stares down at him. "But you did it! You couldn't hold onto the one good thing in your life! You didn't even want to, did you?" she demands.

"Mind if I eat?" he finally asks.

"No one is stopping you," she spits out.

"Who names their kid Vivian anyway?" Jake says, trying to get her to leave, to leave him in peace.

"You're an asshole!" she barks, slapping his check down on the table and stalking off.

"We've already established that," he mumbles at the woman's retreating back.

Jake sits back, staring at the eggs, bacon, and toast on the plate in front of him, trying to decide if he is still hungry enough to eat. A hand holding a coffee pot intrudes itself into his field of vision, the coffee pouring into the cup to the point of slopping over onto the table. The hand and the pot withdraw. Jake looks up to see Vivian stalking off. Even though her back is to him, he can tell she's furious.

'Oh, well,' he thinks as he starts to eat. 'At least I can eat in peace. The asshole is being left alone.'

Chapter 7

Jake's existence reverts to the pre-Jennifer stage. He stays away from people, but this time even his friends. He doesn't want to see the disapproving and pitying looks. And definitely doesn't want to talk about Jen or his state of mind.

Again, he throws himself into his studies. He has scored in the ninety-second percentile on the Graduate Record Exam and has been admitted into the university's master's program in history. He's decided to concentrate on American history. He's just as interested in European and African history, but he knows he's not good with foreign languages so decides he better stay in an area dominated by English.

To avoid everyone, Jake avoids the Student Commons, instead taking refuge in the Student Union, an older off-white stone building about half a mile away. It doesn't have a cafeteria, but it does have coffee. And the chairs are softer, even if there are far fewer of them arranged on either side of a cathedral-size room with windows on both sides. Its major attraction is that he has never used it before, so no one will think to look for him there. He also ignores knocks on his door and doesn't answer his phone or reply to voice or text messages. The constant binging of alerts about those calls and messages becomes so irritating he turns off the notification.

His scheme for hiding works—for a month.

"This is where y'all been?"

Jake looks up from the plush chair he's nestled in to see Karl looking down at him, a quizzical expression mixed with amusement on his face.

"I'm busy," Jake says grumpily, looking back down at the textbook he's reading.

"I can see that," Karl says, adding after a pause, "where've you been?"

"Around. Now will you let me study?"

"Is that what you're doing?"

"Trying to!" Jake's voice explodes with exasperation. "Do you mind?"

Karl looks at him for a moment, then sits in the chair next to his. The two chairs are angled with a small end table between them, like the other forty chairs arranged down both sides of the long stone hall. Jake has a coffee cup on the table, his backpack leaning against his chair. Karl drops his backpack on the floor next to the chair he takes and stretches out his legs, relaxing as he contemplates his friend.

He doesn't say anything. Just looks at Jake.

Minutes pass.

"What!" Jake snaps, slamming his book closed at the same time.

The two men stare at each other for a long moment.

"Why are you avoiding everyone?"

"Why not?"

"We're all worried about you," Karl says softly, sitting up and leaning slightly forward. "Why are you ghosting your friends?"

Jake stares at him for a moment, then looks away. "Because you guys won't stop hammering me about"—he swallows hard—"about Jen. Yeah, I know I screwed that up," he says, looking at his friend, sadness in his eyes, "but you know, I don't think I was ready for … for … that. I think I sabotaged myself … I can't stop The Dream; I can't stop thinking … missing … Charley …"

"Maybe Jennifer wasn't the right woman to make you forget," Karl offers.

Jake looks away again. "I'm not sure anyone is."

"You may be right," Karl says quietly, "but that's no reason to ghost your friends."

"It is if they won't quit going on about her."

"OK, I'll take care of that," Karl offers.

"How?" His voice carries a great sense of suspicion mixed with doubt.

"I'll tell everyone to back off."

"Yeah, right. That'll work with Setareh."

"I'll make it work," Karl says, a hardness in his voice that Jake seldom has heard.

Jake just nods in response and looks down at the book in his lap.

"OK, I'll leave you to your … whatever," Karl says, standing up, picking up his backpack. "See you tomorrow?"

Jake looks up at him. "You know where to find me," he says, with some exasperation.

"No, I mean back in the Commons."

"I'll think about it."

"I won't tell the others where you are," Karl offers.

Jake nods. "I'll think about it."

Karl leaves without saying another word. Jake goes back to reading.

A few minutes later, someone sits in the chair Karl had been in. Jake doesn't look up, keeping his focus on the eighteenth-century colonial history he's been studying.

After a bit, the woman in the next chair asks in a sweet voice, "What are you studying?"

Jake looks up to find a beautiful woman, blonde hair and blue eyes, radiant face, and a sweet smile, looking back at him.

Without saying a word, Jake closes his book, scoops up his backpack, and leaves.

The semester ends two days later—and Jake has yet to go back to the Student Commons. He decides to put that off until the new semester begins in January, two and a half weeks away. The town will empty out and the university shut down in the interim. He will have those two and a half weeks to himself, with no one to bother or question him.

Just him—and his battle to forget.

CHAPTER 8

The university's bookstore is jammed as students descend on it for the books they will need for the new semester—with texts running up to $600 each. Jake has learned to buy off campus when he can. The books cost about half in an off campus bookstore or online. The only difference from the university's store is the cover. And his history books, while expensive, usually don't top $200 each. The exception is a workbook one professor puts out, rearranging pages more than anything, and charging $250. Still, that's cheaper than the science and economics texts, for the most part.

With his backpack full and more books tucked under his left arm, Jake starts to head toward the Student Union. He comes to a sudden stop, remembering his promise to Karl. With a disgusted sigh, he turns on his heel and walks reluctantly toward the Student Commons.

When he walks in, he scans the room. Every table looks to be taken, and the line at the cafeteria area extends well into the room. *'Typical for the start of a semester,'* he thinks. Jake walks slowly into the room, his gaze concentrating on the area where his friends usually congregate.

Finally, he spots them—except four people are at the table: Samee and Setareh, Karl and a woman he doesn't know. Jake makes his way through the crowded room to the table and then just stands there, not sure what to do or if he is welcome.

"Hey, stranger," Karl says with an upbeat tone.

"Hi," "Hi," come in near unison from Samee and Setareh, both smiling. "It's good to see you," Setareh says. "How have you been?"

"OK," Jake responds, looking around for a chair to use.

"May I?" Samee asks the two people at the table next to theirs as he puts a hand on an empty chair.

"Sure," says one of the guys, waving his hand.

"Here," Samee says as he swings the chair over between him and Karl, both of whom scoot their chairs a bit to make room.

"Thanks," Jake says as he drops his backpack on the floor and puts the books under his arm on top of it. He looks over at the line by the cafeteria–it isn't much different from when he came in. "So much for coffee."

"How's your head?" Karl asks.

"OK," Jake responds. "I came prepared." He reaches down to his backpack and pulls out his travel mug from a side pocket. He pops the sipping stop open and takes a swig of the now cool coffee. "What's new?" he asks before giving anyone else a chance to talk.

Setareh waves the back of her left hand at him, but before he can react to that, Karl says, "This is Michelle. We've been dating for a while. She's a forward on the women's basketball team." Karl is obviously proud of her.

Jake looks over at her, "Hi," he says to the tall, thin woman who has been carefully studying him.

"Hello," Michelle responds. "Karl has been telling me all about you."

"I bet he has," Jake says with a shake of his head, but his attention is wrenched back to Setareh's left hand, which is now palm down on the tabletop.

"Engaged?" he asks, realizing the silliness of the question as it comes out of his mouth.

"Yes," she says, like she just revealed a secret to him.

"Who's the lucky guy?" The stupidity of that question hits him immediately.

"Who do you think?" Samee blurts out, half in outrage and half in amusement.

Setareh looks offended. "How could you ask that?"

"Sorry," Jake says, ashamed. "Stupid question."

"You think?" Karl asks.

"Wait a minute!" Jake says as a thought hits him. "How are your families taking this?"

"They're good. Well, as good as can be expected," Samee says.

"They're relieved, sort of," Setareh says, overlapping with Samee. "They were afraid I'd marry outside the faith."

"Mine, too," Samee adds.

"But you're Sunni," Jake says, pointing at Samee, "and you're Shiite," then pointing at Setareh. "I didn't think those two mixed well."

"My father brought that up," Setareh says.

"Both my parents mentioned it," Samee adds.

"But I think all the parents," she says, gesturing toward Samee, "were just so relieved we had found a Moslem to marry in what my father calls 'that crusader nation' that they were willing to overlook that other problem."

"They were worried about where we would live and how we would raise our children," Samee says.

"What did you tell them?" Jake asks.

"We made both families unhappy," Samee responds with a crooked smile.

"We told them we were staying in America and would raise our children as Moslems," Setareh pronounces. "We didn't say whether as Sunni or Shiite."

"And we plan to raise them as neither, so they will accept both," Samee says.

"And when we go to visit, we will go with our new American passports and our Moslem American children, who will learn the differences between them are not important."

Jake gives them a skeptical look. "I hope it works out for you."

"It will." Karl's voice carries authority and conviction.

Jake just looks at him, his eyebrows raised. "Whatever you say, boss."

"Are you always this cynical?" Michelle asks, joining the conversation.

"Yep," Jake responds, his body drawing in on itself, his face losing all expression. "It comes with years of practice and experience with things not"—his voice drops to a barely audible level—"working out."

The table goes silent.

"I think I'll get something to eat," Jake says, although he is not particularly hungry, and the line has not shortened much. He gets up and heads off, escaping from a conversation that has suddenly become uncomfortable.

It takes more than half an hour to get through the line, a trip that usually takes no more than ten minutes, if that. When he gets back, Karl and his girlfriend have left. Setareh and Samee are in deep conversation, their hands clasped together on the table, their heads a fraction of an inch apart.

Jake watches them for a moment, envies them their love, and feels the pain of his own loss, and his loneliness. He wraps the hamburger and fries in napkins and stuffs the food in a pocket, then scoops up his backpack and books, and heads out, without saying a word. The two lovers are so engrossed with each other they don't even notice.

CHAPTER 9

$\mathcal{F}$riday evening a month later. The Garage. Jake has gone to the student hangout for his usual beer and peanut dinner. The place is a long, somewhat narrow hall, with a high ceiling and a bar at the end. Booths line the walls on either side with some tables scattered about the floor in between.

To the right of the bar is a slightly raised square platform, about twenty feet on a side, for dancing. Usually, the music is piped in through a PA system, although sometimes on Friday and Saturday nights, a DJ provides the entertainment—music and commentary. Tonight, it's a DJ. He's a particularly obnoxious one who makes running comments while the music is playing. And his playlist doesn't particularly excite Jake. But the beer and peanuts do, so he's willing to ignore the talk and concentrate on the music that he does like.

Besides, the DJ won't be on for two more hours. Jake gets there about 7 p.m., early enough that the bar is not crowded yet and he can enjoy his dinner in peace. He parks himself in a booth about halfway up the room with his back to the wall, his legs stretched out in front of him, sipping a beer and shelling peanuts as he eats them, the pile of shells growing in the middle of the picnic-style table. He watches as the crowd begins to grow, looking at the boys and girls as they filter in, trying to figure out who's actually twenty-one and who snuck in—or got the bouncer at the door to look the other way. Like a lot of bars that cater to young people, the staff tends to look the other way for pretty girls—it helps to draw a bigger male crowd.

"What's happening?" Karl asks as first Michelle and then he slide into the booth on the opposite side of the table. It's just a bit past 8 so the music isn't as loud as it will become later in the evening, allowing conversation, even if it is at a higher decibel level than normal. Karl's often stated belief is that college bars play the music so loud so conversation is not necessary—on the theory that most people, especially guys, don't have anything intelligent to say, so it spares everyone from the awkward necessity of thinking, or of saying something stupid.

Jake raises his mug in salute as he nods to the couple, takes a sip, and replies, "Not a hell of a lot."

"Do you always come here?" Michelle asks, obviously trying to start a conversation.

"Only on Friday nights, usually, but sometimes on Saturdays, too," Jake replies.

"I've never been here before," she says.

Jake looks at her. "You twenty-one?"

She blushes and looks away. Karl squeezes her hand gently to reassure her.

"Don't worry about it," Jake says. "No one is going to care, least of all the bartenders and servers. Just let Karl do the ordering, which reduces the chance of someone asking. Besides," he says after a pause, "you look like you could be twenty-one."

"I'm twenty."

"Close enough." Then Jake looks at Karl. "Robbing the cradle?"

Karl starts to smile but then forces himself to look outraged. "Hey, I'm twenty-four. That's not a big age gap, you know."

"I don't know," Jake says, shaking his head and trying to sound serious and doubtful—and failing miserably as he begins to laugh. "I've got to get more beer and peanuts. Either of you want something?"

"Beer," Karl says. "You know what I like."

"Do they have wine?" Michelle asks.

"Yep, they do," Jake says.

"Chardonnay then, please."

"Chardonnay it is." Jake heads off to the bar. The crowd is building fast now, so Jake has to maneuver his way through and elbow space at the bar. He waves at the bartenders several times before he gets one of the four to come over.

"Yep, what do you want?" He knows the woman opposite him, and she knows him, but neither one knows the other's name. He just knows her as the most pleasant one back there. She knows him by what he orders.

"Two beers"—she turns to walk away—"and a glass of chardonnay." She stops as if a leash has just been pulled and looks back over her shoulder at him.

"Chardonnay?"

"Yeah," he says with a shrug, "my friend's new girl."

She smiles at him and goes off to get the drinks. While he waits, he grabs a small burlap bag hanging from the side of an old-style wooden barrel filled about a quarter of the way up with peanuts.

A platform has been inserted about a quarter of the way down so the barrel looks like it is full of peanuts. He uses the scoop laying on top of the peanuts to fill the bag.

He gets back to the bar just before the bartender comes back with the drinks.

"Are you going to be able to get those over to your table?" she asks.

"I'll manage," he says as he slides a $20 bill across the bar to her. The peanuts are free. The drinks aren't. "Keep the change."

"All $2.15 of it," she says with a smile.

"Better than nothing," he shoots back in their usual exchange. He takes the handles of the two mugs in his left hand, and the wine glass and bag of peanuts in his right. With his elbows out and a lot of "Excuse me," he carefully works his way through the crowd that is now jammed around the bar. Fortunately, it is early enough so that no one is drunk yet, so people are willing, and able, to give him the space he needs to navigate his way back to the table without spilling anything, either on the floor, himself, or someone else.

He puts the beers on the table, then hands the wine glass to Michelle and pours the peanuts onto the middle of the table where they can all reach them.

"And that, my friends," Jake announces, putting a beer in front of Karl, "is my last trip to the bar tonight. From now on, we use the servers."

Karl immediately begins shelling a nut. Michelle looks at the pile, watches Karl for a moment, gives a little shrug and sigh, takes a peanut, and starts working on it. Soon she is keeping up with the two men.

"Why?" Michelle asks looking at Jake. "Why not go back to the bar?"

"Two reasons," Karl says before Jake has a chance to answer. "First off," he says in his deep, soft voice and waving his peanut-bearing left hand toward the bar, "the crowd is so jammed in there that by the time you work your way in and then get your beer and work your way out, you've wasted an hour, when the servers have their own section at the end and you can get your drink in about fifteen minutes, assuming you can catch their attention."

"They'll even bring you peanuts, if you ask and they know you'll tip them," Jake throws in.

"And the other reason?" Michelle asks.

Jake and Karl look at each other for a moment. Jake gives a bit of a laugh, while Karl just smiles.

"What's so funny?" she demands, now having to really raise her voice as the volume of noise in the bar jumps.

"Not really funny," Jake says. "You tell her," he says to Karl.

"OK," he says, then turns to Michelle. "As the night goes on, the beer consumption goes up. And the drunks come out. It's not only harder to get through the crowd, especially carrying drinks, because so many are, shall we say, not particularly steady on their feet, but then there is the matter of the mean drunks. Those assholes are looking for a fight. If you bump one of them, you're likely to find yourself in a battle."

"Oh," she says thoughtfully. "What about the servers?"

"They're all women," Jake says. "Usually, the worst that happens to them is some bastard plays grab ass, or tit, as the case may be. If the server or one of the bouncers sees who it is, the perp gets thrown out on his ass. Literally."

"And if not?"

"The asshole gets away with it," Karl says with a shrug. "Although there is that one …"

"Which one?"

Karl looks around the room for a moment, finally settling on a slender blonde on the other side of the room. "No one messes with her, even when they're drunk," he says, pointing her out to Michelle.

"Why not?"

"About six months ago, some idiot grabbed her breast while she was working her way through the crowd," Karl says, giving a little laugh. "Without dropping the tray or spilling anything, she broke his wrist and his nose. Turns out she's into martial arts and boxing."

"And no one has seen that guy back in here since," Jake adds.

"Oh," is all that Michelle says.

The trio falls into silence as the DJ takes over and the volume explodes.

"Want to dance?" Karl asks, his mouth inches from Michelle's ear. She nods. As they get up, Jake uses his right forefinger to circle the glasses as he looks at Karl. He nods.

Jake settles into the booth with his back to the wall, watching the servers until he catches the eye of one. When she comes over, he holds up two fingers and points at the empty beer mugs—he and Karl are regulars, so she knows the kind of beer they drink—and yells, "Chardonnay!" at the top of his voice. She can't hear him, but she's able to read his lips. He also holds up the empty peanut bag. She nods and takes it from him.

Ten minutes later she's back—with four beers, two glasses of wine, and a bag overflowing with peanuts.

Jake looks at her quizzically.

She leans into the booth as he leans forward so she can yell into his ear.

"You know you're going to want them eventually," she screams, with him barely able to understand her, "and with this crowd, things are only going to get worse."

Jake sits back laughing, pulls the money out of his wallet and pays her. She starts to make change, but he waves her off—as she knew he would.

Sipping his beer, eating peanuts, he goes back to watching the crowd. A girl slaps a guy who grabs her butt. He slinks off, rubbing his cheek. A bouncer gets between two drunks who are about to come to blows, about what, they probably don't know. A girl jumps on a guy, giving him a deep, full mouth kiss—and, based on his body language, he responds with great glee. For the most part, though, the men and women in the bar are milling around, trying to talk, holding hands, drinking. A gay couple in a booth opposite Jake are making out. A couple of guys stare at them, but before they can say or do anything, a huge bouncer takes them both by the arm—they look at him, obviously deciding not to contest his grip—and, with a little push, he gets them moving on.

After about half an hour, Michelle and Karl come back, sliding into the booth, both looking hot and thirsty. Karl looks quizzically at the two beers and two wine glasses on their side of the table. Jake just smiles at him. The music is too loud for anything to be heard beyond a couple of inches away—and they have a table between them. Karl just shrugs and takes a long guzzle of beer, while Michelle downs her wine rather quickly in an attempt to quench her thirst.

"Head. I'm going to the head," Jake screams across the table. Karl can't understand him, but he gets the gist by reading lips.

Jake slides out of the booth and starts to make his way through the crowd to the restrooms, which are just off the dance floor. A line has formed outside the women's room, while Jake goes right into the men's room. He has a fleeting thought about why women's rooms are never made larger than men's rooms; you can get more urinals in a given space than you can toilet booths.

Coming out, his hands still a bit damp from the blower that never really gets hot or powerful enough to do the job, he is suddenly forcefully pulled onto the dance floor, nearly falling over the small lip of the raised platform.

"What the fuck?" Before he can say anything more or even react, a woman is wrapped around him, her hands on his butt as she grinds her midsection into him. Her head's lying on his shoulder, her mouth an inch from his. He can smell the alcohol on her breath. *'She's smashed,'* he thinks.

Her grinding movement gets his hormones kicking in, and on one level, he finds the experience exhilarating. He also feels uncomfortable as her motion pushes her dress up her legs. He reaches back and moves her arms up to around his neck and then wraps his arms around her back, pulling her slim body close to him. Every time her hands start down, he moves them back up. She keeps grinding her midsection into his, but without her hands on his butt, it isn't as awkward.

The music is in a fast, heavy beat, but she stays pressed as close to Jake as she can get. So close he can feel her heart beating, her chest rising and falling with each breath, her breasts pressed against his chest. The song coming to an end segues into the next. Several songs later, Jake decides he's had enough. He disentangles himself as gently as he can. He steps back holding her shoulders at arm's length to make sure she is steady enough to stand on her own. Convinced she is, he lets go and quickly heads back to the booth.

As he leaves the dance floor, a guy stops him. "Mind if I dance with your girlfriend?" he yells into Jake's ear.

"She's not my girlfriend," Jake yells back and pulls away.

Sliding in, he gets a quizzical look from Karl and Michelle. He raises his eyebrows and shrugs. Karl shakes his head. Michelle looks confused, mainly about the culture of this bar. Jake just shrugs again, picking up his beer for another slurp. While he was gone, Karl—or maybe Michelle, although he assumes it was Karl—ordered more beer and wine. The pile of peanuts has not been replenished. That's fine with Jake; he's just about had his fill of them.

It's just after midnight. The crowd is beginning to thin out. The DJ is gone, and the music level is down to the point that conversation is again possible. Jake gets out of the booth to pay another visit to the restroom. As he stands up, he sees the guy who stopped him as he left the dance floor supporting the obviously drunk woman—she doesn't look like she can stand on her own—heading for the door. As they near the door, the guy looks over his shoulder, apparently checking to see if anyone is watching.

An alarm goes off in Jake's head. He quickly walks after them, catching up just before they reach the door.

"Where are you taking her?" he demands as he grabs the guy's shoulder. The two bouncers at the door turn to watch in case they have to intervene.

"What do you care?" the guy shoots back. "She's not *your* girlfriend!"

Jake has to think quickly. "But she is my friend," he blurts out, hoping he said it with enough conviction to convince the guy.

It works. The guy looks a bit confused and concerned. "OK, OK," he finally says, letting go of her and almost running out the door. The woman starts to drop to the floor. Jake grabs her by the shoulders and steers her to a chair at a table near the door and sits her down. The bouncers have turned their attention to other people now that the situation has resolved itself peacefully.

Jake stands over the woman, whose name he still doesn't know and about whom he knows nothing, as she lays sprawled across the table, moaning softly.

"What's this?" Karl asks as he and Michelle walk up, their coats on.

Jake looks at him with a worried expression. "Some guy was about to take her out, and I just, well, I just wasn't sure what he was going to do. So …"

"What are *you* going to do?" Michelle challenges him.

"You can't leave her here," Karl says.

"I know," Jake replies looking down at her.

"Who is she?" Michelle asks.

"I have no fucking idea," comes the exasperated reply.

"Check her wallet," Karl suggests. "Y'all might find her address, but at least you'll know her name."

Jake thinks a moment. "No," he says firmly. "That could end badly."

"What're you going to do?" Karl asks.

Jake thinks for a moment again. "Take her home, I guess," he says, rolling his eyes and shrugging.

"You're what?" Michelle demands.

"I won't touch her," Jake assures her. "But at least I can make sure she's safe until she sobers up."

Michelle starts to say something, but Karl stops her. "Don't worry," he tells her, putting a hand on her arm, "he really won't touch her."

"If you say so." She looks dubious.

"He won't, outside of the fact he is going to have to support her all the way there."

"Is it far?" Michele asks.

"No," Jake says. "About a quarter of a mile. We'll make it all right, as long as she doesn't pass out."

"Come on. Let's go," Karl says to Michelle. "We'll leave this idiot to his burden."

"All right," she says, still doubtful about what Jake is going to do.

"Thanks. Thanks a lot," Jake says, looking down at the drunk woman he has taken responsibility for. Giving an exasperated sigh, and wondering what he's gotten himself into, he manages to get her to her feet. Her purse slips off her shoulder, so he puts it over his, and with his right arm wrapped around her and under her right arm as she leans heavily against him, he guides her to the door.

The air outside The Garage is cold compared to the heat and humidity generated by all those bodies inside. The change in temperature rouses her a little bit, but not enough to bring her back into the conscious world.

The woman, who is a head shorter than he is, leans heavily against Jake as they make their way toward the corner. She nearly slips down a couple of times, but he manages to keep her vertical, if at an angle. She mumbles something.

"What?" Jake asks, trying to understand what she's saying.

She mumbles again.

Jake realizes whatever she's trying to say is not coming out in the form of words. So, he concentrates on getting her down the street. At the corner, as he maneuvers her into a right turn, she suddenly stumbles heavily in that direction. The sudden movement catches him by surprise, and he almost loses her, just managing to grab her left arm to pull her back just before she goes careening into a building. She rebounds with such force that she nearly knocks him into the street. Regaining his balance, he steadies her as they start to head down the gentle slope of the hill toward his apartment.

Near the bottom of the hill, the woman starts retching. Jake knows what's coming. He gets her over to the curb and holds her by the waist, bent over the gutter, and pulling her hair back from her face. When the vomit explodes, she spews into the street, missing her shoes and clothes. When she's done, she straightens shakily up, but Jake keeps them standing there for a bit. Sure enough, she wasn't done. Jake pulls her back a bit so that she barely misses her shoes, the vomit hitting the curb and grass where she had been.

"You done?" he asks, grinning. He's been there himself.

Predictably, he does not get an intelligible response. Something else he is familiar with.

"Well, come on, lady. We're almost there," he says as he gets her moving again down the street.

Some students pass them, walking around them, giving them cursory glances as they go. A cop driving in the opposite direction slows down and stops, rolling down his window.

"She's drunk," Jake calls, waving with his left hand. "I'm getting her home. It's just over there." He waves toward a random apartment house on the opposite side of the street.

The cop watches them intently as they stumble down the street. Finally, he rolls his window up and drives on. Jake glances over his shoulder, relieved to see him go. It would have been awkward explaining what he's doing with a drunk woman he doesn't know, not even her name. A woman who has no clue who she is with, why she is with him, or where they are going. That could have turned ugly really fast.

Opposite his apartment, Jake turns left to cross the street. The curb nearly creates a disaster as she stumbles badly stepping into the street, nearly bringing them both crashing down. Jake just barely keeps them both upright as the near fall propels them into the street. The driver of a car zipping down the street blows the horn at them and swerves, even though the car is on the other side of the street. Jake wonders if the driver has been drinking, then dismisses the thought as he concentrates on getting them across the street. Having learned his lesson, he is careful about making her step up over the curb, supporting her.

When they reach the apartment house, he gets her inside, and then confronts the problem of getting her up the stairs to his second-floor apartment. He studies the problem for a moment, and then tries to get her to step up. He quickly discovers that won't work—she is just too drunk to manage a flight of steps. He looks at her, deciding that she can't weigh more than 130 pounds. And since he can bench 250 pounds, he decides he can carry her. As he lifts her in the cradle of his arms, her right shoe falls off. He carefully bends down so she doesn't slip off, picks up the shoe and heads up the steps, thankful that none of the other tenants are around to see this.

At the top of the stairs, he goes to the first apartment door on the left. Easing her down onto her feet, he leans her against the wall, holding her up by pressing her shoulder to the wall with his left hand as he fishes his keys out of his pocket with his right hand. Just as he gets his keys, she starts slipping down the wall. It takes two hands for him to catch her. He props her back up, this time putting his left hand just under her neck while he unlocks the door.

Opening the door, he maneuvers her inside and supports her into the living room and into his bedroom down the short hall, immediately on the right. He has a two-bedroom apartment, but the second bedroom has been void of furniture ever since his roommate graduated and moved out. Jake sees no point in replacing the bed and dresser. That will be a problem his new roommate will have to deal with, when he finds one. As for the couch John left behind, well, he might replace that someday. But it's comfortable and the only one in the apartment.

Getting his drunk charge next to the bed, he pulls the blanket back with one hand while holding her up with the other, and then gets her onto the bed. He pulls off her shoes, leaving her beige coat on, and then covers her up. He stands looking down at her for a moment. She looks peaceful. And she is beautiful in an odd way he can't explain. He puts her purse at the foot of the bed.

"If only you weren't drunk," he says softly.

He turns the light off as he leaves the room, shutting the door quietly behind himself. He goes into the kitchen, takes the scotch bottle out of a cupboard, and pours himself a large drink. He carries it back into the living room, turning off all the lights in the apartment except for the lamp by the chair he's sitting in. He takes a swig of the liquor and puts the glass down on the table next to him. He leans back and looks at the ceiling.

"What the fuck have I gotten myself into?"

CHAPTER 10

The slamming of the front door jerks Jake out of a deep sleep. He sits upright in the chair he has spent the night in, wondering for a moment what is going on. Then it hits him—the drunk woman. He jumps up from the chair and quickly crosses to the bedroom.

The bed is empty, the covers thrown back. As he turns to go, he notices her shoes on the floor. He raises his eyebrows as he turns and strides to the front window. Looking out, he sees her fleeing up the street, her coat flapping around her, toward the main drag.

"Oh, well," he says out loud. "I hope she doesn't hurt her feet."

Turning back into the room, he realizes two things: the tumbler of scotch is nearly full, and he didn't have The Dream.

"Son of a bitch!" he says, wondering what happened.

Looking at his phone, he realizes it's 8 o'clock on a Saturday morning, and he's hungry. He gets his jacket off the hook by the door as he heads out.

As he enters the Delightful Chew, he comes to a sudden stop. Karl and Michelle, Samee and Setareh are all there, arranged around a table for four with another table pulled next to it. The remains of their breakfasts still sit on the table.

"See," Karl says to no one in particular as he waves Jake to come over. "I told you he'd show up."

Jake slowly walks toward the group, taking a seat at the table that has been pulled over.

"To what do I owe *this* honor?" Jake says, the sarcasm dripping from the question.

"Wait a minute!" Karl says. "What's wrong?"

"What do you mean what's wrong," Jake retorts.

"You are not hungover!" Samee says as Vivian comes over to put a cup of coffee in front of Jake.

"The usual?" she asks.

"Yeah," he says, nodding in reply. Turning back to his friends, he says, "Can't I be sober once in a while in the morning?"

"You can," Setareh says, "but you never are."

"Well, welcome to the brave new world!" he replies, his arms spread wide.

"What changed?" Samee asks.

"Wait a minute!" Michelle interjects. "What happened to the girl?"

"What girl?" Jake asks innocently, irritated enough to want to play games.

"What do y'all mean what girl?" Karl asks.

Jake just shrugs and smiles at them. *'It is wonderful how much fun you can have when you're not hungover,'* he thinks.

"Spill it, mister," Setareh says.

"What is this? An intervention? An interrogation? You guys don't have enough to talk about? I have to become the center of conversation?"

"When you take a drunk girl home with you, yes, you do," Karl says.

"What happened to her?" Michelle persists.

Jake takes a sip of his coffee as he decides whether to keep them in suspense. Looking at them all, he decides the better part of valor is to tell the truth.

"I don't know," he finally says with a shrug.

"What do you mean you don't know?" Michelle challenges him as Vivian comes with his breakfast.

"Thanks," he says, looking up at her as she turns on her heel and stalks off. "She is still mad at me," he says, shaking his head.

"Well?" Michelle persists.

"She slept in my bed. I slept in a chair," he says, shrugging again. "She ran out of the apartment this morning without saying a word. I didn't wake up until the front door slammed."

"You didn't get her name? Or anything?" Samee asks, incredulous.

"Nope," Jake says, shaking his head as he takes a bite of egg.

"You don't know anything about her?" Karl persists.

"The only thing I know about her is that she's brunette and likes knee-length red dresses and slip-on shoes."

"Slip-on shoes?" Michelle says quizzically. "Most women wear slip-on shoes."

"Yeah, well, she left them behind. Went home in her bare feet," Jake says matter-of-factly.

"Oh, brother," Karl says.

"Maybe she'll come back for her shoes and then you can find out about her," Setareh says.

"And maybe not," Samee says. Setareh hits his knee with hers under the table, prompting him to grin at her.

"I guess we'll find out," Jake says.

"And if you do," Michelle says, "you'll have to let us know who she is."

Jake looks at her, and then at Karl. "Is she always this nosy?"

"She's a communications major. What can I say?" he replies, laughing.

Jake just shakes his head as he continues to eat, and the conversation drifts off onto other topics, none of which, happily, involve him.

CHAPTER 11

When Jake gets back home, he spends the rest of Saturday studying and working on a paper that is due Friday, making sandwiches for lunch and dinner. That evening, he kills a good portion of a bottle of scotch and stumbles off to bed.

The next morning, he finds his way into the kitchen, downs a pot of coffee and a lot of aspirin. When his head is somewhat clear, he collects his dirty clothes and towels, pulls the sheets from the bed, piling them all in a clothes basket. Securing the basket under his left arm, he sticks a couple of textbooks on top and heads for the laundry room in the basement. He likes doing laundry on Sunday mornings because no one else is usually down there, so he can use all three washing machines and dryers. That speeds things up.

He spends the next hour and forty minutes getting everything clean—and his head clear. He occupies his time by studying the political machinations that went on among the European countries working to get rid of Napoleon, and how that impacted the young United States. When the last dryer stops, he pulls his clothes, sheets, and towels out of the three dryers, piles them into the basket and heads back up the stairs.

As he nears the top of the stairs to the second floor, Jake sees a woman standing in front of his door, her hand raised as if she's going to knock. But the hand does not move. It takes him a moment before he realizes she's the drunk girl from Friday night. She's exchanged her dress for tight white jeans and a loose-fitting red blouse. And today she is wearing sneakers. Inexpensive ones.

'*Must like red*,' he thinks. Aloud, he says, "Come back for your shoes?"

His voice makes her jump away from the door and turn toward him. She gives him a quick glance and then looks down at the floor.

"Yes," she says meekly.

"OK," he says, pulling his keys from his pocket. He looks her up and down quickly, then opens the door. "Come on in," he says, leading the way. She stops in the middle of the living room. Jake goes into his bedroom down a short hall to the left, drops the clothes basket on the bed and scoops up her shoes as he heads out.

"Here," he says, handing them to her.

"Thanks," she says, taking the shoes, but not otherwise moving. She had been looking around the room when he comes back in, but now she is avoiding his eyes, her head tilted down, her gaze shifting from the furniture to the floor over to the kitchen, back to floor.

Jake is standing a few feet in front of her, staring at her, not sure what to say. The silence between them stretches into minutes.

"You took off like a scared—" he starts to say, only to be cut off.

"Do you mind if I ask you a question?" she says, quickly, glancing up at him and then back at the floor.

"Sure," he says, shrugging, a bit surprised and curious.

Silence. A minute or more passes.

"Well?" Jake finally says.

"Umm, are you … are you …" Her voice trails off.

"Am I what?" he says rather impatiently.

"Gay." The word comes out quickly and softly.

"Gay?" Jake repeats.

She nods. "Or impotent?"

"That is *none* of your *damn* business!" Anger rises inside him. "Whether I like girls, boys or both is none of your *damn fucking business*! What the fuck are you asking that for? And whether I can do anything about it is none of your business!"

Silence again. Jake forces himself to calm down as he glares at the woman standing less than two feet in front of him. Her face has turned red, the color even going down her arms, as her eyes dart around the floor. Jake is glaring at the dark hair because her head is cast down.

"I better go," she whispers, obviously intimidated by his anger.

"Wait a *fucking* minute!" Jake barks. The order freezes her in midturn. She slowly turns back toward him. "Why did you ask that?"

Silence.

"Talk!" he orders.

She swallows. "My roommates ..." her voice trailing off.

"Your roommates!"

She nods.

"What about your roommates?"

"They think you're gay. Or impotent. They wanted me to find out."

Jake stares at her for a moment. "Where is that coming from? And why would they even care?" He's a bit curious and completely confused, not to mention angry.

"Because ..." she starts to say, her voice trailing off again.

Jake waits a bit. "Because?"

"You didn't ... didn't ... have sex with me." The last comes rushing out, each word tripping over the next one. She catches her breath, then goes on, this time it is coming more forcefully. "Why would you help me? You don't know me! Why bring me to your home and not have sex with me? I think I vaguely remember some guy taking me out of the bar before you. He would have had sex with me. I couldn't have stopped him. But you ... When I woke up, I had all my clothes on ..."

"Except your shoes," Jake inserts.

"Yes," she says, "except my shoes. Even my underwear. So you didn't want to have sex with me?"

Jake is taken aback and just stands there staring at her. She is still avoiding his eyes, but her eyes have darted up to as high as his chest, pulling her head almost straight up since she is nearly as tall as he is.

"I suppose I helped you because once I couldn't help someone I loved," Jake says slowly and quietly. "As for not taking advantage of you, I don't sleep with someone who's drunk. That's a rule I follow," he says, forcing his voice to be calm and reasonable. He is now to the point of wondering where this is going to end up.

She licks her lips. "So you're not gay?"

"I didn't say that. I was just stating a rule. Anyway, my sexual preference is of no concern to anyone but me and whoever I'm with. I'm not accountable to anyone else. And so what if I'm gay? That doesn't change me as a person."

"I have to find out," she pleads, reverting to her submissive side. "They won't let me alone unless I have an answer for them. They'll just keep at me until I find out."

She moves toward him tentatively. Jake stands there rooted to the floor, wondering what will happen next. Her movements take on a fevered pace as, her eyes closed, she presses herself hard against him and reaches up to kiss him.

He starts to return the kiss. Then freezes. Grabbing her shoulders, he pulls his head back and pushes her to arms' length.

"What the hell is that?" he demands.

Her eyes are locked on his chest. "I was just trying to find out. My roommates have demanded that I find out. I have to do what they say or they will make my life miserable."

Jake contemplates her for a few seconds, wondering about the hold those roommates have on her. For some reason he can't identify, he's intrigued by this woman and wants to find out what makes her tick. "OK. If you want to discover my sexual orientation, you'll just have to hang out with me for a while."

"What?" she says, finally looking up at his eyes, her surprise evident.

"That's the only way to find out," he says, matter-of-factly.

"What … what do you mean?"

"I hang out at the Commons with some friends between classes. If you want to know, you can join us—on the condition that you don't ask them," he says mischievously.

"What?" She is really looking confused now.

"That's the deal. Take it or leave it."

She stands there for a minute, thinking. "I guess that's OK." She pauses and then turns to leave.

"Wait a minute! Don't you want to know when we'll be there?"

"Oh, yeah," she says.

Jake is a bit exasperated. "Do you want some coffee?"

"What?"

"Coffee. I'll make some coffee, and we can talk a bit."

"OK," she says, nodding.

Jake pivots and heads into the small kitchen on the right of the dining area, which is open to the living room. She stands there a moment and then follows. While he makes the coffee, she leans against a counter, watching.

"What's your name?" he asks as he pours the water into the coffee maker.

"Kathy."

"With a *c* or a *k*?"

"K."

"Short for Katherine?"

"Yes. What's your name?"

'That's more like it,' Jake thinks. *'She's getting relaxed.'* "Jake. With a *j*. Short for Jacob."

"I sort of figured that out," Kathy says, more energy and firmness in her voice now.

"Yeah, well, I just thought I'd throw it all out there all at once," he says, turning to smile at her—a smile that is returned.

They stand silently looking at each other from opposite sides of the kitchen as the smell of the brewing coffee drifts into the room.

"Do you," Jake says, finally breaking their eye lock as the coffee stops running into the pot, "take milk or sugar?"

"Both, please."

He pours her a cup, leaving room for the additions. Then he pulls the milk out of the refrigerator, the sugar out the cupboard, and a spoon out of a drawer. Setting it all on the counter, he steps back.

"I don't know how much of either that you like," he says, motioning her to help herself.

"Oh, yes," Kathy says, moving across to the coffee cup. She quickly adds some milk and a little sugar, stirring the cup before looking at him.

"Let's go to the table," he says, reaching past her to get his black coffee, then leading the way to the small dining room table that sits in the living room under the bank of windows.

Jake sits in the chair facing the window and motions for her to take the chair diagonally from his.

They spend the next few minutes sipping coffee and glancing at each other.

"You a grad student?" Kathy finally asks, confidence and self-assurance now in her voice.

"No. A senior."

She looks a bit surprised. "You look older than that."

He gives a snort of a laugh. "Four years in the Navy."

"Oh. What's your major?"

"History. ... Yours?"

"Physics," she says, a hint of pride and defiance in her voice.

"Good. Grad or undergrad?"

"I just started the master's program," she says.

"I'll start the history master's in the fall."

Kathy nods as she sips more coffee.

"So how do I find you?" she asks.

"You know where I live."

"I mean in the Commons."

"Yeah, I know." He tells her to look for him on the right side more than halfway back and gives her an idea of when he is there. "Will that fit your schedule?"

"I think so."

"Where do you live?"

"Why?" she asks sharply, suspicion evident in the narrowing of her eyes.

"You know where I live. I think it's just fair that I know where you live."

She thinks about that for a moment. "Let me have your phone."

Jake reaches into the pocket of his cargo pants and pulls out his phone. Unlocking it, he hands it to her. As she puts her name, phone number and address in, he wonders about the transition he has just witnessed—from a subservient woman to an assertive one. She does a quick check to see how many other women are in it. She doesn't find many.

"Thanks," he says as he looks at it after she hands it back. "What's your number?"

Without a word, she takes her phone out of her purse and hands it to him. He puts his number in and gives it back to her. She glances at it and then puts it back in her purse.

"I guess I better go," she says. "I have studying to do."

"OK," he says, "but one last question."

"What?" she responds, suspicion in her voice.

"Do you care about my sexual orientation?"

"No, not really."

"Why do your roommates care?"

"I, they ..." Her voice trails off.

Jake realizes she is not going to answer him, and although he would like to push the issue, he decides this is not the right time. So he stands up.

She stands up as well, looks at him for a moment, then shoulders her purse and heads toward the door. He follows her. She turns, says goodbye, opens the door and walks out.

"By the way," he says as she leaves, "you ought to put a security lock on your phone so no one else can use it if you lose it or it's stolen."

Glancing back at him, Kathy nods as she walks toward the stairs.

Jake stands in the doorway watching her go, wondering about who she is: a mousey, frightened girl under her roommates' thumbs or a self-assured woman working on her master's in physics?

Chapter 12

*T*wo weeks.

Kathy has not shown up. Jake thinks about calling her but decides against it. If she wants to come, she will. If not, then he won't bother her.

He deflects questions about her from his friends. Both Michelle and Setareh have asked whether she came back for her shoes. Jake says yes, describes how she looked, mentions her name—and then lies, just saying she took her shoes and left. He doesn't want to get into a discussion about whether she will show up—he's sure all four will hang around the whole time he's in the Commons, providing an audience he doesn't want—or debating whether he should contact her.

Lying is the simplest way of avoiding that drama.

Besides, Kathy obviously isn't coming.

Jake has mixed emotions about that. On the one hand, he doesn't need, or want, any emotional entanglements. He showed with Jennifer that he would just make a mess of it. On the other hand, Kathy intrigues him. He thinks about her a lot: a woman who appears subservient and unsure of herself, while at the same time has gotten into a physics master's program that is almost impossible to get into because of the fierce competition for the few available spots, and in a field still dominated by men. It's like she has a split personality. And that fascinates Jake. That and something else he can't put his finger on.

So here he is, sitting at a table with his friends at the end of a Tuesday. Samee and Setareh have just left. Michelle and Karl are making noises about leaving.

"You staying?" Karl asks.

Jake looks up from his book and nods. "Yeah. I want to get through this chapter before I head out."

"You're not hungry?" Michelle asks. "We're going to get a bite."

"Thanks, but no," he replies, smiling. "I'll get something later."

"OK then," Karl says. "We'll see you on the flip side."

"Bye," Michelle adds as they both get up from the table.

"Have fun," Jake says, waving at them as he returns to his studies.

About ten minutes later, Jake is engrossed in his studies when he becomes aware of someone standing across the table from him. He looks up—and freezes. Kathy is standing there, smiling down at him.

The silence between them is thick when Kathy finally breaks it. "May I sit?"

Jake just nods yes, still unable to speak.

Kathy sits down opposite him, sliding her backpack onto a chair—and looking directly at him. No diverted gaze this time.

"Have you lost the power of speech?" she asks, humor in her voice.

Jake shakes his head no. "I wasn't expecting to see you," he finally manages to blurt out. "I'd given up on you coming."

"Well, here I am."

"So I see," he says with a bit of a laugh. "Why now?"

She shrugs, shifting her gaze to the tabletop, then off into the distance. "I've been in several times, but you were always with other people."

"That was a problem?"

She shrugs again. "We really didn't have a chance to get to know each other, and I want to feel comfortable around you before I meet your friends."

"I thought you wanted to find out if I'm gay or straight, or impotent."

"I do, I guess. Not really," she says with a sigh. "The main reason I'm here is because my roomies won't drop the subject," she says, rolling her eyes.

"I told you, you won't find that out unless you hang around with all of us. And remember the ground rules: No asking my friends directly."

"I was thinking about that," she says, her eyes fixed down. "We could just sleep together." She glances up at him quickly before diverting her gaze.

Jake is taken aback by the suggestion. "No!" he says emphatically.

"Why not?"

"I'm not having sex with you to prove my sexual orientation! Or ability! Besides, how do you know that a gay guy can't get an erection with a woman? Maybe he can and just not enjoy it as much as with another guy. Or maybe I'm bi. Ever think about that?"

"No," Kathy says thoughtfully. "I haven't."

Jake sits back in his chair and stares at the woman across the table from him. "Well," he finally says, raising his eyebrows as he breaks the silence, "you might want to."

"I guess," she says, making movements as if she's going to leave.

"What a minute!" he says. "You can't leave!"

She stops, holding her backpack partially off the chair. "Why not?" A challenge is in her voice.

"Because," Jake says in a conversational tone, "you came here so we can get to know each other better before you meet my friends. That'll never happen if you leave."

Kathy looks at him contemplatively.

"And if that doesn't happen," he says, "you will never find out, and your roomies will never let you alone. So, you might as well stay and get it over with."

The backpack goes back onto its chair, and Kathy relaxes.

"OK," she says. "What do you want to talk about?"

"How about you?"

"What about me?" she says defensively.

"All I know about you is that you're a beautiful brunette with beautiful brown eyes, who can get really wasted, and is intelligent enough to get into one of the hardest physics master's programs in the country."

"You also know where I live and my phone number."

Jake gives her a disgusted look, which she doesn't see because her gaze is still averted.

"And that's not much!" he says emphatically. "I don't know who you are."

"Why would you want to know?" The question is asked defensively.

He sits back, startled by the question. "Because," he says after a brief pause, "you intrigue me."

"Why?"

"For a whole variety of reasons, most of which I don't even know, and the rest I'm not sure of," he says with a short, sharp laugh. "But you intrigue me. I want to know who you are. Where are you from? What are your interests? Who are you as a person?" Left unsaid is his curiosity about what he had begun to think of as her split personality.

"Oh," comes the weak reply.

"Tell you what. Let's start out with what you like to eat. Let's go to dinner together."

"Where?"

"You pick the place."

"What about what you like to eat?"

"No, tonight is about you. Besides, I like just about anything." He thinks for a moment, then adds, "Except curry and mushrooms."

That brings a bit of a smile to her face. "OK, I know a place I like to go."

"Good. Let's get going," he says, putting his books in his backpack. Kathy swings her backpack onto her shoulders as she gets up, and they head for the door.

"Where are you from?" Jake asks as they leave the building.

"Columbus."

"Columbus," he repeats. "Any siblings?"

"A sister and two brothers."

"Big family," he comments. "Where are you in the pecking order?"

"Number three. An older sister and brother and a baby brother. He's still in high school."

"And what do the older two do?"

"My sister's a secretary. My brother's a mechanic," she replies.

"Cars?"

"Cars and trucks, diesels mostly."

"Your parents?" he asks.

"Why do you want to know all this?" she says, growing more defensive.

"As I said, to get to know you."

She falls silent as they walk off campus, turning right onto a side street. After a five-minute walk, in silence—Jake doesn't want to press her for information she doesn't want to give but is still curious—Kathy announces, "Here we are." She gestures at a restaurant with the name Green Dragon painted in a curve around a green dragon on the front display window.

"Chinese," Jake says, stopping in front of the window, looking at it and inside. The interior is decorated with fancy carved dark woodwork dividing sections of the large dining room, and what looks like red velvet on the upper half of the walls. "It's red inside." He looks at Kathy. "Shouldn't it be green?" he asks, grinning.

She gives him an irritated look. "Come on, smart-ass," she says, leading the way in. They are greeted at the door and shown to a table.

When they are seated, and looking at the menu, Kathy tells him, "They have great sushi."

"And if I don't like sushi?" Jake asks, curious about how she will respond.

"Then order something else." The irritation in her voice is palpable.

"That's OK. I like sushi."

"Then why …" her irritation growing.

"Because I'm an asshole," he says quickly, a small smile crossing his face.

"You can say that again!" she says, glaring at him.

"Because …"

"Shut up!" she snaps, smiling a bit despite herself as she looks at the menu.

"OK, OK," Jake says, enjoying himself.

Silence descends as they peruse the menu.

"You going to get sushi?" he asks.

"Yes."

"So, will I."

The server returns and they order, including green tea.

Another server comes quickly with some soup.

"It's all part of the meal," Kathy tells him.

"Fine with me." As they eat the soup, Jake returns to her history. "Your parents together? Still alive?"

"Yes and yes," she says. "Let's talk about something else."

From her tone of voice, it's obvious her parents are a subject that will have to wait for another day.

"Why physics?" Jake asks, changing the subject.

"Because I like it. I find it fascinating and challenging."

"What kind?" he asks.

"Theoretical."

"Wow," Jake says, never suspecting this seemingly mousey woman has it in her to tackle such a demanding field.

"Wow what?" she says, suspicion in her voice, pausing with her soup spoon over the bowel.

"Tough field," he responds as he quickly swallows some soup so he can answer.

"And?" It's more of a challenge than a question.

"And nothing. I'm impressed, that's all," he replies. "You have to be in the top, what, 5 percent to get into that program?"

"Two percent," she says matter-of-factly as she swallows some of the soup.

"As I said, impressive."

They fall silent as they finish the soup and take sips of the hot tea.

"Where did you do your undergrad?" he asks, trying to elicit more about this woman who intrigues him more and more.

"Here."

"How long have you been with your roommates?" he asks, venturing into her personal life again.

"Four years with Ashley; a couple with Kaitlyn."

"Three-bedroom apartment?"

She nods.

"You get along with them?" he asks, then rushes forward with, "I guess you must if you've lived with them that long."

"They're OK."

"Just OK?" he asks, wondering about the defensive tone and her pulling into herself a bit.

She looks irritated at him. "What do you want?"

"Just curious."

"Humph."

"What's your favorite color?" Jake decides to get off what is obviously another sensitive topic.

"Red."

"Favorite song?"

"I don't really have one."

"OK. Favorite singer?"

She thinks for a moment, "Adele, I guess."

"Never heard of her."

"You're a guy. She appeals mostly to girls, I think."

"Good enough," he says, smiling. "Favorite book?"

"*Lectures of Field Theory and Topology.*"

"Should have known," Jake says with a bit of a laugh as their sushi arrives. "This looks good."

"It is," Kathy says as she pours soy sauce in the little dishes on the table, putting one in front of him.

They fall silent as they eat.

"I haven't had sushi this good in a long time," Jake says.

"Told you," she says, a bit of "I told you so" in her voice. "Where are you from?" she says as they eat.

"All over," he says, accepting her turning the tables on him. He finds himself willing to open up to Kathy more than he has with anyone since Charley. "My father's a civil engineer, and we moved around a lot. Usually, we were in a new town every couple, three years."

"You didn't want to be one?"

"One what?" he asks, not grasping where she's going.

"A civil engineer," she answers, waving her chopsticks at him.

"That's not how I roll; took after my mother, I guess," he answers matter-of-factly.

"They alive? Still together?" she asks.

"Yes and no. They got divorced, oh, thirteen years ago," he says, losing his grip on a piece of sushi as it slips from between his chopsticks.

"Why?"

"Dad had a midlife crisis, I guess. Decided he needed 'more room,' was how he put it. That's bullshit, but that's what he said as he left."

"Were you still in school?"

"I was thirteen, just about to start high school."

"Oh," she says. "Siblings?"

"A younger sister. It hit her hard," Jake says reflectively. "But Mom got her through it. That is before she baled on us too. My sister's in college now, majoring in mechanical engineering of all things. She wants to be an architect."

"Why of all things?"

"Because she blames Dad for what happened with Mom and to us, so I thought she would stay away from engineering in any form," he says between bites. "But that is where her talent and interests are. So …"

Their server brings the check. Jake starts to reach for it, but Kathy stops him. "We pay for ourselves."

"OK," he says, picking it up and looking at it. "You owe, let's see, $12.45 plus tip."

"Here," she says, handing him $15 from the wallet she digs out of her purse. "I don't need change."

"Big spender," he says with a laugh, while he pulls his part out of his wallet, leaving all the money in the small tray with the bill. As they get up, he motions to the server. "We don't need change." He gets a nod and smile in response.

Leaving the restaurant, Jake says, "I'll walk you home."

"OK. I live close to here."

They walk about a block in silence.

"What's your favorite color?" she asks.

"Blue," he says as they stroll down the street and he decides not to try to hold her hand.

"Favorite book?"

"Don't have one," he says, thinking about it. "I like a lot of different books. Same with music. And movies."

"Sounds like you can't make up your mind."

"I guess, maybe something like that," he replies. "I have eclectic tastes. I like mostly sci-fi and fantasy, with the occasional mystery thrown in. And history, of course. Lots of history."

"No romance?" she ask, a bit mischievously.

"No, I'll leave that to you."

"How do you know I like romance novels?" she replies in mock indignation.

"I apparently have fallen victim to a stereotype."

Kathy laughs. "Got you."

Jake gives a sour look. "Yeah, you did."

"A car?" she asks.

"Yeah, and it even runs. You need a ride?"

"No, I have a car. This is me," Kathy says as she stops in front of an old, large wood-frame house that's been divided into two apartments, a porch extending across the front. "I'm on the second floor. The door is the one on the right side," she says, indicating the door next to another that leads into the bottom apartment.

"OK," Jake says, looking over the house. "You going to come by the Commons tomorrow?"

"Maybe," she says, giving him a quick kiss on the cheek and then fleeing up the walk to the steps and through the door.

He watches her go in, amused. Then he turns to walk home, thinking about Kathy and what has just happened—and when, and if, he will see her again. He's confident he will. The question is when.

CHAPTER 13

Jake is sitting at his usual table. He has gotten through his first morning class in his usual haze. Now he's staring down at his usual cup of coffee, waiting for the additional aspirin he has just swallowed to kick in.

Slowly he becomes aware that someone's standing on the other side of the table.

"Karl, you're early," he mumbles.

No response.

He glances up. It isn't Karl.

"Oh, hi," he says. "Haven't seen you in, what, nearly two weeks?"

"Good morning, I guess," Kathy responds, sitting down. "You don't look like you are in very good condition. Actually, you look like shit."

"Thanks. I feel like shit." His voice is flat, devoid of emotion.

"What's wrong? Are you sick?" she asks, worry in her voice.

Jake carefully shakes his head no, trying not to move so fast his headache gets worse. "Hungover. … It's a morning thing."

"A morning thing?"

"Yeah."

That's all the reply she gets. She contemplates him for a moment, wondering about the difference between the guy who rescued her at the bar and who she spent a great evening with, and this sorry specimen who looks like a refugee from a drunk tank.

"You get drunk a lot?" she finally asks.

Jake shrugs.

"Just about every night," Michelle says as she slides into a chair across from them. "Hi. I'm Michelle," she says, looking at Kathy with a smile.

"Kathy," comes the reply. "He gets drunk every night?" she asks, incredulity in her voice.

"Just about. He says that's the only way he can sleep."

"What?" Kathy sounds confused. "Why?"

"He feels g—" Michelle begins to say.

"Stop!" Jake barks. The effort costs him a surge of pain in his head. He squints his eyes and then immediately reopens them as the wave of pain washes over him.

Michelle looks over to find him glaring at her.

"I guess that's something for Jake to ex—" she starts to say.

"This the mystery woman?" Karl interrupts her as he swings a chair next to Michelle. He sits down, happy to end what was apparently becoming an awkward moment. "Hi. I'm Karl," he tells Kathy.

"Karl, Kathy. Kathy, Karl. Now everyone is introduced," Jake says, taking a long sip of his lukewarm coffee.

"Hi, Karl," Kathy says quietly, her gaze slightly averted from him. "I've never been called a 'mystery woman' before."

Karl smiles at her. "I'm assuming you're the lady this sorry excuse for a human took home with him."

"Yes. I am," she says, looking down at the table, her face flushing with embarrassment.

"It's no reason to be embarrassed. We've all been there," Karl assures her.

Michelle smacks him in the arm. "All of us?" she says accusingly.

Karl looks at her with smile. "Well, most of us. I have."

An awkward silence descends on the table.

"Why 'mystery woman'?" Kathy asks.

"We started calling you that when Jake wouldn't tell us anything about you," Karl says.

"We were wondering what happened to you, but he really wouldn't say," Michelle adds.

"And since we didn't know your name, the tag 'mystery woman' seemed to fit," Karl continues.

After a pause, Kathy says quietly, tentatively, "He really didn't know anything about me until recently."

"This her?" Samee says as he slides into the chair between Jake and Kathy.

"Yep," Karl says as Kathy looks surprised, and Jake irritated.

"Hello," Samee tells her.

"Hi," she responds meekly.

"Nice to finally meet you," Samee says.

Kathy just nods.

"Tell us about yourself?" Michelle asks.

"I have to go," Jake announces. "I'll be late for class." He gathers his books and his backpack as he gets up.

Karl looks at his watch. "Not really. You have a good twenty-five minutes."

"I have to do something before I go," Jake says defensively. He rushes off before anyone can say anything else.

"OK," Karl says, drawing out the word, to his friend's retreating back. "Where's Setareh?" Karl then asks, turning to Samee. "That's his fiancée," he adds, looking at Kathy, who has glanced up and then looked back down.

"Her mother's coming into town to help her find a wedding dress, so she's cleaning the apartment."

"Do they know you two are living together?" Karl asks.

"Yes," comes Samee's abrupt reply.

"And they're OK with that?"

"No." The dejection obvious in his voice.

"Her parents? Your parents?" Karl asks.

"Especially her father, but none of them are happy with us living together."

"Are they going to do anything about it?" Michelle asks, worry in her voice.

"There is nothing they can do," Samee says. "Except maybe not come to the wedding. Setareh's father is threatening to do that.

Mine talked about not coming, but Mom made Dad back down. She told him that I have become an American and they have to accept American customs."

"I take it Setareh's parents aren't as understanding?" Karl asks.

"Her mother wants to see her daughter married, and she accepts the fact that we are going to live our lives as we see fit, that we don't have to follow the customs of the Arab world," Samee says, throwing his hands up in exasperation.

"And her father's not so understanding," Karl says as a statement of fact.

"Not yet," Samee says, "but I think he'll come around. It would break Setareh's heart if he doesn't come to the wedding, but we are not going to change how we live just to suit him."

All three look over at Kathy as she starts to gather her stuff. "I'd better be off."

"You have a class?" Michelle asks.

"In a while."

"How long of a while?" Karl asks.

Kathy looks over at the clock on the wall. "About an hour."

"Sit back down and tell us about yourself," Karl says, making it sound like an order.

Kathy quickly sits down, dropping her backpack on the floor and averting her gaze from any of the three.

"What's your major?" Samee asks.

"Physics. I'm in the physics master's program," she says meekly.

"Good job!" Karl says.

"That's great!" Michelle says over top of him.

Samee just looks at her for a moment. "That is really impressive. How far along are you?"

"This is my first semester."

"What else can you tell us about yourself, Wonder Woman?" Karl asks.

Kathy gives an abbreviated version what she told Jake.

"You know about Jake?" Karl asks when she finishes.

"What about him?"

"Wait!" Michelle says. "I started to tell her about what happened, and he stopped me. He was upset that I was going to say anything."

Karl thinks about that for a moment. "He probably wants to tell you himself. Assuming he can work up the courage." He thinks a moment again. "Look," he tells Kathy, "I think you should know so you have some understanding about what is going on with him. I will tell you, but you have to agree not to tell him that you know. You good with that?"

"Yes." A certain firmness enters her voice.

"You can act like you have never heard the story if and when he tells you?"

"I think so," she says tentatively.

Karl considers that for a moment. "OK," he finally says. "Several years ago, Jake was engaged. He was deeply in love. I mean completely and utterly in love. He and Charley—Charlotte—were driving into campus in the early morning for her last final of the semester when a drunk ran a red light at high speed, T-boning their car on the passenger's side. ... Charley didn't survive."

"And Jake blames himself," Samee continues.

"Even though he did nothing wrong," Karl continues. "He seems to think that if he had been paying closer attention to the road, he could have avoided the accident, and Charley wouldn't have died." Karl pauses for a moment. "It didn't help that Charley's mother blamed him for her death. She was really nasty to him. But then she didn't approve of him anyway. Charley was from a well-to-do family. Jake, well, let's just say he's not. The fact that he's a veteran and dependent on the GI Bill didn't do anything to endear him to Charley's family." Karl pauses in the story.

"And the drinking?" Kathy asks.

Karl sighs heavily. Samee starts to speak, but Karl waves him off. "He has this dream. He calls it The Dream. He has it every night when he's not passed out drunk. It's about the accident and what happened after, at the hospital, with her mother, at the funeral."

"The funeral?"

"Her mother wouldn't let Jake come. Either at the service or the graveside. He watched her burial from a distance, then went to the grave after everyone left."

"He was so depressed we were afraid he was going to kill himself," Samee says.

Kathy looks startled at that. "That's just terrible."

"That's one way of putting it," Karl says. "We tried to get him to get some help, counseling. But he's a *guy*. He said he was all right, he could handle it himself. But he cut himself off from his family and all of us for about a year. He still really hasn't come all the way back. We're his friends, but it can be hard to be with him because he shuts us out. He even shuts out his family, including his sister. We found his way of handling it is to get drunk every night so he won't have The Dream."

"None of us," Samee adds, "have been able to convince him that her death wasn't his fault. He just can't forgive himself."

"So," Kathy says reflectively, "he gets drunk every night to forget."

"That's about it," Karl says. After a pause, he goes on. "He did date a girl some time ago but that didn't last."

"Why not?"

"She couldn't handle his drinking every night."

Kathy nods, reflectively. "I can understand that. … You know, I've never seen him drunk or even drinking heavily. This is the first I've heard of it."

"Spend more time with him," Samee says. "You will."

Karl gives him a nasty look. Samee drops his gaze and looks embarrassed.

Kathy glances at the clock. "Crap! I'm going to be late!" She grabs her stuff and almost runs for the door, her mind racing over what she has just learned.

She knows what can happen, how violence can erupt when a man gets drunk. She has seen that with her daddy many times. How he becomes angry when he gets drunk, how he slaps her mother and her and her siblings around over any perceived slight or mistake, no matter how small. But her daddy is mean and domineering even when he's sober. Jake is kind and thoughtful. At least when he's sober. Does his personality change when he's drunk? She really doesn't want to be around him when he's drunk so she can find out. But she is drawn to him. She finds comfort and support from him that she has never known before. The question she faces is this: Does she risk the one to hold onto the other? She doesn't have an answer. Yet.

CHAPTER 14

Jake has been standing on the sidewalk looking up at the second-story apartment Kathy shares with her roommates for nearly fifteen minutes. It's his third attempt to see her since that morning almost a week ago in the Commons. He wants to see her again. Why he doesn't really know. All he knows is that he feels drawn to her. He has tried to phone her nearly every day but never is able to push the call button.

Now for the third time he's trying to work up the courage to go up the walkway and knock on her door. The only things the first two attempts produced were strange looks from people walking by.

The simplest solution would be for her to come out. His timing, however, always seems to be off—she either isn't home or is not going anywhere. Or perhaps, she saw him through a window and just didn't want anything to do with him. That thought depresses him—and is what makes him fearful of going any further. So long as he doesn't know, he can fantasize about her reaction.

As he's standing there, debating with himself, a guy emerges from the first-floor apartment. A girl comes out right after him. She stops at the top of the porch, her arms folded across her stomach, while the guy marches quickly down the sidewalk glaring at Jake.

Not that Jake notices. He's too absorbed with staring at the second-story windows and his own thoughts.

"Hey!" the man says, stopping about three feet in front of Jake. "You!" The yelling shakes Jake out of his reverie. "Yeah, you!"

Jake just looks at him. "Yeah?" he says tentatively.

"What the hell are you doing? Why the fuck do you keep hanging out here?"

Jake just looks at him, not able to say anything.

"You're scaring the shit out of my girlfriend! You need to get the fuck out of here! And stay away! She's about to call the cops on you!" he says, gesturing behind him. His girlfriend waves her cell phone above her head, a scowl on her face.

"Sorry …" Jake manages to say at last. "I … I …"

"You what?" the guy challenges him.

Jake sighs heavily. "I'm trying to go see a girl in that apartment," he says, waving his right hand toward the second floor.

The guy glances over his shoulder, then turns back to Jake, half scowling, half smirking. "Fuck! Man, you either do that or get the fuck away from here! Make up your fucking mind … or we will call the cops."

Jake just nods.

The guy turns on his heel and walks quickly back to his girlfriend. They have a short, animated conversation, punctuated with arm waving toward Jake and the upstairs and glances at him. Finally, they go back inside.

And Jake is left standing in limbo on the sidewalk, feeling humiliated. But the ultimatum leaves him an immediate problem: He has to decide what to do and decide now.

He turns to leave and walks a few steps before he stops as if he's run into a wall. He takes a deep breath, turns back around. After pausing a few seconds, he takes another deep breath—and heads up the sidewalk. He pauses in front of the door to the second floor. He doesn't see a doorbell.

He at last works up the courage to knock, steeling himself for Kathy to answer the door.

No answer.

He knocks again. A bit louder.

No answer.

He knocks again. Louder still. His courage rising.

No answer.

A thought hits him. He tries the doorknob—the door opens onto a stairway that runs steeply up to another door. 'Should have known,' he tells himself, disgusted and amused at the same time.

He climbs the stairs and pauses in front of the door at the top. He raises his fist to knock. Pauses again. Thinks about what he'll say when she opens the door. Then he knocks, gently. He hears footsteps coming to the door. He takes a deep breath, readying what he plans to say.

The door swings open.

"Yes? Who are you?" the short, plump blonde in the doorway challenges.

Jake's caught unprepared. It's not Kathy.

"Well? Cat got your tongue?"

"Is … is Kathy here?"

The blonde looks him up and down before responding. "What are you?"

"Jake," he responds, wondering why the *what* and not the *who*. 'Does she think I'm a thing?' he wonders, bemused.

"Hey! Kathy!" she yells over her shoulder, keeping her eyes on him. "Some guy named Jake is here to see you!" No immediate response. "Kathy! You hear me?"

A bedroom door on the far side of the large living room swings open. Kathy emerges, her hair held up by a large hair clip. A pencil is stuck behind her left ear. She walks into the center of the room and just stares past her roommate at Jake.

Jake looks around the woman in front of him. "Hi," he tells her. "Can we talk?"

Kathy just nods. The blonde has been looking back and forth at them. Seeing the nod, she steps out of the way, allowing Jake to come in.

He walks to Kathy, who seems to have shrunk into herself, her gaze fixed on the floor.

"This way," she mumbles, starting to turn toward her room.

"Hey!" her other roommate, a short brunette, yells. "Aren't you going to introduce us?"

Kathy pauses a moment. Without lifting her eyes, she says, "Ashley, Kaitlyn, this is Jake."

"Is he the guy?" the blonde, Kaitlyn, asks.

"Yes," Kathy mumbles after a brief pause.

"So is he?" Ashley asks.

"Is he what?" Jake asks, irritated by what appears to have become an interrogation. He assumes they are still trying to find out about his sexual orientation and he's not about to help them. It irritates him that they would even care.

Kaitlyn and Ashley are taken aback by his challenge. Without lifting her eyes, Kathy grabs his hand and pulls him into her bedroom, shutting the door behind them as soon as he's in. The rectangular room has a queen-size bed in the middle and a desk under the windows spanning the outside wall, allowing in a breeze that brings a soft, fresh smell, softly moving the curtains, in contrast to the stale air in the living room, which only has two small windows at the front of the room by the door.

"What the hell!" Jake says, both about what Kathy has just done and what her roommates are asking.

"They still want to know about you," Kathy says, regaining a bit of her composure.

"You haven't told them, obviously. Good."

Jake walks up to her, pulls her into his arms, and gives her a deep, long kiss, running his hands over her back and down to her butt. She responds eagerly, wrapping her arms around his neck, which gives him hope.

Finally, he steps away a few inches, his arms still around her. "There. Now you can tell them, if you want. But if it were me, I wouldn't give them the satisfaction."

Kathy gets a mischievous look. "That really doesn't prove anything. A gay guy could kiss like that."

An exasperated look crosses Jake's face at having the tables turned on him. Then he ventures a guess: "Karl told you all about me and ... and ... my past."

"No, he didn't," she says, a bit too quickly.

Jake takes a step back, hands on her shoulders as she avoids his look. "Come on! He couldn't resist telling you. And he made you promise not to tell me that he told you, didn't he?"

"Yes." Kathy smiles meekly, looking at him directly for the first time. "Do you mind? Are you angry?"

He stands farther back. "No. I knew Karl couldn't keep his mouth shut. And it may be a good thing. … Is that why you've been avoiding me?"

She shrugs, looking back down.

"Or is it the drinking?"

She nods tentatively. "That worries me." She looks up at Jake.

Now it's his turn to divert his gaze. "I was afraid of that." He decides not to bring up the night they met—and how drunk she was and why she got that way.

A silence falls between them: Kathy looking intensely at him, Jake looking forlornly at the floor.

"I know why you do it," she finally says. "But it's not healthy. You have to stop."

He glances up at her. "Will you help me?"

She considers the question for a moment. "How?"

"I'm not sure," he says softly. "But being with you helps. I don't know why but it does. The night you spent in my place, I didn't have The Dream and didn't get drunk. And the night we went out together … I drank a little, not enough to get drunk, and I didn't have The Dream."

"I'm not moving in with you," she says firmly. "But," she says after a pause, "I will hang out with you."

Jake brightens up immediately. "Great. Let's get out of here."

"Let me get my jacket." She grabs her jacket from her closet, and Jake holds the door for her as they head out into the living room.

"Where're you going?" Ashley asks in a challenging tone.

"Out," Kathy says, becoming meek and withdrawn again. She grabs Jake's hand and quickly pulls him through the apartment door before anyone can say anything else, almost running down the steps, through the bottom door, across the porch. She doesn't slow down until they are on the sidewalk, leaving Jake wondering what that was all about. He decides he doesn't need to know right now. There will be time enough for questions.

"What way?" she asks.

"Hungry?"

"I could eat."

"Any preference?" he asks.

"You choose?"

Jake smiles. "I am not falling into that trap."

"What trap is that?"

"The one where the girl says, 'You choose,' and then rejects every choice the guy makes," he responds.

She smiles at him. "Oh, that trap."

"Yes, that one."

"Make a suggestion," she says.

Jake thinks a bit. "Chinese or Italian?"

"Either one."

Jake thinks a moment, knowing he'll probably be wrong no matter what. So, he picks the one he isn't really in the mood for. "Italian."

"Sounds good."

"What? You agree?"

"Surprised?"

"You could say that."

"We can go Chinese if you prefer."

"No, no, Italian it is," he says, unwilling to admit the game he was playing.

She smiles at him as they head up the sidewalk toward downtown. He reaches out and takes her hand, feeling the welcome pressure as she squeezes his hand a bit.

CHAPTER 15

*J*ake and Kathy make the ten-minute walk to the restaurant in near silence.

"You know …" Jake starts to say, trailing off as they near their destination.

"Know what?" Kathy asks after a moment.

"Oh, never mind," he says quickly, not really wanting to get into the past but realizing she probably has questions about it.

"No. I want to know."

"It's nothing." Jake wants to ask her about what just happened at the apartment but is afraid this is not the time for such a question.

"No, please, tell me," she insists.

"How are your classes coming?"

"My classes?" Kathy looks at him sharply from the corner of her eye. Jake is looking straight ahead. She doesn't believe that is what he wants to talk about, but she's not sure she wants to press the issue. "My classes are fine."

"You carrying a full load?"

"Twelve hours. I wanted to take one more class this semester, but my adviser said twelve hours was the max in the grad program."

"Are you in a hurry to finish?" he asks, holding the door for her as they enter the restaurant.

"Two, please," she tells the greeter.

"This way," the greeter says as she takes two menus and leads them to a table near the front window.

"Yes and no," Kathy says over her shoulder as they follow the greeter.

"Here you are," the greeter tells them, placing the two menus at seats opposite each other. "Your server will be with you in a moment."

"Thanks," Jake and Kathy say in near unison.

"What's the 'yes' part?" Jake asks as they settle into their chairs and start to peruse the menu.

"I'm anxious to get to my doctoral program and out the other side so I can start my career," she says, turning menu pages.

"And the 'no'?"

"Would you like something to drink?" the server says as he comes up.

"Yes," Jake says and then motions to Kathy. They both order wine. The server pauses, looking a bit quizzically at Kathy. Her return look and Jake loudly clearing his throat prompts him to decide he doesn't need proof of age. He turns and leaves. Jake and Kathy go back to their menus.

"And the 'no'?" Jake repeats.

"I enjoy being in school, learning. I always have, and in a way, I don't want it to end," she says, putting the menu down.

"OK," Jake says, putting his menu down as he sits back in his chair, giving her a small smile.

The server comes back, puts down their wine, two glasses of water, and some bread with dipping sauce. "Are we ready to order?"

"Yes," says Kathy, launching into her order, making enough changes in the dish to make Jake wonder whether it will resemble what's on the menu to any extent.

When the server is finished writing, he turns to Jake. "And you, sir?"

"I'll have the spaghetti with marinara sauce and the house salad with oil and vinegar."

"Yes, sir," the server says and turns to leave.

"What about you?" Kathy asks.

"What about me?"

"How many hours are you taking?"

"Twelve," he says, grinning at her. "Two classes and two seminars. I finished my bachelor's last spring and now going strong for a master's."

"Are the courses interesting?"

"So far, though I doubt you'd find them challenging," he says, a touch of humor in his voice.

"Why do you say that?" she responds, curious about his reasoning,

"No advanced math. No math at all," he replies, mirth in his voice. "Isn't that what you theoretical physicists specialize in?"

"I guess it is," she replies, catching onto his humor. "So why history?"

Jake thinks about that for a moment. "I'm fascinated by what people do and why they do it. What, for instance, made Adam Burr tick? Would he really have tried to split off part of the country to create his own? How did Woodrow Wilson's racism impact his presidency? What kept Elenore Roosevelt going despite all the attacks that were launched against her? And why did FDR not rein her in? … And Andrew Jackson. Was he a power-hungry megalomaniac? Or was he just a man of his times and his culture? And why did people support him? FDR? Wilson?"

"Those are a lot of questions," Kathy says as he finishes his tirade.

"I guess," he says, looking up and sitting back as the server comes with their dinners. They eat in silence for a time.

When he is nearly finished, Jake decides to try to explore Kathy's history. "So, you're the only one in your family to go to college?"

"Yes," she says, the defensiveness back in her voice.

"Sorry," he says, drawing back. "I didn't mean to offend you or go where I'm not supposed to."

"No, no, it's all right. It's just that …" Her voice trails off. Jake decides not to push. "It's just that," the words come rushing out, "my parents didn't think education was important … especially for girls. Daddy always said, 'Schooling's wasted on girls. They just get married and have kids, so why waste the time and money on them.'"

"An *enlightened* point of view," Jake says sarcastically, instantly regretting opening his mouth.

Kathy nods, a weak smile flirting across her face. "Momma didn't say much of anything. She just followed whatever Daddy said and did what he told her."

"What does your father do for a living?"

"He's a mechanic."

"Like your brother." It wasn't a question but a statement.

"Yes. That's why Bobby became a mechanic."

"And your sister's a secretary?"

"Theresa works for an insurance agency. She just got married."

"What made you different?" Jake asks, immediately regretting again that he couldn't keep his mouth shut, afraid he'll either offend her or drive her into silence, or both.

"I have a brain and I want to use it!" comes the defiant reply. "I love learning. I always have. I got straight As in school. Momma would tell me. 'Good job.' … Daddy just got another beer, muttering about wasted time and energy," Kathy says, a slight drawl slipping into her usual crisp, clear English. "He kept telling me that I had easy teachers and would fail later on, that I should just be satisfied with being someone's wife and having babies. That's what women are for. He would point at Momma and say that if that is good enough for her, it should be good enough for me. He told me over and over again that I was wasting my time on 'book learning' and would never amount to anything, that men rule the world, they always have and always will, and that women should learn their place and keep it."

"Despite that, here you are, in one of the toughest programs in the country. You should be proud of yourself," Jake says, admiration for what Kathy has overcome slipping into his voice.

Kathy looks around, as if searching for something. "Do you think I did the right thing?" she says, her voice almost pleading for affirmation. "Was I right to go against Daddy? Can I really do this?"

Jake sits back, a bit horrified by the outburst. "You are doing it," he finally says. "That should be answer enough."

"But I love Daddy and Momma. I don't want to disappoint them. I want them to be proud of me."

"Kathy! Look at me!" Jake orders, the force of his words dragging her eyes to his. "Love them all you want, but you have to live your life. You have a first-class brain to use and a dream to fulfill. You can't give that up to please your parents. You owe it to yourself."

"And Daddy and Momma?"

"They will either accept you or not," Jake says intensely, leaning forward on the table, taking her hands. "But if you tailor your life to meet their expectations, you'll spend the rest of it miserable. What are you going to do? Drop out of school and marry some guy you don't love to keep them happy? You're not going to do that. You know it. You've already started down your own road. Stay on it."

Kathy starts to quietly cry, looking down at the table.

"I think you're stronger than you know," he says, sitting back a bit. "But you have to accept yourself for who you are and who you want to be."

"Is everything all right?" the server asks, coming up to the table.

"Yes," Kathy says quietly, waving at him.

"May I have the check?" Jake says, looking up at him.

"Sure," the server says, collecting their dishes and heading off.

"Sorry," Jake tells her. "I didn't mean to upset you."

"No, no, you didn't," she says, using her napkin to dry her face. "I needed that. I've been trying to escape my childhood. But it's hard when you hear nothing but women are baby machines at the service of men."

"You do know that's bullshit," Jake says as calmly and kindly as he can.

"Yes, but it's hard to escape."

"I suppose it is. … Have you had counseling?"

"At the clinic," she says, nodding, referring to the university's student health clinic.

"Does it help?"

"Some. I guess."

"Keep trying."

"That's funny, coming from a guy. Coming from someone who refuses to go to counseling when he needs it so badly." It is Kathy's turn to regret saying something as soon as she says it.

Jake takes a deep breath, leans back in his chair, and looks at the ceiling. Looking back at Kathy, he says, "Karl told you about that too, did he?"

"Yes," she nods.

The server comes back with the check. Jake looks at it and hands it back with his credit card. Then he looks out the window.

"He's right, I guess. And I don't have a good explanation why I don't," he says, pronouncing each word carefully.

"Then why don't you?" she asks as kindly as she can.

"I'm not sure. Maybe I'm afraid of looking weak. Maybe I'm afraid of what I'll find out. Maybe I don't want to know. I … just … don't know."

The server comes back with his card and slip to sign. Jake puts on the tip, signs the slip, and puts the card back in his wallet.

"Come on, let's go," he tells Kathy.

"OK. Where do you want to go?"

"Go?" he says as they get up and head for the door.

"I'm not ready for tonight to be over," she says. "Is that OK with you? Or do you want to be alone?" she says, worry coming into her voice as her confidence evaporates.

"I'm not ready for tonight to be over either," he says reassuringly. He thinks for a moment. They could go to The Garage or another student hangout. But what he really wants is just to be alone with her. "How about my place? No one else is there. We can listen to music and talk."

"Sounds good," she says as they walk away from the restaurant.

Jake slips his arm around her. In response, Kathy snuggles up against him.

CHAPTER 16

"I remember this place," Kathy says, laughter in her voice, a small smile on her face as she looks over her shoulder at Jake as they walk into his apartment.

'Ms. Hyde's back,' Jake thinks. He's begun to think of Kathy as a Dr. Jekyll and Ms. Hyde character, only in this case Dr. Jekyll is meek and deferential, a sadness running through her, while Ms. Hyde is determined and assertive, and happy. He prefers Ms. Hyde. Definitely.

"I guess that's a good thing. It proves you have a memory that works," he tells her, returning her smile and happy tone of voice.

"You had doubts?" A playful challenge is in her voice.

"I wouldn't dare doubt you," he shoots back. "I'm afraid of what might happen."

"Smart man. … What now?"

"A drink?"

Kathy immediately gets serious. "Is that right?"

Jake is taken aback by the swift change in her tone. "Don't worry. I'm not going to get drunk."

She gives him a long, hard look, the unspoken question hanging between them.

"I promise," he finally says. "As long as you are here, as long as I am with you, I promise I won't drink heavily."

"And when I'm not with you?"

Now it's his turn to divert his gaze. He stares out the window for a moment. "I don't know," he finally says.

Kathy keeps him under her steady, steely gaze. "At least you're honest."

Jake looks at her. "It's all I can offer."

The silence is thick between them. Jake finally looks away again.

"Do you have any tea?" she finally asks.

"I ..." Jake starts to say, the question catching him unprepared. He looks back at her, a slight frown on his face as he thinks. "I might," he says slowly. He turns on his heel and heads for the kitchen where he starts rummaging through the cupboards, digging around among the contents, some plastic bottles and paper containers falling onto the counter during his mad search.

Kathy follows him and leans against the doorframe, her arms folded across her stomach, smiling, amused by the chaos she has unintentionally sparked.

"You don't have to destroy your kitchen for my sake," she says as he starts on the second cabinet.

"I'm sure there is tea in here somewhere," he says over his shoulder as he destroys the neat order in the second cupboard he searches. "My old roommate used to drink tea a lot, and I don't think he took it with him."

"How long has he been gone?"

"Let's put it this way: The tea is well aged," Jake replies, moving to the third white cupboard. "But it still should be good. Tea doesn't really go bad." He pauses a moment. "At least, I don't think it does," he says as he returns to his search. "I know my sister wouldn't drink it, but she's a tea snob." He pauses and looks over his shoulder at her, afraid he has just said something wrong. "You're not ..." He thinks better about the way he's going to frame the question. "Are you particular about your tea?"

Kathy laughs and steps a bit closer to him. "Not tonight."

"Are you sure?" The anxiety in his voice nearly physical.

"Yes," she says kindly. "Whatever you have will be fine. Assuming you have some."

"Right," Jake says as he goes back to searching. "Got it!" he announces in triumph. He brings out a box that is still in reasonably good condition. "Is this OK?" he asks, holding the box so she can see it.

"That will definitely do," she announces.

"Great," he says, then fishes a kettle out of one of the lower cabinets. He looks at it a moment, then starts washing the dust and crud off the outside and scrubs the inside. After he is satisfied it is clean and all the soap is rinsed off, he fills it halfway with water and puts it on the stove.

"Your roomie left the kettle?" Kathy asks.

"Yep. Guess that turned out to be a good thing," he says, pulling two cups out of the cupboard.

"You like tea too?" she asks.

"I guess we'll find out."

"You've never had tea?"

Jake gives her a quick look, rolling his eyes and raising his eyebrows. "Guess I never had a reason to try it."

"And you do now?"

"I can't let you drink alone. It wouldn't be polite."

She just smiles in response as she watches him put a tea bag in each cup. Jake then looks at the mess he's created on the counter and in the cupboards. He picks up a box of spaghetti to put back.

"Do you want some help?" Kathy asks.

"Ahh, no," he says hesitantly. "I'll take care of this later," he says as he puts the box back on the counter. "It'll be a few minutes before the water boils."

"Oh, you know this from your vast tea-making experience?" The question carries no challenge, just humor.

"I have boiled water before, you know!" he replies with equal humor.

"I'll take your word for that."

"You'll just have to," he says in mock seriousness. "Want to listen to some music?"

"Sure. What've you got?"

"All kinds of stuff. What do you like?"

"You pick."

Jake is having no part of that—he already has been burned once today playing that game. "No, I suggested the restaurant. It's your turn."

"OK. How about Adele?"

"Good, I like Adele too," Jake says, although he has no idea who that is or even if the singer is male or female. "I have all my music on my phone, so give me a minute." The kettle's whistle goes off as he searches for the music. He looks up from his phone toward the kitchen.

"I'll get that," she says, heading off, deciding not to mention that he has already admitted to not knowing who Adele is.

"Thanks," he says, relieved that he has some space to find the music. He does a search and finds four albums—*Adele 19*, *Adele 21*, *Adele 25*, and *Adele 30*. He's downloading as much as he can as Kathy comes back into the room, carrying a cup in each hand, the strings of a tea bag hanging over each cup's lip. She puts the cups on the dining table as the last of the two albums finishes downloading. Jake gives an internal sigh of relief.

"OK, I have to turn on my speaker and get the Bluetooth connected."

"I would never have guessed," she says with more humor than real sarcasm. Jake just looks at her and makes the connection.

"What album do you want to hear?" he asks her.

"How about *Adele 28*?" she says mischievously.

"Twenty-eight?" Jake says, confused. "I …"

"You don't know who she is, do you?" There is a *gotcha* quality to the question, although she is giving him the biggest smile he has ever seen from her.

"It's that obvious?" he says sheepishly.

"Painfully. Don't worry about it," she says, reassuringly. "Play *25*."

"Thanks," he says, putting on the first song on the album. "What are the numbers about?" he says, looking up at her. "Since I've shown my utter ignorance about this, I might as well go all in."

Kathy laughs. "As I understand it, the numbers correspond to her age when the album came out. She was twenty-one for one of them and twenty-five for another."

"Oh … that's a big gap, four years," he observes.

"I've been told she took some time off to get married and have a kid," she says, turning reflective. "It's funny. Her husband never heard her sing before they were married, or so I have heard."

"Weird."

"Yes, but at least she knew he loved her and not the idea of her."

"The idea of her?" Jake asks.

"You know, when someone wants to be with you not because of who you are but because they want to be with the star they fantasize about."

"Good point," he says, a bit thoughtfully. "I knew a guy in high school who had all the girls throwing themselves at him. He was a really nice guy, but what attracted the girls was he was really handsome. It messed with his mind big-time. I've known beautiful women who had the same problem, and the same messed-up minds. On the good side of that, I've never had to worry about that problem."

"Neither will I."

"Oh, don't be so sure of that. I can see a Nobel Prize in physics in your future. Besides, you're already beautiful."

"No, I'm not," Kathy says quickly and defensively, adding, "and that'll never happen!"

"Don't sell yourself short," Jake responds, enjoying being with this self-confident, funny woman.

"Well … What kind of music do you like?" she says, changing the subject that has become uncomfortable.

"All kinds," Jake says with a shrug. "Want to dance?"

She looks at him quizzically. "This really isn't dance music."

"We'll fake it. Come on," he says, holding a hand out for her. She pauses for a moment before joining him in a slow dance in the middle of the living room floor. He pulls her close, just enjoying feeling her against him. She relaxes in his arms, content to be held and to stop talking for a bit. They dance through three songs, before they step away from each other by mutual consent.

"That was nice," she says.

"Yes, yes it was," his voice a bit husky.

She looks at him and starts to laugh.

"What?" he asks defensively as he flees to one end of the couch.

"Oh, nothing. Nothing at all," she says, looking away from him as she gets her laughter under control, finally sitting down in an armchair.

Jake clears his throat. "Should we try some different music?"

"Sure, but you pick this time. I want to hear something you like."

"OK, but don't laugh."

"Why would I laugh?" she asks a bit suspiciously.

He just raises his eyebrows in response, giving her a quick smile, as he searches his music menu. "Here, this one," he says and pushes the play button.

As "The Dock of the Bay" begins to play, Kathy looks at him quizzically. "It's pretty good. ... I've never heard this guy before."

"I'm not surprised. It's Otis Redding from back in the sixties."

"The 1960s?" she asks, somewhat incredulous. "You listen to music that old?"

"It's my granddad's fault," he says, smiling.

"Your grandfather?"

"Yeah. After my parents divorced, my sister and I were sent to live with my mother's parents. I spent the next four years there, until I graduated from high school and went into the Navy."

"He forced you to listen to this stuff?"

"Well, he didn't force us. It's just that he played it all the time—all kinds of music, rock, blues, jazz, country ... and what he didn't play, Grandma played. We sort of got used to it and even started to like it."

"They wouldn't let you listen to music you liked?"

"Oh, no, we could listen to any music we wanted to, but they couldn't understand the lyrics in most of the heavy metal songs. Besides, they hated a lot of our music and wouldn't let us play it around them, so I guess even if they could understand the lyrics, it wouldn't have mattered."

"That seems unfair—not allowing you to play your music."

Jake shrugs. "Not really. Well, maybe, I guess. Well, some of ours they did like. I think they'd like Adele. But they saved us. Dad's an alcoholic, which is why he and Mom divorced, and which is the real reason he left."

"And your mother?"

Jake swallowed hard. "She … she didn't want us after Dad left."

"Really?"

Jake just nods.

"And your dad?"

Jake shrugs. "I don't know. He was never sober enough for us to find out." He smiles at her.

"But he was an engineer?"

"Yeah. He was sober when he went to work, but when he got home, he drank his dinner, and he was usually drunk by early afternoon Saturdays, Sundays and holidays."

A silence falls. "Is that why you drink?" she asks, tentatively, afraid she might have ventured into a topic she shouldn't have.

"No, no," he responds quickly. "He's the reason I never drank heavily … until …" his voice trailing off.

"I see," she says gently, going over to where he's sitting on the couch. She sits next to him, putting her arms around him and drawing him in. She can feel his tears as he softly cries, his head on her shoulder.

CHAPTER 17

The sunlight hits Jake in the face. His eyes flutter open. He squints as he stares out the bedroom window.

'Forgot to close the blinds again,' he thinks. He glances at the clock on the night table next to the bed—8:16. His class starts at 9:30 a.m. *'I better get moving.'* As he starts to move, he feels his left arm is pinned. Then he feels the body moving gently against him, a comfortable murmur coming from the warm softness as she snuggles against him, disturbed a bit by his movement.

He looks over to see a pile of brown hair covering the head resting on his chest. He feels her naked body lying against his, her leg thrown over his, her left arm across his chest. He feels her soft breathing.

He concentrates on a spot on the ceiling as his mind clears of sleep. Last night comes flooding back into his memory. He remembers the soft gentleness of her touch. Their lovemaking. Their bonding. His feelings for her come flooding back in.

"Kate," he says softly.

No response.

"Kate," he says a bit more forcefully, gently shaking her shoulder a bit.

"Hmmm?"

"I have to go to class," he softly says, kissing the top of her head.

"OK," she says, not moving.

Jake smiles. "I have to move."

"OK," she says, snuggling closer to him.

"I don't think you quite understand. I have to get up."

"OK," she says. "You need a bigger bed," she adds as she snuggles under the covers of the twin bed.

"Here goes," he says as he pulls his arm out from under her as gently as he can, a bit amused about the bed comment. He swings out of bed. For a moment, he stands looking back down at the mop of hair with a nose poking out, the rest of her body snuggled under the covers. It's only then that it hits him: The only thing he had to drink last night was tea. Not his favorite substance. But still, no alcohol. And he didn't have The Dream. In fact, he slept more soundly than he had since … he let the thought go.

Jake closes the blinds so Kate can sleep and heads to the bathroom for a quick shower. He brushes his teeth while the water warms up and then jumps in, washing quickly. He learned to take fast showers on board ship where fresh water was at a premium.

Turning off the water, he reaches for a towel. Drying himself quickly, he steps out of the tub—and collides with a still naked Kate, who wraps her arms around his neck and kisses him deeply. He wraps his arms around her, the towel slipping to the floor.

Finally, he pulls his head back, "I can't—"

"I know," she says, cutting him off. "You have class."

"You got it," he says, stepping around her and heading into the bedroom. She follows him, pulling a towel around herself.

"Kate?" she says.

"What?"

"When did you start calling me Kate?"

Jake thinks for a moment, pausing with his right leg in his pants and the left out. "This morning, I guess."

"Why Kate?"

"I'm not sure?" It came out more as a question than a statement. "I guess when I woke up this morning, I saw you differently. Do you know what I mean?"

"No, not really."

"Good," he replies, "because I don't either. The only thing I am sure of is that this morning when I woke up, you were Kate. Are you mad? Upset? I can go back to Kathy if you want," he says as he slips his shirt over his head, worried he did something wrong.

"No, no," she says, her voice sounding perplexed. "It's OK. I just wasn't expecting to get a new name. … Kate is fine. In fact, I like it."

"That's a relief," Jake says, visibly relaxing.

"A relief?" humor creeping into her voice.

"Yeah, for a moment there I was afraid you'd be mad."

"No worries about that," she says, smiling.

"I have to run," Jake says as he gets off the bed after putting on his shoes. "When's your first class?"

Kate looks at the clock by the bed. "Two hours. I have time to go home and change."

"You can shower here if you want," Jake offers.

"Hmmm, thanks, but all my shower stuff is at home."

"OK. Will I see you later? Today?"

"Of course, silly. I'll meet you in the Commons this afternoon."

"Great," he says, kissing her as he rushes out of the bedroom. He quickly stuffs the books and other material he'll need into his backpack and runs out the door.

Kate wanders out of the bedroom and watches him as he flies out the door. She stares at the door for a few minutes, thinking about what has happened since yesterday evening and how her life seems to be changing. She wrenches her mind off those thoughts, goes back into the bedroom, and dresses. As she is about to leave the apartment, she looks into the kitchen and the chaos that is still scattered around. She pauses for moment, thinking about whether she should put stuff away, and then realizes she doesn't know where anything goes. Besides, Jake made the mess. He can clean it up.

She heads out the door and back to her apartment. She's not sure how her roommates will react. Her self-confidence, her self-assurance, drains away like water in a shower.

When she gets home, she is relieved Kaitlyn and Ashley are not around. Whether they are in their rooms or have gone somewhere, she doesn't know and doesn't care. Kate quickly showers, skipping washing her hair, dresses quickly and leaves. When she is well away from her apartment, she finally relaxes, realizing that at least for the rest of the day, she has avoided a confrontation with those two, whom she is beginning to think of as her prison guards. And in the back of her mind comes the stirrings of the need for a prison break.

CHAPTER 18

"Hey," Jake says, looking up from the book he's reading when he realizes someone is standing across the table from him in the Commons.

Karl stares at him for a moment, then slides into a chair opposite him. "Who are you and what have you done with my friend?"

"Come again?"

"Are you all right?" Karl asks as he sits down.

"Yes. Shouldn't I be?" Jake responds, uncertain about what is going on.

Karl's piercing stare bores through Jake. "You're not hungover?" comes out as half question, half statement.

"Don't appear to be," Jake says, catching on to what Karl is confused about.

"How did that happen? Why did that happen?"

Jake just shrugs, not willing yet to talk about Kate and last night, holding on to the warmth of his, their, private time.

Before Karl can say anything else, Samee and Setareh come up, sliding into seats at the table.

"How's the hangover?" Samee asks as he sits down.

"He doesn't have one," Karl says before Jake has a chance to respond.

"What?" Samee blurts out, looking back and forth at the two men.

"This is truly a miracle," Setareh chimes in, her voice rich with sarcasm.

"Thanks, guys," Jake says in a flat, deadpan manner.

"Hi. How's the invalid this morning?" Michelle says as she pulls up a chair next to Karl.

"The invalid is not an invalid this a.m.," Karl responds.

"Not possible," Michelle says. "How did that happen? They close all the bars and liquor stores?"

"Funny," Jake says, "real funny. Look, I didn't get drunk last night. That's all there is to it."

"What about The Dream?" Karl asks, worried.

"Didn't happen," Jake declares flatly.

"That's a first," Karl observes.

"Well, all good things must come to an end," Jake says.

"Is The Dream really gone?" Karl asks, worry in his voice.

Jake shrugs. "Only time will tell, I guess."

"I, for one, am glad you didn't get drunk last night, and I hope that awful dream is gone forever," Michelle says.

Samee and Setareh second the thought.

"Thanks, guys," Jake says, looking at the clock on the wall, realizing he still has fifteen minutes before he has to head out. "I have to go. Got a seminar."

"Wait a minute!" Karl says, holding up a hand as if to stop him. "You haven't told me what made this happen."

"Don't have time now. Maybe later." Jake grabs his book and backpack and makes his way toward the door, happy to avoid a discussion he's not ready for.

CHAPTER 19

*J*ake wanders out of the classroom building, deep in thought. And not about the seminar he just left. Or the class that will start in three hours. He strolls over to the Quadrangle, a grassy area surrounded by the campus's original brick buildings. Tree-lined sidewalks run around the outside of the grassy area, cut in the middle by a walkway connecting the two long sides of the rectangle.

Jake finds an empty bench and, checking for any birds that might be perched right above it, sits down. He watches the students hurrying to class or just strolling by, and the occasional faculty and staff member. But he doesn't really see them. He is too deep in thought—wondering about Kate, about why he is drawn to her, why she seems to have this calming effect on him, who is she really: the insecure, damaged little girl or the self-confident, brilliant woman? But most of all, he wonders why she is with him, what she sees in him, whether she will stay with him. And what if she won't?

He turns off his brain to give his overactive imagination a rest, concentrating on the world that is passing before him, trying to guess about the lives of the people walking by. Especially the couples, the ones holding hands. Some are talking to each other, sometimes the girl dominating the conversation, sometimes the guy, while others walk in silence together. Watching them makes him think about Charley, and what he had with her, and what he lost in a split second. He takes a deep breath, forcing his mind back to the present, back to Kate and what he has, might have, with her. He's trying to decide if he's falling in love with her, or is it just lust or loneliness? He's afraid it's one of the last two. He's afraid that it's the first. He's just afraid.

"Hey, you." Jake looks up to see Kate's roommate Ashley standing in front of him.

"Hi," he says as she plants herself next to him on the bench. She sits there, her body angled toward him, just looking hard at him.

Silence.

"And you want?" Jake finally asks, the annoyance coming out strongly, both because he wants to be alone and because he doesn't know this woman and resents her intrusion.

"What's this with you and Kathy?" she demands. "She spent the night with you, didn't she?"

Jake frowns, his irritation growing. "What business is it of yours?"

"She's my roommate." Her tone of voice carries a sense of ownership.

"So what?" Jake can't keep the hostility out of his voice. He doesn't like the subservience Kate shows her roommates. He worries about whether they dominate her and to what extent. And he doesn't like being grilled—which this feels like—by someone he doesn't know, and he doesn't think he'll like. Actually, he realizes he already doesn't like her. He's not sure why, but he doesn't.

"She's fragile," Ashley announces. "We have to protect her. So, I have to know: What are you doing with her?"

"Why don't you ask her?" Jake shoots back, becoming confrontational. "Last I looked, she has her own mind and can answer for herself."

"Look," Ashley says in a calmer tone, trying to regain control of the conversation, "Kathy is weak. She can't think for herself. She depends on us to protect her."

Jake just stares at her. "You're serious? You have to think for her?"

"Yes," Ashley says, calmly but forcefully. "If we don't protect her, she would have no idea what to do."

"Are we talking about the *same* woman?" Jake challenges her. "The one I know seems quite capable of thinking for herself."

"You're wrong. I've known her a lot longer than you have, and I can tell you she is not all there mentally. She needs our help."

"Who is *our*?" Jake asks in exasperation.

"Me and Kaitlyn."

Jake sits back on the bench, looking at Ashley. "Let me get this straight: Kate—"

"What did you call her?"

"Kate."

"That's not her name," Ashley says in a tone more demanding than anything.

"Really?" Jake shoots back. "OK. Kathy, then," he says, using the name Ashley will accept so the conversation doesn't degenerate into the absurd, "is able to get into one of the top physics programs in the country but isn't capable of thinking for herself?"

Ashley considers him for a moment. "Just leave her alone. You're not right for her."

"That is for her to decide."

"No, it's not!" she spits out harshly. "We have to protect her from domineering bastards like you!"

"Excuse me," Jake says, laughing. "I think you've got that label backwards."

Ashley gives him a look of hate. "You won't be seeing her again!" she declares as she launches herself from the bench and walks quickly away.

Jake watches her go, trying to figure out what just happened. And whether Ashley could really stop Kate from seeing him.

He looks at his watch—twenty minutes before class. Not enough time for the conversation he needs to have with her. He pulls out his cell phone and calls Kate.

"Hi, Sweetie," comes the cheery answer.

"Hey," he says quietly, worry in his voice.

"What's wrong?" His tone of voice worries Kate.

"Can I see you right after class? Before you go home?"

"Of course," she says reassuringly, not even aware she called him Sweetie. "What's going on?"

Jake takes a deep breath. Exhaling, he says, "I just had a very strange conversation with one of your roomies. I need to talk to you about it."

"What happened?" Kate says, worried and sounding unsure of herself.

"No, not over the phone. It's not that kind of conversation, and I have to get to class. Please meet me in the Commons. Let's say, five?"

"If that's what you want," the worry growing in her voice.

"I'll see you then. I love you." The last three words just pop out. Jake has no idea why he said that or where it came from.

"I … love … you too," Kate replies, unsure why she answered that way, unsure of how she feels, and unsure about how Jake really feels about her.

"Bye."

"See you," she replies, now wondering about their relationship.

CHAPTER 20

Kate is sitting at what has become their table in the Commons. She's worried and confused. She's worried about what Jake needs to talk to her about, about how her roommate fits into this. She's doesn't even know which roommate he's talking about. And she's confused about how the conversation ended. He said he loved her. And her own hesitant reply—did she really mean it? Or was it just a hollow response to what he said, to a guy she cares about and who has become important to her?

"Hey, lady," Karl says as he slides into a seat at the table.

"Oh, hi," Kate says.

"What's up?" Karl asks.

"Not much. I'm just waiting for Jake. He wants to talk to me about something."

"Oh," Karl says, looking at her closely, seeing the worry on her face and hearing it in her voice.

"Hi, everyone," Michelle says, planting a kiss on Karl's cheek as she sits down.

"Hi," Kate replies, somewhat distractedly.

"Are you—" Michelle starts to say.

"Honey, we have to go," Karl says, cutting her off.

"What? Why?" Michelle looks questioningly at Karl.

"We have that appointment," Karl tells her, his tone of voice carrying more meaning than the words.

Michelle looks at him, at Kate and then back at Karl, catching on to what he is trying to say without saying it. "Oh, yeah, I forgot," she says, picking up the backpack she just put down. Karl gets quickly to his feet, putting one arm around her as he slings his backpack over his shoulder. They tell Kate goodbye and navigate their way around the tables as they head to the other side of the cavernous room, finding a table near the front. They intercept first Samee and then Setareh as they come in, Karl explaining what little he knows about what is going on—only that it is serious, and Jake and Kate need to be left alone. They speculate a bit about what could be going on before Setareh puts an end to the discussion by pointing out that none of them really have any idea about what is happening, so they might as well stop creating scenarios that probably bear little resemblance to reality.

"Hey, look," Samee says, gesturing toward the door. They all turn to see Jake walking in. Since they are in an area none of them ever sit in, he doesn't notice them; instead, his gaze is fixed on the other side of the room. His pace picks up when he sees Kate, who waves at him.

"Hi," Kate says as Jake silently slides into a seat next to her, his gaze fixed on her, making her a bit nervous. He reaches out a hand and takes hers, still not saying anything. She feels his gentle squeeze and responds.

They sit there, just gazing at each other, both reluctant to break the warm mood that has settled on them.

"Ashley found me when I was sitting in the Quad," Jake finally says with a sigh.

"And?" Kate asks nervously to prompt him to continue speaking.

"It was a really weird conversation, if you can call it that. ... She says we can't see each other anymore, that she and your other roomie have to protect you because you are," he says, taking a deep breath and exhaling before going on, "you are too weak to make decisions for yourself." He looks at her quizzically as she looks away, tears forming in her eyes. "What's going on?"

The question hangs in the silence between them. Kate grips his hand a bit harder. Tears run down her cheek.

"Kate?" he asks gently. "I don't know what is going on, but whatever it is, I want to help."

She looks at him, sorrow painted on her face. "I don't think you can," she finally says.

Jake's concern is growing. "You may be right, but at least let me try," he pleads. "Tell me what is going on."

Kate takes her hand back and dries her eyes and face with a napkin. "I … I told you about my family, about my daddy, about how I was raised, how I was taught that girls are subservient to men." She stops talking, looking at the floor.

"Yeah, you did. What has that to do with now?" he says, coaxing her to continue.

Kate looks at him, silently crying. "You'll hate me," she says flatly, looking back at the floor.

"No," he says definitely. "I don't see how anything you have told me or can tell me will make me hate you."

"Are you sure?" she says, hope in her voice.

"Yes," Jake says flatly.

Kate sighs, glances at him, and then looks back at the floor. "It's like I'm two people. When I'm working, I have all the confidence in the world, I'm in control. … But when I'm around people … I don't know … it's like I can't decide for myself. … I … I just … do what I'm told."

"I have noticed that about you," Jake says as Kate stops talking. "But you don't seem to be that way with me. In fact, you're quite the opposite. You're bossy with me," he says with a forced laugh. "You don't seem to have any trouble making up your mind that I can see. It's one of the things I love about you. And I definitely don't hate you."

"You will," she says dejectedly.

"Why do you say that?"

"Because … of … what … happens … at home," she says slowly, sorrow in her voice. "What used to happen sometimes before I met you."

Jake sits back in his chair, studying the sad woman in front of him. "What happens at home?"

"I don't want to talk about it. Not now. Not with you." The words come out in a rush.

"Why not?" Jake leans forward, taking her hand again, this time holding it gently in both of his.

She looks at their hands together, and sighs. "Because I don't feel helpless around you. I feel more like I do when I'm working on my project." She looks at him, questioning. "Why is that?"

Jake shrugs. "Not a clue. All I know is that you make me feel calm. I don't have to drink when I've been with you. Why is that?"

Kate looks at him, calming down. "I do?"

"Most definitely. And I can't figure out why. And I don't really care why. It makes absolutely no sense to me. Do you know?"

"No," Kate says, her spirits lifting. "I've never had that effect on anyone before."

"So, what are we going to do about this?" he asks. Then he goes on, trying to hide the fear in his voice. "Do we stop seeing each other?"

Kate takes a deep breath. "Can I spend the night with you?"

"Do we need to stop by your place first?"

"No. I can go back in the morning."

"OK. I have stuff at my place we can make for dinner if you're up for cooking."

"Will I like it?" she asks mischievously.

"How in the hell am I supposed to know that?" he says, welcoming back the woman he is attracted to.

"Then let's go find out," she announces.

'Welcome back, Ms. Hyde,' Jake thinks, taking her hand as they walk out.

CHAPTER 21

ate and Jake walk toward his apartment in silence, his arm wrapped around her shoulders, pulling her close as they huddle under the large umbrella she holds as rain comes down in a steady drumbeat. The trees lining his street help a little.

Jake wants to ask her about her relationship with her roommates— why she's subservient to them. But he's afraid to broach the subject, fearful she will pull away from him and retreat into her Dr. Jekyll persona.

Kate—she likes her new nickname; it signifies the person she wants to be—is torn by opposite desires. She wants to tell him about the situation with her roommates, wants to unburden herself and seek his … she isn't sure what she wants from him. She also does not want to tell him about it, fearful he'll reject her.

When they reach the apartment, they get under the entry overhang. Kate turns around, shaking the water off the umbrella while Jake holds the door open. She closes the umbrella, going through the open door into the lobby, with Jake following. He follows her up the stairs to the second floor, fishing out his keys as they go.

"Hey, Jake," another denizen of the apartment house says as Jake starts to open the door.

"Hi, Scott," he responds, turning to look at who is talking. Kate looks at the floor, shrinking into her coat.

"How's the weather?" Scott asks, slowing a bit and glancing at Kate.

"Raining," Jake answers matter-of-factly.

"Great," comes the unenthusiastic reply.

Scott disappears down the stairs as Jake gets the door open. He goes in, holding it for Kate.

"What do I do with this?" she asks, holding up the still wet umbrella.

"Bathtub, I guess," Jake replies.

He stops her as she starts to head to the bathroom. "Let me have your coat first." She strips off her coat while still holding the umbrella. Handing it to Jake, she heads off as he hangs their coats in the small closet by the door.

He reaches the living room at the same time she comes out of the bathroom.

"Dinner?" she asks.

"Ah, yes. Let's see what I have."

"You mean you don't know?"

"Well, I know sort of," he says as he leads the way into the kitchen. "I haven't taken inventory lately."

"Inventory? Is that what you call it?" she says, laughing.

"Yup. Let's see," he says, looking into the refrigerator. "There's … let's see … hamburger," he says, taking the meat out to sniff it, "that's still good. Bacon, eggs, cheese, lettuce, still reasonably fresh, green beans, a tomato, some milk." He sniffs it and puts the cap back on, returning it to the refrigerator. Closing the refrigerator door, he opens a cabinet. "And up here, we have spaghetti, a variety of spices, some spaghetti sauce, roasted garlic," he says, pulling the bottle down and reading the label. "And potatoes and an onion," he says, closing the cabinet door. Gesturing to the vegetables on the counter, he gives the potatoes a hard look. "Looks like they're beginning to sprout. Guess they better be used soon. … So, what's your pleasure?" he says, turning to Kate.

She thinks for a moment. "Do you have any bread?"

Jake hesitates briefly. "Yes, yes I do." He pulls a loaf out of another cabinet. Looking at it, he pronounces, "No mold."

"You do realize that if you keep it in the fridge, it won't go bad as quickly?" Kate asks, laughing a bit at him.

Jake looks a little confused. "Is that a physics principle?"

"No. Biology … and common sense."

"Oh," comes his sheepish reply. "Guess I'll start."

"You do that."

"OK, now why did you want to know if I had bread?"

"Well, we could make hamburgers or grilled cheese, maybe a salad to go with it," she says, thinking. "You do have salad dressing, don't you?

"Vinegar and oil is all."

"That'll do. Which do you want?"

Jake thinks for a moment, wary of guessing wrong. "Grilled cheese?"

"OK, but that hamburger has got to be aging if you had to smell it to make sure it's still good," Kate points out.

"Yeah, right," he responds, realizing that he's been tripped up again, and schooled. "I guess it's hamburgers."

"If you want," Kate says, smiling.

"If I ..." he says, before cutting himself short. "Let's get cooking."

He pulls out the hamburger, and as he mixes in spices and makes four decent-sized patties, Kate finds a frying pan, puts it on the stove with some oil and starts heating it.

"Let's skip the salad," Jake suggests as he puts the hamburgers in the pan. "We can use the lettuce and tomato on the hamburgers."

"OK," she says, finding a knife to slice the tomato as Jake pulls leaves off the lettuce.

"Cheese?" Jake asks as he checks the burgers.

"That sounds good."

Jake puts a slice of cheddar on top of each patty to let the cheese soften. Then, putting a slices of bread on each of two plates, he slides the burgers on, puts the tops on and carries the plates to the table. He turns around to see Kate rummaging through the cabinets. "What are you looking for?"

"Ketchup and mustard," she says, not stopping her search.

"Fridge," he says.

She stops, dropping her arms to her side. "Should have known." She finds the condiments in the fridge door. "Any relish?"

"No. Sorry."

"That's OK. We can get some later," she says without realizing the implications of that comment. But it makes Jake pause. He looks at her with raised eyebrows as she comes to the table.

"What?" she asks when she sees the quizzical look on his face.

"Nothing," he says, shaking his head a bit and smiling a little.

It's her turn to look quizzical, but she lets it pass.

The meal passes with no talk about the question hanging between them. Instead, they talk about their classes, the football team, tuition and fees, their professors, the weather, and politics—they are on the same page there. Jake finishes the last two burgers, Kate declining a second one.

"Now what?" Jake asks, after they've cleaned up from dinner.

"There is a song I heard when you were playing those oldies, something about clouds? It was sung by a woman. Judy or Joanie or something like that. Do you know the one I mean?"

Jake thinks about it for a moment. "I think so," he says, picking up his phone and scrolling through the song list. "Judy Collins. 'Both Sides Now.' I don't think she wrote it, but it's her version. Do you want to hear it?"

"Yes."

Jake turns it on. *"Rows and flows of angel hair. And ice-cream castles in the air ..."* the song begins.

"I would like to learn that song," Kate says as they listen.

"You sing?"

"I've been known to."

"All right then," he says, picking up his laptop from where it's leaning against the couch they are sitting on. He opens a search engine as the song goes on and soon finds the lyrics, then prints them.

"Do you play an instrument?" he asks.

"What?" she responds, irritated by the interruption.

Jake just shakes his head as she goes back to listening.

"Here, this is the part I really like," she says intensely, sitting up straighter: *"I've looked at love from both sides now, from give and take and still somehow it's love's illusions that I recall. I really don't know love, don't know love at all."*

She looks at Jake, near tears, as the song ends.

"Here," he says quietly, handing her the lyrics. "It was written by Joni Mitchell back in the sixties."

"Thanks." Kate studies the lyrics, humming to herself as she regains control of her emotions.

"Do you play an instrument?" Jake ventures to ask again.

"What?" She looks up, distracted at first. "Yes, guitar," she says as the question sinks in and she goes back to the lyrics. Jake sits back on the couch, just watching her as she studies the lyrics with an intensity he has not seen from her before. After about five minutes, she looks up at him, a sheepish grin on her face. "Sorry."

"Don't worry about it," he says reassuringly. "What about that song captivates you so much? I never gave it much thought."

Kate looks at him thoughtfully. "It's about me. It's about my life. It's about what I'm dealing with. Do you know what I mean?"

"Not really," Jake says, with a small smile and shake of his head. "Can you explain it to me? I mean, what in your life is like this? Do Kaitlyn and Ashley fit into this?" He immediately regrets bringing them up as he sees her sinking back into herself, closing up. "I'm sorry. I shouldn't have gone there."

Kate waves him off. "It's all right. I … I just don't want to talk about that now."

"OK," he says. What happens next catches him by surprise: Kate scoots close to him on the couch.

"Hold me," she pleads, snuggling into him. He wraps an arm around her. "Don't talk," she whispers. "Just hold me."

He doesn't say a thing, just holds her tighter.

The music plays on, going through a variety of songs. He can feel her quiet, slow breathing as she slips into sleep. He's getting tired as well. He kisses her gently on the top of her head.

"Let's go to bed," he says quietly.

Kate stirs and looks up at him. "OK. … Can we just sleep?"

"Sure," he says out loud, while thinking, *This is not going to be easy.*

As they go into the bedroom, Kate just stops. "You got a new bed. A bigger bed."

"You told me to," Jake says as he stands behind her, his hands on her shoulders.

"I did?"

"Yes, ma'am. The first time you spent the night. Don't you remember?"

"Not really," she says, a bit bewildered. "But that was a small bed you had."

"It's in the other bedroom now, if you care to use that instead," Jake jokingly suggests.

"You're an ass," comes the humorous reply.

"Yep," Jake says as he moves past her to get a T-shirt for her to wear. She strips to her underpants, then puts the shirt on. He watches her undress covertly as he pulls out his pajama bottoms and slips them on. When they get into bed, she kisses him and turns to face away from him, backing up until she is snuggling against him. She reaches back, pulling his right arm around her waist, then pulling his legs up against hers to the point that there is no room between them.

Kate is soon in a deep, contented sleep.

Jake is wide awake. The erection their cuddling has produced is uncomfortable in the extreme. And what's worse is there is nothing he can do about it. At first, he hopes she can't feel it. Then he realizes that she is fast asleep, her breathing slow and regular. Her only motion is to snuggle closer to him if that's possible. He can feel the warmth of her body.

Finally, he decides he has to make himself sleep. And if something happens … well at least he's wearing pajamas. Somewhere in the night, he drifts off to sleep.

CHAPTER 22

*S*mells of cooking bacon mixed with coffee slowly make their way into Jake's consciousness. He blinks his eyes open. As the pleasant odors bring him slowly awake, he realizes he's hungry and that he's in bed alone.

Contentedly, he rolls out of bed. Standing, he's suddenly thrown into a panic. Checking his pajamas, he finds they're still clean. Relieved, he puts on a T-shirt and goes into the kitchen.

"This smells great," he says, coming up behind Kate, and wrapping his arms around her middle, gives her a hug.

"Hey, I'm cooking," she replies in mock anger, shrugging him off.

"I see. What brought this on?" he says, stepping next to her and looking into the pan.

"Can't I cook?" The tone in her voice daring him to contradict her.

"By all means. I don't mind a bit. Anything I can do to help?"

"Get out the eggs and make toast."

"Right." He pulls them out of the refrigerator, saying, "How do you want to cook the eggs?"

"How do you like them?" she responds.

"We have toast, so over easy."

"OK, let me have them."

"Two each?" he asks.

"Sounds right."

When the eggs—hers are scrambled—are done, Kate slides them and the bacon onto two plates she has by the stove, while Jake butters the toast. He adds the slices to the meal, then picks up the plates and heads for the table, where he has already put forks, napkins, milk, sugar and a spoon for Kate to use. She follows with two cups of coffee.

As they start to eat, Kate suddenly stops, dropping her fork onto the plate. "I don't know why I let Ashley and Kaitlyn run my life and order me around, use me." Tears start flowing as she stares intently at her plate, avoiding Jake's eyes. "I guess," she resumes after a pause, now looking intently at Jake, "it's how I was raised, not to challenge people who boss me around. My momma," the words now come pouring out, "never went against my daddy, but she ran my life from the moment I got up in the morning to when I went to bed. I had to do anything and everything she said … unless Daddy said something different. Then we both did what he said. Momma would never look directly at him and always spoke meekly to him. With me, it was completely different: She spoke harshly to me, would slap me if I even seemed to be hesitating to do something she told me to do. You learn to do what you're told, not to argue, just comply."

Jake has stopped eating as well, sitting straight in his chair, watching her intensely. "I had no idea," he finally says quietly.

"I know," Kate says, the tension going out of her body, her shoulders sagging. "How could you?"

"I guess," he replies. "What I don't understand is that you are anything but that way with me, or from what I hear, in the lab or during class."

"When I'm working, I feel like a different person, like I'm in charge. I don't really see other people so much. I see a problem that needs to be solved and I attack it. I guess the other students have never seen me any other way, so that's how they think of me."

"And with me?"

Kate looks at him, her head cocked to one side a bit, her expression relaxed. "That is a mystery. Perhaps because of the way we met? Perhaps the way you treat me?"

"How I treat you?" he asks, taken a bit aback.

"You never order me around or talk down to me. You treat me … like an equal."

"Why should I treat you any differently?"

"You shouldn't, I suppose."

"Why do you let other people, like your roommates, treat you that way?" he says, gently challenging her.

Kate thinks for a long moment. "Habit, I guess. Training."

"You have to stop," Jake tells her. "It's not healthy and it's not you."

"In a way it is me. It's how I was brought up."

"Change."

"Easier said than done. Will you help me?"

Jake leans forward and takes her hand. "I will do everything I can, anything you want."

"Thanks," Kate says, breaking their eye lock. "We better eat. Breakfast is getting cold. I hate cold eggs."

They eat in silence, both lost in their own thoughts. Kate thinks about the possibilities of her changing; Jake about the woman he's sitting with. He looks at the time on his phone.

"I have to get out of here or I'll be late for class," he says, pushing back from the table, picking up his plate. "What are you going to do?"

"I don't have a class until this afternoon, so I'll go by my place. I need a shower and clean clothes."

"What about your roomies?"

"They're not home now," she says quickly before he says anything else.

"OK, I've got to go. You can stay if you want," Jake says, looking at the time on his phone. He digs around a drawer in the kitchen. "Here it is," he announces from the kitchen where they had gone to take the plates to the sink. "Here," he tells her, handing her a key. "Lock up when you leave. I have to run."

Kate takes the key, with some hesitation. "Thanks," she finally says, looking at the key in her hand, and then at him questioningly. "Are you sure?"

"Yep. Got to run," Jake says as he grabs his backpack, then his jacket, and heads out the door, leaving her standing by the table, a bit perplexed by what just happened.

Just as he reaches the door, he stops and turns around. "See you later in the Commons?"

"Yes, of course."

"Great. See you later," he says, smiling at her as he turns and runs out the door.

CHAPTER 23

Jake has a seminar followed by a class. As he walks out of his class, which was two hours after the seminar, he realizes he's been on automatic pilot the whole time and doesn't remember anything that was said. *'Good thing I take detailed notes,'* he thinks. Ever since he left home, he can't get Kate out of his mind. He keeps coming back to her and her situation with her roommates who seem to control her, or at least want to, and her seemingly split personality. He can't help a feeling of helplessness because he doesn't know how to help her, although she seems to want to break away from Dr. Jekyll.

At the root of his problem is that he doesn't really understand what is going on because Kate has not been completely open with him. Jake believes what she has told him is true, he is confident of that, but her story seems to have major gaps in it. He realizes that until he knows the whole story, any help he can offer will probably be lacking.

With his mind working overtime, he makes his way through the Commons, sitting down at the table where Samee, Setareh and Michelle already are. They are in an oasis of silence as they study amid the hubbub surrounding them. Jake silently sits down, still lost in thought, his gaze fixed somewhere off in space, his eyes not focused on anything in particular.

"Hello?" Setareh finally says.

Her voice snaps Jake out of his reverie. He blinks, shaking his head a bit, and looks around at the three faces staring at him. "Hi," he says.

"Welcome back to earth," Michelle says with a smile and a little laugh.

Jake just shrugs, raising his eyebrows a bit and tilting his head.

"So where were you?" Samee asks.

"Me?" Jake says, collecting his thoughts, getting his mind back to the here and now. "I was just thinking about something."

"Or someone?" Setareh suggests.

Jake gives her a weak grin. "Yeah, that."

"Anything we can help with?" Michelle asks.

"No, not really," Jake answers quickly. "It's just something we have to work out."

"Your relationship?" Michelle persists.

"No," Jake says.

"Then what?" she asks.

"Never mind," he says. "It's something I need to help her work out. But that's just between us. OK?"

"How about them Cubs?" Samee throws out, using the classic line to indicate the topic is closed.

Michelle looks unsatisfied but accepts the change in topic.

"I have to study," Setareh says, turning back to her laptop.

"Me too," Samee adds, picking his book back up.

Michelle just sighs, accepting defeat, as she goes back to reading.

Jake relaxes, relieved his friends have given up on the question and fishes some notes for a paper out of his backpack. He sits there, but doesn't see them, his mind still fixed on what he has begun to think of as the Kate Problem.

He isn't aware of the passage of time, and hasn't gotten any work done, when her voice cuts into his consciousness.

"Jake?" Kate says softly.

He looks up, seeing her standing next to him. He glances around the table. Michelle is gone. Samee and Setareh have both glanced up, exchanged "hellos" and then gone back to their studying.

"Hi," he says, looking back up at Kate.

"Can we go somewhere else?" she asks, looking nervously around the room.

"Sure. What's the matter?"

Kate glances at him and then the others at the table. "Not here."

"OK," he says, gathering up his stuff and standing up, not saying goodbye to the others, leaving them with questions that will have to go unanswered, at least for now.

"Not that way," Kate says, stopping him with a hand on his arm as he starts to head toward the front door. She heads toward the back of the room, leading him down a long hall where the restrooms are and out the back door that is seldom used because it leads to no place in particular. It's sort of an emergency exit because it only allows leaving the building, not coming in.

Jake is surprised by the route they are taking but says nothing, just following Kate out the door into a paved area used by delivery trucks bringing food and other stuff to the kitchen, the double doors of which are nearby to their left as they walk out. As they leave heading to the right, he catches up to her, taking her hand. She gives his a light squeeze but does not look at him.

"Where are we going?" he asks as they leave the asphalt, heading down a sidewalk that leads toward the College of Medicine.

"Shhh," she says.

Jake looks at her but stays silent as they walk about fifty yards. When they reach a small park area, Kate leads him off to one side, finally sitting on a bench under a big oak. Jake stands for a moment, just looking down at her. That's when he sees the tears running down her face.

"What's going on?" he asks, sitting beside her.

She looks forlornly at him, then away. "They told me I can't see you anymore," she says through sobs. "They grilled me about where I spent the night. I lied. But they didn't believe me."

"Who? Ashley and Kaitlyn?"

Kate just nods, staring at the ground.

"What gives them the right to tell you what to do?" Jake says, jumping to his feet, outraged.

"Nothing," Kate says. "I don't want to do what they say, but I … I don't know if I can resist. I know I want to keep seeing you," she says looking up at him.

"Well then you *will*!" he declares. "They have no right to tell you what to do!"

"That doesn't stop them," she says unhappily. "Or make it easy for me to resist."

"Did they give you a reason?" Jake asks in frustration.

"Not really. Ashley said something about me not knowing what's best for myself."

"Bullshit!" Jake nearly yells in anger, frustration, and disbelief. "Do you believe that?" he asks, forcing his voice to sound calm, as he sits back down next to her.

"I don't know," Kate says after a brief silence.

Jake sits back, looking at her, holding her hand in his. "Why not?"

"I don't know," she says again, sighing, looking at him, the misery on her face apparent. "I guess because of the way I grew up. I'm hardwired to do what I'm told."

"Except in the lab," Jake says quietly but firmly.

"Yes, except in the lab," she says, almost like a question.

"And with me."

"Yes, with you," she responds with a weak smile, the tears still running down her cheeks.

"You're not so hardwired after all. You *can* change your wiring."

"How?" she asks, looking at him, more in pleading than questioning.

"Hmm," he says, thinking. "How about you start by keep seeing me?" he says after a moment, a faux smile brightening his face.

"How can I do that without them lecturing me?"

"You probably can't forever, but we can start by not letting them know you are seeing me. We'll sneak around until you are comfortable enough with defying them that you can tell them to go to hell and make it stick."

Kate looks off into the distance. "I don't know if I can do that."

"I'll help you. Besides, I've always enjoyed doing what I'm not supposed to," he says, a lightness in his voice he doesn't feel.

Kate sits back on the bench and looks at him. "OK, if you help me," she says, drying her face with a handkerchief he gives her. "We won't be able to go into the Commons for a while."

"Why not?"

"I told you that they didn't believe me when I said I didn't spend the night with you, so they will be checking to see that I broke up with you. We'll have to go places they don't go to and won't look."

"OK," Jake says, thinking. "Any suggestions?"

"Let me think."

"OK," he says. "By the way, what did you tell them about where you spent the night?"

She gives a deep sigh. "I said I got drunk and woke up in some guy's place, that I don't know him and don't remember his name."

Jake nods, thinking back about how they met. "And they didn't buy that?"

"I'm a rotten liar," she says. "And I don't do that anymore," she quickly adds, an earnestness in her voice, "not since we've been together."

"Good to know. On both accounts," he says, laughing a bit as the tension begins to leave him. "Are you hungry?"

"Famished!"

"Where do you want to eat?"

"I want to cook for you," she announces.

"So they won't find us?"

"Partly," she responds sheepishly.

"How about we cook together?" he offers.

"That sounds better."

"We'll have to stop at the grocery store. I don't really have anything to cook."

"We can decide on the menu on the way," she announces, confidence and determination returning to her voice as she stands up.

Jake shoulders his backpack as he stands. They walk off, hand in hand, taking a route that will keep them away from the usual routes taken by students. It's longer but safer, and they enjoy walking together, discussing how much cash they have between them and what they will make for dinner. The meal has to be cheap. And they discard anything that will take time to cook since both are hungry. They settle on hamburgers with french fries and a lettuce salad, since Jake has salad dressing—vinegar and olive oil—and canola oil for frying at home, along with the necessary pans. At the store, they buy hamburger meat, half a dozen eggs, buns, lettuce, an onion, relish, and a couple of russet potatoes to turn into fries.

All the way to the grocery store, then back to Jake's apartment, they talk about everything but Kate's dilemma—happily chatting about classes they are teaching and taking, sports, movies, and music.

Working in the tiny kitchen, they quickly develop a kind of dance as they maneuver around each other. Jake makes the french fries, while Kate cooks the hamburgers. As she fries them, Jake reaches past her to get the potatoes into the hot oil.

Getting the food on their plates, fixing the burgers how each of them likes, they go to the table.

"Beer?" Jake asks.

"Sure," Kate responds, getting napkins.

They both sit down, clink the necks of the beer bottles together to celebrate their accomplishment, and concentrate on their food, eating in silence, with music playing in the background.

"How do we do this?" Jake asks as they finish eating and start to clean up.

Kate looks at him, her eyebrows raised, her head cocked to one side. *"This was your idea!"*

Jake laughs. "That doesn't mean I have a clue about how to pull this off."

"Well get a clue!" she orders.

"Yes, ma'am. Let me think a moment," he says, drying his hands after putting the last of the dinner dishes in the dish drainer. "How about … we pretend you have a boyfriend, or better yet a husband; you are cheating on him, and I'm the evil interloper who has seduced you into an affair," he says triumphantly, pleased with the scenario he has created.

Kate looks at him in disbelief. "That has *got to be* the dumbest idea I have ever heard!"

"Now, wait a minute," Jake says a bit defensively, not ready to give up on a story line he is proud of dreaming up. "I mean we just approach it like that. If we do, if we act like getting caught will be the end of the world, then we will be really careful and probably won't get caught. Besides, if we're sneaking around, we might as well have some fun doing it. We can make it a game."

Kate looks at him as if he has lost his mind. "You're crazy, you know that?"

"What's your point? Some of the best plans come from crazy people!"

"Name one?" she challenges him.

"One what?" he responds, thrown off his line of thought by the question.

"Name a great plan that came from a crazy person!"

"That's not the point."

"You can't, can you?" she challenges him.

"That's not the point," he persists. "The point is we can have some fun playing a game while we're doing this. Look, this sneaking around thing is a real pain in the ass. It can make us miserable. So why not make it a game and have some fun while we're doing it?"

Kate looks at him, dubious about the whole plan.

"So," he says, now pacing about the living room and avoiding looking at her, "your imaginary husband …"

"Wait a minute, I have a husband?"

"Don't worry; he's just imaginary. You have to have a husband to make this work," he says, flashing her a smile. "His name is … let's see … Kevin Ash."

"Kevin Ash? Where did that … oh, no, no you don't," she says, coming off the couch as she realizes that he is playing off her roommates' names.

"Why not? He has to have a name. Might as well be that as any other, Mrs. Ash."

"Don't call me that … *ever!*" she says sharply.

"OK, I won't," he says, taken aback by her tone.

"I don't like the idea of cheating on my husband," she says defensively.

Jake stops in midstride. "He's just imaginary."

"But we have to pretend he's real, don't we?"

"Yeah, I guess."

"I don't like the idea of cheating, whether he's imaginary or not," she says defiantly. "And why does it have to be me with a husband? Why can't you have a wife you're cheating on?"

Jake almost falls back on the couch, laughing.

"You find this funny?" Kate says sharply.

Jake just nods, unable to stop his laughter. "I'm sorry," he finally manages to gasp out, looking up at the angry woman standing in front of him. "We're not talking about a real person, you know?"

"It's the principle of the thing," Kate says, relaxing a bit as the humor of the situation filters in.

"Well, we'll just have to be unprincipled for the duration," he says, looking up at her, smiling. "Just in make-believe. And you have to be the one with an imaginary spouse because you are the one the private eye is following."

"The private what?" she asks, a bit confused by this addition to the story line.

"The imaginary detective your imaginary husband hired because he suspects you." He leaves out the words "of cheating" so as not to set her off again.

"All right," she says, returning his smile, "as long as it is clear that I don't like it."

"Clear as a bright, sunny day," he says, struggling to suppress his laughter.

Kate sits down beside him, starting to smile. "It is kind of funny, isn't it?"

"Yes," he says, his laughter breaking through.

"Oh, stop!" she says in mock anger, slapping him lightly on the arm.

"Ow!" he says, pulling back a bit, but his laughter actually increasing.

"Stop!" she says, smacking him again a bit harder.

He holds up both hands in a token of surrender.

They look at each other a moment with straight faces before dissolving into mutual laughter.

"I didn't know you were so moral," he chides her.

The comment is like a switch being thrown—all humor drains from her as Kate shrinks into herself, pulling away from Jake. The change is so swift and dramatic that it throws him. In his turn, Jake becomes serious, realizing he has said something wrong. What, he doesn't know.

"I'm … sorry," he says, not knowing what he is apologizing for.

"It's not your fault. It's mine," she says, tears rolling down her right cheek.

Jake reaches out and gently takes her hand. "What is?" he prompts her.

She looks at him as tears roll down both cheeks now. "You'll hate me," she says through sobs.

"That's not possible," he assures her.

"Yes, you will!"

"What did you do? Kill someone? Torture pets? Abuse children? What can be so bad?"

Kate collapses against him, crying softly. "I let them use me."

That confuses Jake. "Who uses you? Kaitlyn? Ashley?"

He feels her nod against him as she buries her face deeper in his chest. "How do they use you?" he asks. To his surprise, the question just makes her cry harder. He gently takes her shoulders in his hands and pushes her away from him so that he is looking into the eyes of this distraught woman. "There is no way I could hate you. Ever," he tells her, becoming intense. "Just being with you is, has healed me. I no longer have The Dream. Even when we are not together at night, I don't have it. I don't have to get drunk to sleep anymore. I can think about Charley without falling apart. That's all because of you. *You.* Whatever those two bitches are doing to you doesn't matter. Well, it does *matter* but not in how I feel about you. OK? This is a problem we will solve together. You and me. Me and you. Us. You understand?"

Kate nods. She wipes away her tears with the palms of her hands. Looking down at his shirt, she says, "I think I got you soggy." Then she wipes her hands on his shirt.

"Thanks," he says in mock sarcasm. "I guess I won't have to wash this now."

Kate smacks him lightly and then puts her head against his chest again. "I love you," she says quietly. "I feel safe."

"You are, and I love you too."

As they sit there, Jake begins to feel her breathing becoming deeper and regular. He realizes she has fallen asleep. He also realizes his right leg, which is pulled up beneath him, also has fallen asleep. It's uncomfortable, but he is afraid to move, so he doesn't, letting her sleep.

After about twenty minutes, Kate jerks awake, almost in a panic, sitting up. "I better go."

"Why?" he asks, straightening his numb leg.

She gives Jake a wry look. "I can't use the same excuse two nights in a row. I have to leave," she says, getting up. She heads into the bathroom to wash her face. Jake just watches her, straightening out his numb leg so it will regain feeling. Kate comes out and just stops, looking at him. "I'm sorry … I'm so weak."

"You're not weak," he says. "You're just healing. You have all the strength you need. You just have to find it."

"I will. I hope."

"You will."

Kate sighs. "I'll see you tomorrow?"

"You better," he says, looking at the clock. It is 11:38. "What are you going to tell your roomies about coming in so late?"

"They probably won't ask. I work this late a lot. If they do ask, I'll just tell them I was in the lab."

"And if they don't believe you?"

"Screw them!" she says defiantly, the emotion surprising herself.

Jake doesn't say anything, just enjoying the statement of defiance. 'It's a first step,' he thinks.

"Where will we meet?" he asks.

Kate thinks for a moment. "Here?"

"When?"

She looks at him wide-eyed, the expression on her face carrying more meaning than words ever could.

"OK, OK, it was a dumb question. You'll call me," he says, laughing as he stands, the feeling having returned to his leg.

He walks over to her. The two tightly hold onto each other in a long, deep kiss. Kate finally pulls away. "I have to go."

"Right. Do you want me to walk you home?" he asks.

"That's another dumb question."

"How about partway?"

"That works."

"Most of the way?" he offers.

"OK."

"To within sight of your place?"

"Quit while you're ahead," she orders him.

"Yes, ma'am," he says, grabbing his jacket as they head out the door.

Chapter 24

The next few weeks pass with Jake and Kate avoiding each other on campus, then meeting in the late afternoon or early evening at his place. They have dinner together, sometimes going out to places she doesn't think her roommates ever frequent, but more often cooking simple meals together or ordering in. Most of the rest of the time is spent studying, as they would be doing if they were in the Commons. The difference now is the occasional trip to the bedroom.

Kaitlyn and Ashley make periodic sweeps through the Commons. Since they know where Jake usually sits, they know where to look. What they don't know is Jake's usual pattern for occupying a table with his quartet of friends, so just seeing him in the morning and afternoon doesn't raise any alarm bells for them. But his friends notice that he is no longer there most late afternoons and never in the evenings. And they never see him at The Garage anymore.

Kate has disappeared from the Commons, but they are all reluctant to quiz Jake about it—afraid of what bringing up the topic may mean. What they also notice, which explains their reluctance, is he is not hungover in the morning; he isn't drinking. At least not heavily. No one wants to say anything that may get him going again.

But after three weeks have gone by, Karl can no longer restrain himself.

"So," he says casually, looking at Jake sideways early on a Thursday afternoon, "how's Kate?" The other three at the table all perk up, listening intently while trying not to be obviously listening, their faces buried in their studies.

"Hmmm?" Jake replies just as casually, not looking up from the book he's studying. "She's fine."

Now everyone looks at Jake, no more pretending.

"So," Michelle says, "you're still seeing her?"

"Seems so," Jake says, still looking at the textbook resting on the table.

"We never see her here anymore," Setareh says.

"Nope," Jake responds.

His four friends exchange questioning looks.

"Doesn't she like us?" Michelle asks.

Jake sighs and closes his book. "No, that's not it," he says without looking at them.

"Then what?" Karl asks, breaking the seconds-long pause.

Jake sighs again and looks at him, then others in turn, before going back to Karl and then looking off into space, trying to come up with an acceptable answer without telling them the truth. He doesn't mind them knowing; what he does mind is the embarrassment it could cause Kate.

"Is it something you can talk about?" Samee asks.

Jake sighs again. "No, not really. She and I are fine, and we are seeing each other. But there are reasons why she can't come here. Can we just leave it at that?"

"Is it something we can help with?" Setareh asks, looking intensely at him.

"No," Jake says. "It's ... something ... we have to deal with."

"You're involved?" Karl asks.

Jake's exasperated by all this questioning. "Look, guys, can we just drop the subject? It's not something I can, will, talk about. Kate has to work her way through a problem and I'm helping her. *Enough said.*"

"We just want to help," Setareh says, not willing to let it go just yet.

"I know you do," Jake says, resignation in his voice, "and I appreciate the offer. But it's not something you can help with. So *please* drop it."

"How about them Cubs?" Karl says after a moment of silence as the four digest what Jake just said.

"Well, the offer is always there if you change your mind," Setareh says.

"Why is it the Cubs and never the White Sox?" Samee asks. "No one ever says 'How about them White Sox.' They're in Chicago, too, you know."

"Good question," Karl says. "Maybe it's because the Cubs were so hopeless for so many years."

"Were not the White Sox in the same condition?" Samee counters. "At least that is what I have read."

"You read about the White Sox?" Karl asks in surprise.

"I have read about many American things," Samee says. "I want to learn about my new country."

"Guys!" Michelle interjects. "You can stop now!"

Karl and Samee both give her big grins. Setareh grumbles in frustration. Jake is just happy the interrogation is over. He starts to look back at his textbook; then, for some reason, he feels like he is being watched. He looks up, sweeping the room, until his gaze fixes on Ashley. She's standing halfway across the room, staring intently at him. He wonders how long she's been standing there as he stares back. Their eyes lock for a brief moment. Then she breaks contact and finds a table to sit at—facing him. 'So, I am being watched,' he says to himself. He looks away, to find Karl staring intently at him and then Ashley, then back again. Jake shakes his head. Karl nods and goes back to work. The other three did not notice the incident. For that, Jake is relieved; it would have just provoked a new round of questioning.

After about forty-five minutes, Jake looks up to find Ashley still there. He picks up his phone and texts Kate: "Where're you?"

"Your place," comes the reply a few minutes later.

"'Bout to head out. Ashley's here. Think she's following me."

"I'll stay here."

"Good," he texts back. Jake gathers up his stuff, loading his backpack. "Got to go, guys," he tells the others.

"Say hi to Kate for us," Karl says, a sly grin crossing his face.

Jake gives him a hard look. Karl just waves. The others catch the hint and just say goodbye.

As Jake makes his way toward the door, he glances in Ashley's direction. She is watching him intently and gathering her stuff up. As he pushes through the door, he manages to glance over his shoulder; yep, she is following him. He sets a stiff pace for the walk home, determined to give her a workout. As he approaches his apartment building, he sees the blinds have been pulled down. He wonders if Ashley will find that suspicious. But then, she doesn't know his habits, and probably not which apartment is his. Turning onto the walkway to the apartment building's door, he glances to his left, catching a glimpse of her about thirty yards away trying to hide in the shadow of a tree.

Jake smiles to himself as he goes inside. "Hi, Sweetie," he calls as he enters the apartment.

"Did she follow you?" a nervous Kate asks.

"She sure did. But with the blinds down, she can't see anything so we're safe. Besides, I doubt she knows which apartment to watch. For all she knows, mine could be on the other side of the building."

"I don't feel safe," a depressed Kate says.

"Want me to go out and tell her to fuck off?"

"For God's sake, no!" comes the horrified reply. "You do that, and she'll know I'm in here!"

"She won't know, just suspect," he replies calmly.

"That's bad enough. Just let her stay out there until she gets tired of watching."

"How long do you think that'll take?" Jake replies, fascinated by the dismissive attitude Kate seems to have adopted.

"It shouldn't be too long," Kate says thoughtfully, regaining her composure. "She has a major paper due in a couple of days, and it's going to get cold this evening."

"OK, so what do you want to do about dinner? We obviously are not going out."

"Could we order a pizza? I'm really hungry."

"Sure. The usual?"

"Yes ... unless you want something different."

"Nope," he says, pushing the contact on his cell phone for the local pizzeria they both like. When the phone is answered, he puts in their order for a large red-sauce pizza with extra cheese, onions and peppers, and mushrooms on half of it. He hates mushrooms, but Kate loves them. He gives his credit card information and his cell phone number along with the address.

"It'll be here in half an hour or so. Can you last that long?" he asks her.

"As long as it's not an hour. I'll be dead of starvation by then," comes the reply.

"We can't have *that*," he says, smiling.

Kate keeps staring at the windows. "I wonder if she's still there."

"Want me to look?"

Kate shoots him a look that makes him laugh. "If you'll stop asking that question, I'll stop asking mine," he offers.

"Deal," she says resignedly.

"You want a beer?" he says, going to the refrigerator.

"Juice," comes the reply.

Jake peers inside. "Grape, apple or orange?"

"Grape ... no, apple."

"There's nothing like being decisive," he chides.

"Shut up and get me the juice," she shoots back, happy and relaxed now.

He pours some apple juice in a glass and goes back into the living room with the juice and a bottle of beer. Handing her the glass, he sits next to her on the couch, and they both begin to work on projects on their laptops. Jake is putting together his thesis proposal, which he has found requires a lot of research, which he is doing online at the moment, taking notes as he goes along. Kate is wrestling with some equations that almost work—almost.

They take a break from working when the pizza arrives, adjourning to the dining table. No plates. Paper towels for napkins. They eat slices out of the open box, washing the pizza down with either beer or juice. Both are hungry, so they eat in silence, listening to the music Jake has put on, a mixture of oldies and contemporary, some with lyrics, some without. When they are done, Kate starts collecting the box, but Jake stops her.

"Don't. I'll get it later."

"OK. I guess we better get back to work."

Jake looks at the clock, 7:47, and thinks about the amount of work he has to get done this week. "I guess we should. Couch?"

"Yes."

They sit side by side for a while, then Kate stretches out, her back against the couch's corner, her legs stretched across Jake, who has to rest his laptop on her legs to keep working.

"You know …" Jake starts to say after working for several hours but stops when he looks over at her. Her chin is on her chest, her arms limp, her breathing deep and regular. Kate is asleep. Jake smiles, watching her, thinking about how beautiful and special she is.

He also realizes it's after 11. He gently shakes her legs. "Hey, lady, time to go to sleep."

"I thought I was already doing that," comes the reply, Kate not opening her eyes or moving.

"Yeah, well, a bed is more comfortable."

"I better go home," Kate says, stretching.

"You sure? You can stay here," Jake offers, hoping for a yes, expecting a no.

"No, not tonight," she says as she swings her legs so her feet are on the floor.

"You sure?"

"I'm not ready for a confrontation yet."

Jake looks at her contemplatively. "Will you ever be?"

"I'm getting there. Slowly. But I'm getting there. I'm just not ready yet."

"I'll walk you home."

"Partway," Kate says sharply.

"You know," Jake says as lightly as he can, "I don't know what's holding you back. You have no problem bossing me around."

"Shut up," Kate quips. "Go see if Ashley's still out there."

"After all this time?" he asks, half in humor, half incredulous.

"I know it's stupid," comes the quiet reply. "Please," she says, looking at him, pleading in her eyes.

Jake smiles at her. "Back in a moment." He grabs his jacket and goes out. A couple of minutes later, he's back. "All clear, unless she's hiding in a tree."

Kate has gotten her backpack ready and put on her coat. "You need new material."

"Want to write some for me?"

In response, she pushes him toward the door. "You're a better writer than I am," she tells him. "You come up with some."

"Bossy, bossy, bossy," he says happily as they leave.

"It's cold out here," Kate says, snuggling into her coat as they walk outside.

"Yep. That's why I knew Ashley wouldn't be here. She'd have frozen her butt off, along with other parts of her anatomy."

"True," Kate says, moving closer to Jake as they walk. He puts his arm around her, drawing her closer still.

"I like this time of night," he says.

"Why?"

"It's quiet. Not many are out. The cold keeps windows closed, so no noise from the houses."

"Except on frat row."

"Those guys don't know that speakers don't have to be turned all the way up all the time. I wonder how many suffer from hearing loss?"

Kate just laughs. "Good thing we're nowhere near there."

"Yep," Jake says, as the two fall silent, just enjoying each other's company and the quiet of the night.

"This is as far as you go, mister," Kate says when they come in sight of her place.

"You sure?"

"Yes, for now," she says, turning to face him and then giving him a lingering kiss. "Good night."

"Good night, lover."

She kisses him again, lightly this time, and then turns and hurries off. He watches her until she goes inside. He stares at the door for a minute, wondering what is going on behind that door. Then he turns and heads home.

CHAPTER 25

"Ash following me," reads the text Jake receives the next afternoon.

"Where are you?" he texts back.

"Black Cup," comes the response, Kate referring to a coffee shop just off campus that is popular with students.

"Can you shake her?"

"Don't know. Will try to meet u later. Luv u."

"OK. Sounds good. Luv u 2." Jake puts his phone away, feeling worried, disgusted, and angry all at the same time. He's worried about the impact this will have on Kate, who seems to have been gaining self-confidence; disgusted her two roommates are trying so hard to keep her under their control; and angry this could make her lose some of the ground she has gained.

But there is nothing he can do about it at the moment.

"Something the matter?" Setareh asks, seeing the deep frown on his face.

Jake looks up to find his four friends all looking at him with worried expressions. They are occupying their usual spot in the Commons.

"Never mind," he says dismissively, scanning the room looking for Kaitlyn. He doesn't see her, but that doesn't mean she isn't in the room, watching him. The thought crosses his mind he's becoming paranoid. Or perhaps he already is.

"What's amusing?" Karl asks.

"What?" Jake asks in return, realizing that he's now smiling a bit. "Oh, nothing really. Just a thought I had."

"Care to share?" Michelle asks.

"Paranoia strikes deep, into your life it will creep," he intones, quoting an old song by Stephen Stills.

"What?" Karl asks.

"It's from an old song my granddad used to sing—well, not the whole thing. He wasn't that good of a singer. In fact, he was pretty bad. No, he was awful. He used to play an album that song was on a lot. Buffalo Springfield from back in the sixties or seventies, I think. Something like that."

"And what does that have to do with anything?" Samee asks, confused.

"Yeah, what he said," Karl adds.

"Just remember, just because you're paranoid doesn't mean they're not out to get you," Jake says, gathering his stuff together.

"You realize you're not making any sense," Setareh says.

"Yep. Have to go," Jake announces, a big smile on his face now having decided what to do and leaving his friends wondering what is going on. He takes a few steps toward the front of the Commons, then abruptly turns and heads toward the back door. If Kaitlyn is following him, he will soon know. He walks quickly out the door and makes a sharp right. Hugging the wall, he goes about ten feet, then turns around and leans against the wall, facing the door.

He doesn't have long to wait. Kaitlyn emerges, quickly scanning the area. She comes to a sudden stop, as if she's just run into a wall, her head flipping toward him. Her eyes widen in shock as she sees him staring at her, casually leaning against the building. She quickly turns to go back inside but runs up against the fact that the door is exit only. She drops the hand she had out to grab the handle that isn't there. She looks back at Jake, who is still leaning against the building, still watching her. But now a small smile is on his face, a smile she finds unnerving.

"I can't get back in," she says, the nervousness obvious in her voice.

"Nope," he says after a brief pause. "You haven't been out through this door." It's a statement not a question.

"Ah, no, no I haven't."

"They won't let you go in through the kitchen doors," he drawls, waving his right hand toward them. "You have to walk all the way around to get back in."

"Yes. I forgot a book," Kaitlyn says defensively, looking around for a way to escape from this encounter.

"The shortest way is that way," he says, indicating the direction by jerking his thumb over his shoulder, enjoying her discomfort immensely. It isn't exactly the shortest way, but it is in the opposite direction from where he wants to go.

"Do you usually come out this way?" comes the nervous question as she debates whether to walk past him or go in the other direction.

"I like the solitude," he replies matter-of-factly, still not moving.

"Oh, well, I better go."

"OK." He realizes she wants him to leave before she has to walk past him, but he just stays in place. Her problem is that she's afraid to walk past him but doesn't want to show fear by going in the opposite direction.

"Well, goodbye," she finally says, working up the courage to walk past him, but giving him a wide berth as she goes by.

"Bye," he says, unable to stop himself from smiling, and feeling triumphant, as he watches her walk around the corner of the building. He waits a few minutes, happy in the thought that his paranoia has a basis in reality. *'Not completely crazy yet,'* he thinks as he pushes off from the wall and heads in the opposite direction from where he sent Kaitlyn.

When he comes around the corner to the front of the Commons building, he cautiously peers in the direction she would have come from. He scans the area, finally spotting her trying to look inconspicuous standing behind the fountain in the middle of the square between the Commons and the classroom building across from it. She is staring intensely at the opposite end of the building. Jake laughs to himself and walks quickly away, glancing over his shoulder occasionally to make sure Kaitlyn is still waiting for him. When she is out of sight, he picks up the pace even more to make it harder for her to catch up, should she suspect that he had gone in the opposite direction. When he reaches his apartment building, he stops on the walkway to the front door, looking behind him, searching for her. No Kaitlyn. He wonders if she is still waiting for him, or if she worked up the courage to go back around to find him. He'll never know, and really doesn't care.

When he gets inside his apartment, he pulls out his phone as he drops his backpack and jacket. He finds a message from Kate. "She's still here. I better go home."

"Call when u can," he texts back.

He goes into the kitchen to find something to eat. Pulling out some old spaghetti and sauce they had made a couple of nights ago, he puts some on a plate and sticks it in the microwave. Just as he pushes the button to warm it up, he remembers Kate's lecture about covering food so it doesn't splatter and make a mess as it warms up. He pushes cancel, finds one of the covers she had him buy, and then restarts the microwave. As it warms, he pulls out an open bottle of red wine and pours a glass. Then he carries his dinner and the wine to the table. Pulling out the book he had been studying in the Commons, he settles down to eat and read. Halfway through the meal, his phone comes alive with Kate's ring.

"Hi, Sweetie," he says, chewing quickly and swallowing.

"Hi," comes the soft, sad reply.

"Where are you?"

"In my room. What did you do to Kaitlyn?"

"Nothing," he says in as a matter-of-fact tone as he can muster.

"Oh, you did something," she asserts. "When Ashley came home, Kaitlyn started in about 'that jerk' ambushing her. I assume you're 'that jerk'?"

"Guilty as charged, I guess."

"What did you do to her?"

Jake tells her about feeling paranoid and then setting the ambush that caught Kaitlyn. "It was fun."

"Maybe for you!"

"Sweetheart, I don't give a good goddamn about your fucking roommates!" his anger growing as he talks. "If they don't like what I do, then they should just stay the fuck away from me! I don't like being followed, and they goddamned better know it."

"Calm down, will you," Kate orders him, keeping her voice low so it won't carry out of the room, even though the door is closed.

"Yeah, OK," Jakes responds, getting control of his emotions. "What happened with you?" He hears her sigh over the phone.

"I noticed Ashley following me when I left the science building. So I went to the Black Cup. I was hoping she would give up and leave. Instead, she came in and sat down at my table. She asked me if I wanted company. I felt trapped. I had to say yes, or she would have figured out something was up."

"And then?" Jake prompted her.

"She didn't leave. Finally, I said I was heading out and she said she'd join me. So I came home. I couldn't get away from her," Kate says, her frustration coming through the phone.

"You know, sooner or later, you'll have to confront those two."

"I know," comes the reply after a short pause, Kate's voice subdued. "That day is coming," she says, the strength beginning to return.

"Just not today?"

"Just not today."

"Can you come over? I warmed up the leftover spaghetti."

"I'd love to but not tonight. Not with those two the way they are behaving. And the stunt you pulled with Kaitlyn will make them even more suspicious. That could backfire on us."

'Or force you to confront them sooner,' Jake thinks. "Sorry," he tells her, "I didn't think of that." While that's true, the thought of Kate confronting them sooner, which he also had not thought of, appeals to him. "What do we do now?"

"We play it cool," she tells him. "No more stunts, OK?"

"All right," he says unhappily. "And if one of them follows me?"

"Ignore her. Just go about your business. After a while, they'll give up. I'll do the same."

"All right," Jake says in resignation. "When will I see you again?"

"I don't know," she says, exasperation in her voice. "Don't call me. I'll call you."

"Can I at least text you?"

"Yes," she replies.

"I don't like it, but you're the boss."

"Love you."

"Love you," he says, hanging up. He sits at the table, holding his phone, staring at a wall, not seeing anything. He realizes now that he screwed up by messing with Kaitlyn's head.

CHAPTER 26

Jake is sitting on his couch, his legs stretched out in front of him. It's Saturday morning. He's feeling lonely, and a bit lost. He had gone to The Garage last night and hung out with Karl and Michelle for a while, but it didn't feel right without Kate.

He left about 9 o'clock and wandered around, repressing the urge to call her. He wants to hear her voice, not just read the text messages they have been exchanging multiple times a day for more than a week. Her texts have become increasingly cryptic. He has no way of knowing what is going on with her. As frustrating as it is, he is respecting her edict not to call. But the problem is she has not called him. Several times he has found himself walking toward her place and had to force himself to turn away.

He still comes home every evening instead of spending it in the Commons with his friends, hoping she'll be there.

She never is.

So here he sits on this Saturday morning, with the bright sunlight streaming into the room. It doesn't help; he feels dark. He's staring at the phone in his left hand. He's sitting on his right hand to keep from calling.

He's lost in deep thought when a knocking on the door filters through to his consciousness. Part of him wonders who's at the door as he sits motionless. A few moments later an insistent pounding on the door shakes him into movement.

"All right, all right," he calls irritably, forcing himself to his feet. He puts the phone down on the table as he passes. "What?" he nearly shouts as he flings the door open, only to find himself assaulted by a flying brunette who wraps herself around him, driving him back a foot or two until he regains his balance.

"I'm sorry! I'm sorry!" Kate cries, burying her face first in his shirt and then kissing him all over his face.

"Hello to you too," he says, returning the kisses before they settle on a long, deep kiss. Then she hugs him, putting her face into his chest.

"I missed you," she says softly, resting her head on his chest.

"Me too," he responds, kissing her hair.

Kate unwinds from him, turns, shuts the door, then turns back and kisses him again.

"It's been too long," Jake says.

"Yes."

"What about your roommates?" He didn't want to ask but couldn't stop himself, his curiosity about what has been going on overwhelming any discretion.

"Fuck those two bitches!"

Her response, especially its vehemence, takes Jake by surprise. He steps back, holding her at arm's length. He just looks at her a moment. "What's this? The butterfly has emerged!"

"What are you talking about?" she asks, irritably, shrugging off his hands and hugging him again.

"I've just never heard you talk about them that way. It's nice, actually," he says, returning her hug.

"Well, it's how I feel," she asserts.

"Does that mean we don't have to sneak around anymore?"

"Screw them. If they don't like us being together, they can ..."

"I know, go fuck themselves."

"Exactly," she says. "I'm hungry. I haven't eaten since lunch yesterday."

"Off to the Delightful Chew? They're still serving breakfast."

"Sounds good," she says, taking his hand and pulling him toward the door.

"Wait! I have to get a jacket," he says, turning around. Walking quickly to the table, he pulls his jacket from the back of a chair and scoops his phone from the table. Putting on the jacket, he heads back toward the door, stuffing the phone in a pocket. Kate grabs his hand again, almost pulling him out of the apartment and down the stairs. Outside, she wraps an arm around his waist, snuggling against him as he wraps an arm around her shoulder.

"What brought this on?" he asks as they turn up the sidewalk toward the restaurant.

"Shut up! I don't want to talk right now. I just want to enjoy being with you on this beautiful day."

Jake starts to respond but then snaps his mouth shut, suppressing his curiosity, content for the moment just to be with her.

"But you have to answer one question for me," he says finally, hurrying on before she has a chance to shut him down. "Why didn't you just use your key? Why knock?"

"Because I wanted to. Now shut up!"

Jake's mouth opens and then clamps shut before anything can come out of it.

When they enter, Jake leads her to his spot, sliding into the seat by the wall, while Kate sits across the table from him.

"Haven't seen you in a dog's age," Vivian says to Jake in an accusing tone as she puts a cup of coffee in front of him. "I thought you had finally drunk yourself to death."

"He's stopped drinking for the most part," Kate says before Jake has a chance to reply.

"You his new honey?" Vivian asks her.

"Yes."

"Well, be careful of this one. He can be a real pain."

"I think I can handle him," she replies confidently as Jake just sits back, starting to enjoy the role of spectator.

"Humph," Vivian says. "You want coffee, Sweetie?"

"Yes, please. With milk," she responds, spotting the packets of sugar and sweetener on the table.

"Be right up," Vivian says as she walks away.

Kate looks across at Jake, her eyebrows raised. "You have a fan."

"Yeah, well, I've been coming here for years. Vivian has seen me at my worst."

"So I gather," Kate says, taking the menu Jake hands her from the two that are on the table. She peruses the offerings, then looks up to find Jake watching the world go by through the windows opposite him. "You know what you want already?"

"I get the same thing every time," he says with a shrug, still looking out the window.

"Doesn't that get old?"

"Not if I only come here once a week, which I do. Or used to."

"Aren't you interested in trying something new?"

Jake shifts his gaze to her. "I already have. I'm with you," he says, grinning.

Kate gives him a 'you're a silly ass' look and goes back to the menu.

Vivian comes back with Kate's coffee and some creamers. "You ready to order, Sweetie?" she asks Kate.

"Let him go first," she says, waving a hand at Jake.

"He hasn't ordered anything different in more than four years. Don't expect he'll change today."

"Nope, not today," Jake says lightly.

Vivian writes his order on her pad and then looks at Kate.

"By the way, I'm Kate."

"Nice to meet you, honey. I'm Vivian."

"Hi," she says, looking up a moment and then telling Vivian what she wants.

"OK. It'll be right up," Vivian says, turning to head to the kitchen.

The two drink their coffee in silence, Jake looking out the window, Kate gazing off, not focusing on anything, lost in thought. Jake has decided to let her start the conversation. He really wants to know what has been going on with her but realizes that he has to wait for her to bring up the subject.

"So," Kate says, breaking the silence, "I'm your latest honey."

Jake winces a bit. "Vivian has her own way of putting things."

Kate considers him for a moment. "What number am I?"

Jake stares down at his coffee a moment. "Three," he says in a near mumble. "Number three. After Charley, I was with Jennifer for a while."

"What happened?"

Jake winces again. "I didn't stop drinking."

"But you did with me?"

"Yes."

"Why? What's different?"

Jake sits back, looking at the woman across the table from him. "I don't know," he says very deliberately, pronouncing each word separately.

Before Kate can say anything else, Vivian brings their breakfast, setting the plates in front of them. "Enjoy," she says, looking at them and then turning away, shaking her head, to deal with other customers.

They look at their plates. Kate is hungry and attacks her pancakes and eggs with determination. Jake watches her for a moment, smiles, and then starts eating. Kate finishes well before him. She sits back as Vivian comes around to refill their cups. "Thanks," they both say, nearly simultaneously.

"You're welcome," Vivian replies, throwing a "you be good" look at Jake as she heads off.

Kate watches Jake eat for a moment. "I've had enough of those two," she finally says, steel in her voice.

"Oh?" he replies between bites of toast as he finishes his meal.

"I'm finally at the point where I won't let them, or anyone else, control me or tell me what to do."

"Good," he says, wiping his mouth and hands with a napkin.

"They started berating me about seeing you," she says, tears forming in her eyes. "They figured out we were avoiding them. They kept pushing and pushing. They want to control me, and I've let them. Just like my daddy and momma controlled me. And I let them."

"You were just a child," Jake says as reassuringly as possible.

"But I'm not anymore!" she spits out, anger in her voice. "I should not have let Ashley and Kaitlyn run my life. I should have never been their …"

Jake waits for her to finish the sentence. But she doesn't, her voice just trailing off. "My therapist—I told you I've been seeing one, didn't I?" Jake nods yes. "She told me I would be able to deal with my problems a lot better if I had a support system." She shrugs. "Problem was I didn't have a support system. I couldn't turn to my parents. My roommates were the opposite of help, as you know. Then," she says, looking at him, "I met you. You are the support system I need, or needed."

Jake snorts a laugh. "I've never been called a support system before. My friends would all say that I am the one who needs one."

"So perhaps, you're mine and I'm yours?"

"It would seem so," he says, smiling at her. "But you were saying?"

"I feel safe with you. I feel like you accept me for who I am and want me to succeed. You value my intellect."

"All true. But I still can't figure out why I don't need to drink since I met you, why I don't have The Dream anymore. Why you seem to have healed me. Weird. You're like a medicine."

"And I've never been called *that* before," she says, smiling in her turn.

"Perhaps," he says reflectively, "I needed to be needed. Does that make sense to you?"

"In an odd way, yes," Kate responds.

They both fall silent, just contemplating each other.

"Ready to go?" he finally asks.

"Yes, I'll pay," Kate says, looking at the bill Vivian had left when she picked up their empty plates and pulling money out of her purse. Jake starts to object, then stops—he likes this new Kate and doesn't want to do anything that might change things, such as acting like the dominant male to her submissive female.

"What now?" he says as they start to walk out. "Got work to do?"

"Not today," she says. "Let's take the day off."

"And do what?" he asks. It's been so long since he has spent a day not studying he has forgotten there might be other things to do.

"Anything we want! It's a beautiful day! We can go for a walk, we can go to the state park, we can just go to bed," she says, looking at him a bit shyly.

"We could do all of that," he answers, laughing.

"Let's go down to the river," she announces.

"Let's do it."

They spend the rest of the morning and most of the afternoon, walking along the paths of the river about five miles away in a state park, sitting on some big rocks, watching people fish and the water just flow by, sparkling in the sunshine. They stop for lunch at a dockside eatery.

"How about a movie?" Jake asks as the afternoon moves toward evening.

"Is a good one playing?"

"I don't have a clue," he answers, laughing. "We could go to the theater and find out?"

"Might as well," she says, taking his hands, pulling him to his feet from the rocks they're sitting on. They walk hand in hand back to his car and drive to the theater. None of the movies appeal to both of them, so they have hamburgers at a restaurant nearby.

"Let's go to my place," Kate says as the night's darkness deepens.

That startles Jake. He looks at her, eyebrows raised. "You sure?"

"I couldn't be more sure," she declares, the steel returning to her voice.

CHAPTER 27

Ashley's cold, hard stare and withering silence greet Kate and Jake as they enter the living room.

"Hi," Kate says, returning her look as she squeezes Jake's hand. Jake says nothing, deciding he's there to give Kate moral support, not to get involved in whatever is about to happen.

"Kaitlyn!" yells Ashley, who is sitting on a couch against a wall, not returning Kate's greeting or taking her eyes off her.

"What?" Kaitlyn says, coming out of her room. She comes to an abrupt halt when she sees Kate and who she has brought home with her. "Oh, it's you!" The words come out hard and disapproving. "You're not welcome here," she says, shifting her disapproving glare to Jake.

Jake says nothing, just holds Kate's hand a bit tighter, his jaw clamped shut.

"This is my home," Kate fires back, "and I will have whomever I want here!"

"Look, Kathy—" Ashley starts.

"It's Kate!"

"What?"

"You heard me!"

"You're Kathy to us," Kaitlyn interjects, stepping farther into the room.

"You can call me anything you want, but if you want a response, you'll use Kate. Understood?"

Her challenge is greeted by sullen silence from the other two. The three women exchange glares for nearly a minute before Kate breaks the spell.

"Come on," she says harshly without looking at Jake. She walks toward her room, pulling him after herself. She shuts the door and locks it after they get inside, flipping on the ceiling light.

"That was pleasant," Jake comments dryly.

"Bitches!" Kate spits out as she starts pacing the room, trying to work off her agitation and get control of her anger.

"So, tell me, how do you really feel?" he says as lightly as he can, trying to break her mood.

"How do I really feel?" she shoots back, obviously not responding to his attempt. "I would like to rip them apart! I would like to give them some of their own medicine!"

"I think you just did," he says, a bit of a laugh spilling out.

Kate comes to a sudden stop, glares at him and then her face softens. "I did, didn't I?"

"Yep. How does it feel?"

"Really good." Kate sits down at her desk, looking out the bedroom window. "That's the first time I've really confronted them. I didn't think I could do it."

"Well, babe, you did it," Jake says. "And you did it in style."

"Style?" she says, looking at him.

"Yeah, you didn't back down. Not a bit. You gave as good or better than you got. I think it's going to take a while for those two to get their heads around what just happened."

"You think?"

"Definitely."

Kate smiles at him a moment, then gets up, crosses to him, and wraps her arms around his neck. "Then give me a victory kiss!"

The kiss turns into the two undressing each other and ending up in bed. With their lovemaking finished, they lie curled together, Jake's arms wrapped around Kate's middle, her arms wrapped around his as they doze in and out. It starts raining. Jake listens to the rain and wind against the window, the storm's force coming in waves as he begins to fall asleep.

"I'm not a piece of meat." Kate speaks quietly and with deep sadness. Jake comes fully awake, startled by the words.

"I know," he says quietly and as gently as possible. He feels her starting to cry. He untangles one arm and strokes her hair. "I know," he says again.

"I let myself be used like a piece of meat," she says so softly he has to listen intently to understand her.

Jake stays silent, just holding her a bit more tightly with one arm, stroking her hair with his free hand.

"When their boyfriends brought their friends over, we all would start drinking. Sometimes I would get really drunk, like the night we met." Jake says nothing, just gives her a comforting hug. Kate begins sobbing. "And I let those boys. Do you believe that? I let them. Sometimes two a night. And I let them. I let them use me like a piece of meat." She swivels in Jake's arm, putting her face inches from his. "Do you understand what I'm saying? Do you understand what I did?"

"Yes," he says quietly and calmly, staring intently into the tear-streaked face of the miserable-feeling woman.

"Do you hate me?" she says, looking away from him, pushing him back a bit.

"Hate you? No. I happen to love you."

"Even after what I just told you?" she says, looking at him again.

"Yes."

"How? Why?"

"Look, I'm no virgin, and definitely not a saint. What matters, the only thing that matters now, is what you and I do from now on. We can't change our pasts, but we can make our future."

Kate's response is to give Jake a long, deep kiss and snuggle down into his arms. "I haven't let them get me drunk since I've been with you," she says in a whisper. Soon they are both asleep, lulled by a sense of peace by the sound of rain against the window.

In the morning when Jake wakes up, he is on his back, one arm stretched across the empty half of the bed. He sits up in a panic, but immediately calms down when he sees Kate wrapped in a bathrobe watching him.

"Good morning," she says.

"Yeah, good morning. You sleep well?"

"Yes. You?"

"Oh, yeah," he says with a grin.

"I'm hungry," she says.

Jake looks at her. "I'm sensing a pattern here."

"Good," she says, smiling. "Then you know it's time to feed me."

"Can I get dressed first?"

"That would probably be a good idea. I need to go the bathroom. I'll see you in the living room."

"Right," he says, swinging his feet to the floor and looking for his clothes. Kate grabs some clothes and heads out of the bedroom.

Dressed, Jake walks out into the living room. Ashley is there, sitting in a chair, reading. Jake glances at her and then walks over to the windows to look outside, partly to see what the weather's like and mostly so he won't have to look at her or try to make conversation.

"Do you know what she is?" Ashley says, the acid dripping from her voice.

"Who?" Jake says, not turning around, and immediately regretting having responded to her.

"You know who!"

"No, I don't know who," he responds, not willing to give her an inch.

"Kathy!" Ashley spits out as if she has a bad taste in her mouth.

"Don't know any Kathy," Jake says calmly.

"Yes you do! You just refuse to use her right name!"

"Nope," he says, still looking out the window. "Don't know anyone by that name."

Silence descends for a brief moment. "Oh, all right! You insist on calling her Kate!" The distaste that Ashley says that with is palpable.

"Oh, Kate. She's a lovely, lovable woman," Jake says without turning around, enjoying the small victory he's just won.

"You don't know her!" Ashley spits out the words. "She's a whore. She'll sleep with anything that has a penis. You're nothing special! She'll jump in bed with the next guy who comes along!"

Jake doesn't respond, choosing instead to watch a cat try to catch a squirrel that's running up the big oak next to the house.

"Just wait!" Ashley continues. "You think you know her? You don't know shit!"

Jake turns to look at Ashley. "I'm looking at shit right now," he says calmly. "What happens between us is none of your business." Before either one can say anything else, Kate comes out of the bathroom, dressed and ready to go.

"Ready?" she asks Jake, looking back and forth between the two.

"Never readier," he says, heading for the door. "The Chew?"

"I know another place I'd like to go to," Kate responds.

"Lead on, fair lady," Jake says, holding the door for her as they go out, leaving a steaming Ashley behind.

CHAPTER 28

*O*utside, the ground is wet and the pavement damp from the overnight downpour. The autumn air is clean and crisp, the pollen washed out by the rain. Kate and Jake walk hand in hand, not talking, just enjoying the bright, shiny new day and each other.

Finally Kate can't stop herself. "So, what did you and Ashley talk about?"

"Oh, I don't think she approves of me," Jake replies in a deadpan voice.

"Good."

"Good?" Jake asks, humor in his voice. "Why is that good?"

"If she liked you, I'd start worrying about you," Kate says, snuggling up against him.

Kate leads him about a mile past the campus to a small café with outdoor seating under an awning, a waist-high wrought iron fence surrounding most of the patio. She goes to a table off to one side. Checking to make sure the seats are dry after the rain, she sits down and smiles up at him. Jake is still standing, looking a bit perplexed.

"Kind of cool for eating outside," he observes.

"I like it out here, besides the coffee is good and will warm you right up."

Jake shrugs and sits down next to her so both can see the street. Just as he sits, a server comes out with menus.

"Hi, folks! Coffee?"

"Yes, please," Kate says. "Milk and sugar too."

"You got it," she says, handing them menus before disappearing inside.

Jake is looking around at the café and the area, which he has never seen before. "You come here often?"

"I used to. Not so much anymore … since I met you. But I miss this place, and I want to share it with you."

"I'm glad you did. The Chew's become a habit. Doing something different is nice."

"Here's your coffee," the server says, putting a carafe on the table along with two cups, a small pitcher of milk and some packets of sugar, as well as sugar substitutes. "Are you ready to order? Or do you need a few more minutes?"

"I'm ready," Kate says. "You?" she says, looking at Jake.

"You go ahead. I'll be ready by the time you're done."

"OK," she says, and then orders pancakes and scrambled eggs.

Jake gives her a funny look and then orders the same breakfast he gets at the Chew.

"Isn't that what you always get?" Kate asks.

"Yep. I want to compare the food and the best way I can figure to do that is by ordering the same meal. But tell me," he says, changing the subject, "how can someone as thin as you eat so much and not gain any weight?"

"My momma says I have a hollow leg, but I think it's just a fast metabolism."

"Fast? I'd say runaway." His comment is greeted with a laugh that almost turns into disaster as Kate was taking a sip of coffee, nearly spitting it out.

"Don't do that!" she tells him, wiping her chin with a napkin.

"Sorry?"

She just gives him a happy look in return.

"How did you find this place? It's not exactly on the route between your place and campus or near anywhere you go on campus."

"I like to explore. I found this place just taking a walk one day. No one I know comes over here," she says. "In fact, most of the people I see here are townies and some faculty. It's a good place for privacy, where I don't have to deal with anyone I know who comes along and wants to talk."

"Kind of blew that."

"What do you mean?"

"I know your secret now," he says in mock seriousness.

"You don't count," she shoots back.

"Oh, gee, thanks. It's good to know I don't count."

"You know what I mean," she says, lightly slapping his arm in fake disgust.

"Ouch. That hurts," he says in mock pain.

"You'll get over it," she says, sitting back as the server brings their food.

They spend the next hour eating, drinking coffee, and chatting about everything except Ashley and Kaitlyn, and what had happened that morning. Or what might happen in the future.

"Look," Jake finally says, "I didn't get any work done yesterday. Not that I mind that at all," he hurriedly adds. "I enjoyed yesterday immensely. I really did," he says, reaching out and taking her hand. "But I have to get work done today."

"I do too," Kate says. "I should go to the lab."

"I need to go by my place for my laptop and some other material. You have to go by yours?"

"No, everything I need is in the lab."

"OK, well, I'll work in the Commons. Want to meet me there later?"

"Sure," she says, starting to get up and then stopping, looking at Jake, who hasn't moved. "You coming?"

"I think I'd better pay the bill first," he says as the server comes hurrying out the door, a small plate with their bill on it. "My turn."

"Oh," Kate says, sitting back down.

Jake takes the plate, looks at the bill, pulls some money out of his wallet, enough to cover the bill and the tip, and hands it all back to the server. "We're good," he tells her.

"Thanks. You two have a good day," comes the reply.

"We will," Kate says, getting back to her feet as Jake stands.

"You too," Jake adds.

They walk outside the patio and back toward campus. When they reach the university grounds, they kiss and head off their separate ways.

Jake strolls back to his apartment, a sense of peace and happiness filling him he hasn't felt in years—since Charley died. He gets his laptop and other material, and heads back toward campus at a brisk pace.

CHAPTER 29

It's Sunday, so the Commons is mostly empty. None of his friends are there. Jake goes to the table he usually sits at, happy the area is deserted. He pulls out his laptop and notes, and starts writing. He works for a couple of hours, then goes to get some coffee. He settles back into his chair, pauses as he remembers where he left off. His fingers are about to go to the keys when Setareh comes running up.

"Help! I need your help!" she cries, urgency in her voice, tears streaming down her cheeks.

"You what?" Jake says, startled, his hands frozen over the keyboard.

"It's Samee! He's been arrested!" she says, sitting down next to him, both hands tightly gripping his forearm.

"He's been what?" Jake says, confused, his mind trying to process what he's being told.

"Arrested!"

"Why?" Jake is astounded by even thinking about that happening to a guy who is as peaceful as they come.

"They think he's a terrorist!" Setareh wails.

"Who?"

"The police! The FBI!"

"Why?" he repeats.

"I don't know!" Setareh cries, tears rolling down her face. "They say he's on a list of terrorists! He's not a terrorist! He told them that! I told them that! But they would not listen! They just put handcuffs on him and took him away! They said if I did not shut up and get out of the way, they would arrest me too!"

"Where did they take him?"

"I don't know!" Setareh wails. "I'll never see him again! They'll send him back to Syria! Or to Guantanamo! What can I do?"

Jake sits back, trying to absorb what is going on and to come up with some plan of action.

"Karl!" he finally says.

"What?" Setareh says, sounding uncertain and hopeful at the same time.

"Karl has contacts in law enforcement from when he was an MP in the Army, I think. And he has a poly sci professor who has government contacts," Jake says, pulling out his phone and calling his fellow veteran, knowing it's a long shot but not knowing what else to do. "Hey, Karl! Sorry to bother you, man, but Samee is in a jam big-time and we need your help! … Setareh and I are in the Commons. Can you meet us here? We'll fill you in then. … Great. See you in fifteen." He turns to Setareh, "He's on the way."

"Yes, but what can we do?" the distraught woman cries.

"Whatever we can," Jake says, trying to reassure her but not really having a clue what Karl could actually do.

"But what is that?" she pleads, her grip on his arm tightening.

"I …" Jake starts to say.

"What's going on?" Kate's question relieves Jake of trying to come up with an answer. Kate sits next to Jake and across from Setareh. She quizzically looks at Setareh's tear-streamed face, the panic in her eyes, the vicelike grip on Jake's arm.

"It's Samee," Jake says as calmly as he can. "He's been arrested, accused of being a terrorist."

The comment provokes another outburst of tears and wails from Setareh.

"What!" Kate looks back and forth between the two. "Why? On what grounds?"

"My guess is that the FBI has confused him with a terrorist with the same name," Jake replies.

"Then they'll sort it out," she says, trying to sound confident.

"What if they don't?" Setareh wails. "I'll never see him again!"

Kate stares at her, not knowing what to say or to do. She looks at Jake, who looks powerless.

"What's up?" Karl says, sliding into the fourth seat at the table, surveying the scene and seeing a distraught Setareh and the hopelessness on Kate and Jake's faces.

"Samee's been arrested," Jake and Kate say simultaneously. The comment sends Setareh into another fit of tears.

"OK," Karl says slowly. "Why?"

"They think he's a terrorist," Kate says quickly.

"He's not, he's not, he's not," Setareh cries.

"I got that," Karl says. "Who's they?"

"The FBI, apparently," Jake says. "It looks like he has the same name as someone on their watch list."

"Yeah, I can see how that can happen," Karl says.

"How can you say that?" a teary Setareh challenges him.

"Sometimes people have the same names or really similar ones," Jake interjects. "I know a guy who the cops keep stopping because he has the same name as another guy who is wanted for a whole list of crimes. Larry finally had to get a note from a judge saying it isn't him, but he's still getting hassled."

"That doesn't make me feel any better," Setareh says, sounding dejected and defeated.

"We'll figure something out," Kate reassures her. "Don't give up hope."

Setareh looks at her pleadingly. Kate pulls her chair next to her, wrapping her arms around the distraught woman.

"What," Karl says quietly to Jake, "do you expect me to do?"

"You were an MP. Do you know anyone who could help?"

"You're kidding, right?" he says in a dismissive tone. "I was a corporal, and I've been out for five years. Even when I was in, I was a lousy E-4. You know goddamned good and well I had no pull at all."

"Yeah," Jake replies a bit dejectedly. "I was just hoping. Wait a minute," he says, suddenly brightening, "what about that poly sci prof you are tight with? Doesn't he have contacts?"

"I guess he does," Karl replies thoughtfully. "I know he knows a few congressmen and a senator or two. I could ask him …"

"What's stopping you?" Jake asks.

"I'm not sure he will help. He doesn't know Samee."

"But you don't have to ask him to spring him, just to get someone to make sure the right guy was picked up. Do you think he'll do that?"

"He just might," Karl says, warming to the idea. "It won't hurt to ask. But this is Sunday; nothing will happen until tomorrow."

"But start on him now so he'll be prepped and ready to go first thing in the morning. We need to get Samee out before they ship him deeper into the system."

"Where is he now?" Karl asks.

"I don't know," Jake says, admitting to his ignorance. "Setareh, do you know where Samee was taken?"

"What?" she says, raising her face from Kate's now soggy shoulder.

"Do you know where Samee was taken?" Jake repeats as gently as he can.

"To jail," she sobs.

"Which jail?" he gently presses.

"I'm not sure," she says, confused. "I think it might be the one here. They said something about needing a place to keep him until they could move him."

"OK," Jake says, shifting his attention back to Karl. "If that's true, we at least have that going for us. Can you see if your prof will help? Maybe keep Samee here until this is sorted out."

"I'll see what I can do," Karl says, getting up to leave.

"Thank you," Setareh tells him through her sobs.

"I'll do what I can," he says as he strides toward the door.

Jake watches him go as Kate strokes Setareh's hair, trying to comfort her.

"I know a detective here in town," Kate offers, hesitation in her voice as she struggles to pull herself further into her new persona, to make another break with her past. "He may be able to help."

"How?" Setareh says, pulling back from Kate a bit, a hopeful look on her face.

"I … don't really know," Kate says hesitantly, surprised at herself for suggesting an action that goes against how she was raised, for a woman to tell a man to do something.

"But it won't hurt to ask," Jake says.

"OK," Kate says, slowly fishing her phone out of her purse as she struggles with the question of whether she can actually do this. She stares at it a moment, working up the courage to make the call. After listening a moment, she says, "Hi, Uncle Pete. This is Kate, Kathy. I need to talk to you. It's important. Please call me back as soon as you can." She ends the call, telling the others, "Voice mail." She's almost relieved that the call was not answered.

Setareh's face loses its hopeful look, reverting to her distraught appearance as tears resume their flow.

Seeing her friend deflate so suddenly, Kate pauses, takes a deep breath while working up the courage to try again, and then, doing a lookup, she calls another number. "Hi," she says. "Is Detective Johnston on duty today? … No, I don't need to talk to him … I'm his niece; I want to come up and surprise him … Thanks." Kate ends the call, looking at the other two in triumph. "Let's go!"

"You have an uncle who's a cop?" Jake asks.

"He's not really my uncle. He's a good friend of my Uncle Bobby. I just grew up calling him Uncle Pete. Now can we go?"

"Yes, yes, please," Setareh says, the urgency clear in her voice as she gets quickly to her feet, drying her eyes as she collects her coat and purse.

"Lead on," Jake tells Kate, almost lightly. She gives him a bit of smile and leads the trio toward the door.

CHAPTER 30

$\mathcal{I}$t's a twenty-minute walk to the city's police department. They make it in just more than ten, with Setareh continually urging the other two to move faster, finally driving them into a near jog.

The police department is housed in an older redbrick, three-story building which occupies a bit more than half the block. The rest of the block is taken up with parking for police vehicles and officers' cars.

Leading the way up a short flight of steps, Kate pauses at the double doors of the main entrance, her hand on one door. She turns to Setareh, looking serious, and says, "Don't say a thing. Let me do the talking. OK?"

"Yes, yes, but let's go!" Setareh replies, doing what she can to rush them into the building.

Jake just shakes his head in wonder at the strength Kate is showing as he follows the two women into the building and up another short flight to stairs into the reception area, a large square, brightly lit room.

A sergeant sitting behind a raised wooden desk that nearly spans the length of the room looks up as they enter. "May I help you?"

"Yes, sir," Kate says, almost deferentially, as she reaches the window, which is actually a thick piece of bulletproof plexiglass with a series of holes punched into it, stretching the length of the desk. "I would like to see Detective Johnston, please."

"What about?" comes the challenge through the small holes in the shield.

"I'm his niece."

The sergeant looks at her intently, then picks up the phone. Pushing numbers, he waits for an answer. "Sergeant Willis on the front desk. A woman who says she's your niece is here." Willis looks at Kate, "Name?"

"Kate. Katherine. Kathy."

The sergeant gives her a challenging look. "Which is it?" he demands.

"Tell him Mouse Kathy is here," she responds, swallowing hard and holding tightly to her courage.

Willis looks at her quizzically. "She says her name is Mouse. ... OK." He hangs up and, looking at her, says, "He'll be down in a bit."

"Thanks," Kate says, turning to the others.

"Mouse?" Jake asks.

"It's a pet name he gave me years ago," she replies, somewhat defensively.

"OK. Why?"

"Do you really have to ask?" she demands.

"No, I guess not."

"What's going to happen now?" Setareh asks, a bit hysterical.

"We'll see if he can do anything for us," Kate says matter-of-factly, portraying more confidence than she feels.

"And if he can't?" Setareh asks, panic creeping into her voice.

"Let's not worry about that until we talk to him," Jake says soothingly.

"But ..." Setareh is cut off when a big, heavyset man in a suit comes striding off the elevator and across the room.

"Mouse!" he roars, scooping Kate up and giving her a big hug, which she returns. "Great to see you," he says, putting her back on her feet. "I heard you were at the university, but you never come to see us."

"I'm sorry Uncle Pete. I should have. I just ... I don't know ..."

"That's all right," Pete says reassuringly. "You young folks have a lot to keep you busy. I hear you're in the physics program?"

"Yes, sir. But how did you know? My parents think I'm going to be a teacher."

"I'm a cop. I have my sources," he replies with a huge smile, resting a big paw on her shoulder. "I have to keep track of my favorite niece. And you being in physics is great. I always knew you had it in you if you just worked at it. Glad to see you did. Now," he says, glancing at her companions, "what brings you here on a Sunday? It's got to be trouble of some kind."

"Can we talk in private?" Kate says, staring up at the man who towers above her.

"Sure thing," he says, glancing around. "This way." He leads them into a small conference room off to one side of the reception area. He opens the door and ushers the three of them in, then closes the door behind him. "OK, what's this about?"

"A friend of ours has been picked up as a terrorist," Kate says.

"I don't help no fucking terrorists!" Pete declares.

"Samee's no terrorist!" Setareh cries, flying toward the detective, who instinctively readies for an assault.

Jake intercepts her, pulling her back and holding onto her shoulders as he says calmly but forcefully, "She's right. Samee's no terrorist."

"How do you know?"

"I've known him for three years. All he wants to do is become an American citizen and live here in peace."

"And you're an expert on this subject?" Pete says, looking him up and down. "You some kind of bleeding-heart liberal?"

"Navy. I was a combat corpsman; did two tours in Afghan," Jake says, a hard edge to his voice.

"Yeah?"

"You got a problem with that?"

The detective gives him a hard look, then relaxes. "No. Guess not. I was in the 101st when we went into Iraq in ninety-one."

"Hoorah," Jake says, quietly.

"Hoorah," the sergeant replies, turning back to Kate. "So, Mouse, what do you want me to do about this guy?"

"Wait a minute," she says, looking at Jake in surprise, "you never told me you were in combat?"

Jake just shrugs. "The subject never came up. We can talk about it later. Let's help Samee now."

"We think," Kate says, turning back to her faux uncle but still glancing at Jake a couple of times, "he got picked up because he has the same name as a real terrorist. Can you check it out or have someone else do that?"

"That's not in my jurisdiction," he replies. "That's the feds."

"Please ..." Setareh starts to say before a look from Kate cuts her off by stepping in front of her and giving her a hug.

"Detective," Jake says, "look, I know he's not a terrorist because I've known him long enough to trust him and know what he wants."

"What's that?" Pete challenges.

"He wants to marry this lady," he says, indicating Setareh, "and build a life for them here. Look, he's Sunni and she's Shi'ite. If you spent time over there, you know what that means. On top of that, he's from Syria and she's from Iran."

The detective gives Setareh a look of comprehension, nodding. "That kind of complicates things for them. Their folks can't be happy about that."

"That's putting it mildly," Jake agrees. "And they are already living together. They won't get married until next year."

Pete looks at Setareh. "She's dead." Setareh sinks back at the words.

"Not if she stays here," Jake says. "And life will be miserable and possibly really short for Samee if he's sent back. You know what's going on over there."

Pete nods, looking thoughtful. Then he looks at Kate, who is now standing next to Setareh, an arm around her. "This still isn't in my jurisdiction."

"Uncle Pete, you have to try. You have to do something to save Samee!" Kate's voice is hard and demanding, taking Pete aback even as it surprises her.

"Whoa, what happened to my Mouse?" Pete says, stepping back and looking at her up and down. "You ain't no Mouse anymore!"

"I've grown up," Kate tells him, feeling her confidence and self-assurance growing.

"I guess so," he says after a pause. "It's nice to see. And about time. I always worried about you. You never stood up for yourself. It's really good to see you've grown a backbone."

"Thanks. Now help us," she says forcefully.

"All right, I'll see what I can do."

"Should we wait here?" Kate asks.

"You can, but I wouldn't recommend it. This could take a while. I know some guys in the bureau I can call. Tell you what, you go about your business, and I'll give you a call as soon as I know something."

"How soon will that be?" Setareh says, grasping at hope.

"Don't know," Pete says. "It could be tomorrow or never for that matter. But," he says hurrying on as he sees the impact his words have, deflating Setareh, "I'll find out as fast as I can. OK?"

"Yes, yes," she says, hope returning to her voice.

"Thanks, Uncle Pete," Kate says, reaching up on her tiptoes to kiss him on the cheek.

"Anytime, Mouse," he says, then stops himself. "Can I still call you that? You've changed and for the better."

"Of course you can," she says, smiling at him. "That's been your name for me since I can remember. I would never want you to stop."

"Good," he says, "then I'll be talking to you later."

"Can I see him?" Setareh asks, the desperation in her voice clear to them all.

"No," Johnston says. "If they have him here, he's being held in isolation as a federal prisoner."

"Thanks. Bye," she says, turning toward the door, her head bowed, her shoulders shaking with her sobs.

"I feel sorry for her," Johnston says, watching her go.

"We do too," Kate says. "We better go." Kate reaches up and kisses him on the cheek again.

Jake says goodbye and follows Kate out the door as Pete heads toward the elevator.

CHAPTER 31

The next three days pass in a blur. Setareh stays hold up in her apartment, too distraught to leave or study. Michelle, Kate, and her other friends look in on her every day—when they can get her to come to the door—sometimes bringing her food and offering what comfort they can.

As for Kate, Jake, Michelle, and Karl, they go through the motions of study and work. None of their hearts or minds are in it as they worry about Samee and Setareh. Their conversations center on speculation of what is happening. All they know are the periodic updates from Pete, which usually come because Kate calls him several times a day. But all he can tell her is that he is working on it. He tells her gently that she doesn't have to call all the time, but she does anyway, unable to stop herself.

"What happens if they ship him back?" Michelle asks as the four of them sit at their table in the Commons.

"Don't even think about that," Jake says.

"We have to," Karl says. "We won't be able to do anything for him if that happens, but what do we do about Setareh? We have to have a plan just in case."

"He won't be," Jake says. "Life isn't that cruel."

"Do you really believe that?" Karl challenges him. "We both know better than that."

In response, Jake shrinks in on himself. "Fuck. I know that," he says, his eyes darting around. "It doesn't mean I have to like it. And in this case, think about it."

"I know," Karl says, patting him on the shoulder. "But reality is—"

"What?" Kate shrieks, her cell phone pressed against her ear, jumping out of her chair with such force it flies into the people at the table next to theirs, drawing protests which she and the other three are oblivious to. "You're kidding? When?" she says, forcing her voice to calm down but not her body—she's jumping around, almost dancing in excitement. "Thank you, thank you, thank you, thank you, Uncle Pete. I love you." Without ending the call, and still jumping around, tears coming down her cheeks, she almost yells at the others, "Samee is being freed. He's being released. Uncle Pete is on his way to get him from the jail."

By this time, the other three, sensing it was good news, are on their feet as well. Kate jumps on Jake who twirls her around as they start to kiss each other. It's only then that they realize everyone in the Commons is staring at them. Collecting themselves, they sit down but are unable to sit still.

"What happened?" Karl demands but with joy in his voice.

"They checked and found he has the same name as a terrorist on the watch list, just like we thought. So they are letting him go."

"Took them long enough," Michelle observes.

"Yes," Jake agrees, "but he's getting out. When and where?" he asks, turning to Kate.

"Uncle Pete is going to give him a ride home. He says it's the least he can do."

"Does Setareh know?" Michelle asks. "We have to call her."

"No," Jake says quickly. "We have to get over there. If we call her, she'll just go nuts waiting."

"Let's go!" Karl says, grabbing his jacket and stuff, and just about running toward the door, with the others strung out behind him as they all bump into chairs and tables, offering a quick "Excuse me" or "Pardon me." Those farther away from them, seeing the commotion, get out of the way. They don't know what is going on, but it's obvious these four are in a hurry.

Karl nearly knocks over a couple of girls trying to come in. They jump out of the way as he flies through the door they have partially opened. As they start back in, the other three come flying past them, offering hurried apologies.

The four friends start running toward the apartment Setareh and Samee share, about two miles away. Eventually they slow down to a trot as they all become winded.

"Hello?" Kate says, stopping to answer her phone, which was in a back pocket of her pants. "Daddy? ... I can't talk right now. I'll call you back later. ... No, I'm not disrespecting you. I just can't talk now. Bye." She ends the call.

Realizing Kate has stopped, Jake comes back to see what is going on.

"Everything OK?" he asks, breathing heavily.

"Yes. I don't know," she says, somewhat exasperated. "It was my daddy. He's upset about something. I'll just call him later," she says as she puts her phone away and starts running to catch up to Karl and Michelle.

"Right," Jake says, turning to join her.

The pair have nearly caught up as the other two reach the apartment house door. They race inside, pass the elevator, and run up three flights of stairs and down the hallway. They are all breathing heavily when they reach apartment 3G.

Catching his breath first, Jake pounds on the door. "Setareh! Open up! Setareh! Samee's coming home! Setareh!" He is joined by the other three, Karl pounding on the door with him, all of them calling her. Those in neighboring apartments respond before she does, opening their doors, some venturing into the hallway to see what the commotion is about.

Finally, the door opens slowly. Setareh looks at the four of them in turn, disbelief and hope mixed in her expression, her face wet with tears, her eyes red. "Are you sure?"

"Yes, yes," Kate says excitedly. "Uncle Pete called. He's bringing Samee home. They should be here anytime."

"Oh, I look a mess!" Setareh says, her hands going to her face and hair. "I can't let him see me this way!"

"He won't care," Karl says. "Trust me."

"No, I have to get in a good dress, wash my face, do my hair," she says, looking a bit panic-stricken.

"All he will want to see is you! And you'll look beautiful to him just the way you are," Jake tells her, grabbing her hand. "Come on! The first thing he'll want to see when he gets here is you! We have to get out front!"

"No, I have to look beautiful for him! I'm such a mess!"

"You're beautiful already!" Kate says, grabbing her other hand as the two of them pull her out of the apartment. The four of them usher her into the elevator, Setareh still resisting some.

"I haven't changed clothes in days," she protests, indicating the blouse and jeans she's wearing. "I can't let him see me like this!"

"He won't care what you're wearing," Michelle says, her hands on Setareh's back to keep her from breaking free and returning to the apartment. Finally, they get her out the door and onto the walkway in front.

"I don't see him!" Setareh protests, forgetting about changing clothes and doing her hair. "Where is he?"

"On the way," Kate assures her. "Uncle Pete had to go to the jail to get him. It's about a forty-five-minute round trip, so they should be here in a few minutes."

"I have time to change clothes …" Setareh's protest is cut short by the sound of a police siren.

An unmarked car with lights and siren comes racing down the street to come to a sudden stop in front of the apartment house, facing against traffic. Johnston jumps out of the driver's door, and reaching back, opens the passenger door. Samee comes flying out and into Setareh's arms. The two kiss passionately. The others standing back to give them room.

Kate walks over to Pete and gives him a hug, wrapping her arms around as much of his middle as she can reach. He reaches down to kiss her on top of her head.

"Thanks, Uncle Pete. You're wonderful," she says, holding on tightly.

"Yeah, remember that next time you get pissed at me," he says, jokingly.

"I'll try," she replies, looking up at him and smiling.

"Thanks," Jake says, holding out a hand. "This is a great thing you did. You saved those two."

"Just doing my job," Pete replies. "Besides, I was afraid of what Mouse here would do to me if I didn't," he says jokingly, shaking Jake's hand while still having one arm around Kate. "So, you're going by Kate now?" he asks, looking down at her as they separate.

"Yeah, it fits better."

"How's that?"

"I've grown up. I'm not a doormat anymore. For anyone."

"Anyone?" Pete asks skeptically.

"Anyone!" she says defiantly.

"Good. Don't lose that," he tells her. "I like you better this way."

"Thanks."

"I got to roll," he says, turning back to the car. "You stay in touch now," he orders her as he gets in.

"I will. And thanks again, Uncle Pete. I owe you big-time."

"You can pay me back by making a good life for yourself," he says as he shuts the door and drives off.

"I will!" she calls after him, waving.

"Nice guy," Jake comments as they watch the car disappear.

"Yes, he is," she says contemplatively. "They're going inside," she says, looking toward Setareh and Samee.

Jake looks over at the couple who are holding each other as closely as possible, oblivious to everyone and everything else. "I guess the celebration can wait. Those two want to be alone."

"I'm hungry," Karl says, walking over to them along with Michelle.

"Where do you want to go?" Jake asks.

"That Italian place around the corner. Cheap and lots of food."

"He's always thinking with his stomach," Michelle says, patting his tummy.

"I'm a growing boy."

"Growing which way?" Jake chides him.

"Aww shut up," Karl says jokingly.

"I'm hungry, too," Kate says. "Let's go."

The four of them spend the next two hours eating and talking, enjoying life now that their friends are back together. They decide they'll wait for them to reappear before having a celebration. They also decide they need to get Uncle Pete a thank-you gift. Bourbon being his favorite drink, they pool their money to buy him the best they can find. Kate volunteers to be responsible for picking it out and delivering it. When they leave the restaurant, the two couples walk together for a few blocks before going their separate ways.

"Your place or mine?" Jake asks.

"Yours. I don't feel like dealing with those two tonight. I don't want to spoil the mood."

"Gotcha."

"Shit!" Kate says, coming to a sudden stop. "I forgot to call Daddy back. He's going to be really mad." She pulls out her phone, scrolls through the contact list and pushes the icon.

"Hi, Daddy," she says, standing in the middle of the sidewalk, the night's darkness deepening around them as Jake watches her curiously. "Sorry I couldn't talk earlier. … What? … I did not … No! Uncle Pete was happy to help. … What do you mean it's not a woman's place to boss a man? … That's just not right. … I have every right … That's not fair … Samee is not a terrorist! … Uncle Pete wouldn't have gotten him out of jail if he was. … What? … How dare you! … I don't screw every man I meet! … He and his fiancée are friends. … Yes, she's Moslem, too. … What? I can have any friends I like! … No, I won't come home! … I'm my own person; I'm no one's property! … What? … Don't be like that! I'm your daughter! … Daddy? Daddy?"

Kate looks at her phone, the shock on her face showing even in the dark. She looks up at Jake. "He's says I'm not his daughter anymore." She looks back at her phone and then back at Jake, the tears starting to run down her face. "He says no daughter of his would have anything to do with camel jockeys. He says no daughter of his would disrespect her daddy. He says I can never come home."

Jake wraps his arms around her, pulling her close, feeling her tremble against him. "I have no family," she says softly.

"Yes, you do," he says gently. "You have me. You have Karl. You have Michelle. You have Samee. You have Setareh. And you have Uncle Pete. He's proud of you, you know."

"But my daddy? My momma?"

Jake sighs. "Either they'll come around or they won't. You can't go back to what you were. You're not a doormat for anyone anymore," he says, paraphrasing her. "You will survive and thrive."

"Yes, I will!" Kate says defiantly, pushing away from Jake. "I will survive!"

"Good. Now can we go home. That was a really big dinner, and I need to sit for a while."

"You're a jerk, you know!" she says in a joking tone.

"You're just finding that out now?"

In response, she hits him lightly on the arm, then grabs his hand and pulls him in the direction of his apartment. As soon as he's next to her, she wraps her arms around his left arm, resting her head on his shoulder. They walk the rest of the way home that way.

In silence.

Chapter 32

The joyous mood is spoiled.

Kate sits in a chair staring at the window. She can't see out of it because of the deep darkness on this moonless night. Her eyes are not focused on anything anyway. A look of profound unhappiness is on her face.

But she is not crying.

Jake says nothing, just sits on the couch near her, waiting for her mood to crack, quietly reading a book but holding it in such a way that he can glance over the top of it to keep watch on her.

This silent tableau lasts for more than half an hour. Kate finally stirs and sighs. Swallowing, she looks around until she finds Jake. Smiling weakly at him, she asks, "Have you been sitting there long?"

"No longer than you've been sitting there," he replies, closing the book and setting it on the table.

Kate just nods and looks away, back into space. "I've been thinking …"

Jake is tempted to ask her about what as her voice trails off into silence, but restrains himself, giving her space and time.

"I've been thinking," she says again, giving a deep sigh. "Daddy will either get over it or he won't. But I can't go back to the way I was. I can't be that girl again. Not anymore." She smiles weakly at Jake, who just nods. She looks away again. "Momma and I can talk on the phone when Daddy's at work. … I'll miss seeing them. Even after all they've done … I still love them … but I can't be that girl anymore." She sighs again and looks at Jake. "I'm tired. So very tired."

"Then let's get some sleep," he offers quietly.

Kate just nods. Jake stands up, takes her hand, and gently leads her to the bedroom. Soon they are in bed, with Jake holding her. She quickly falls asleep; he just lies there, feeling her quiet breathing through the T-shirt she's wearing. Somewhere in the night he drifts off to sleep.

When his eyes open, Jake realizes that he's been sleeping and that it's morning; the sunlight is filtering in through the blinds. He and Kate are in the same position they were when they went to bed. He knows they both have seminars this morning, and he doesn't know what time it is. He decides not to worry about that right now. Not after yesterday. Not after last night. He raises his head slowly to look at Kate. Her face is peaceful. At least what he can see of it through the hair that has drifted over it. He smiles to himself and then gently disentangles his body from hers. He gets out of bed quietly and slowly so as not to disturb her. Getting up, he looks at the clock on the night table—6:45. 'Good,' he says to himself. His seminar isn't until 9:40; hers is at 11:40. And that's all either of them have today.

He goes into the kitchen and starts coffee. Then he quietly pulls out the flour, eggs, milk, and other ingredients for pancakes. He's just about ready to start cooking when Kate comes wandering out of the bedroom.

"Good morning," she says, brushing her hair back from her face, her voice content. She looks rested and refreshed.

"Good morning, Sunshine," he says, smiling at her. "Sleep well?"

"Yes, beautifully. But I need coffee. The smell woke me up and drew me like a magnet."

"The coffee is self-serve. The pancakes will be ready in a bit if you want to sit at the table."

"Mind if I stay here?" she asks, getting a cup from the cabinet. "I could use the company."

"I would like that," he says. By staring at the cooking pancakes instead of looking at her, he succeeds in suppressing a nearly overwhelming urge to ask her about her parents and how she feels about them this morning.

"I have a seminar this morning," she says.

"Yeah, so do I. But we have time for breakfast and a shower before heading out."

"That's good. I could use breakfast and a shower. I'm hungry and I feel kind of grungy."

"You don't look it," he says, glancing at her as he puts some pancakes on a serving plate and pours the rest of the batter into the pan.

"You're prejudiced," she observes, smiling.

"Yeah, well, so what? Prejudice ain't always bad," he says lightly. "At least not in this case."

"OK, mister, have it your way."

"I will, my lady." They fall silent. Kate pulls out plates, tableware, and napkins, setting the table. While Jake takes the last of the pancakes out of the pan, she gets butter and syrup from the refrigerator. They sit down to eat, the silence heavy between them. She's still sorting out her feelings and thoughts; he's not willing to broach the subject.

After breakfast, they shower and get dressed. Kate has started leaving some clothes and other stuff at Jake's place. Then while Jake finishes clearing up from breakfast, Kate pulls out two travel mugs. Pouring the last of the coffee into them, along with some milk and sugar in hers, she hands one to Jake as they head for the door on their way to campus, walking in silence.

"You going to the Commons until your seminar starts?" Jake asks when they are halfway there.

"No, I have some work to do at the lab first. I'll meet you there for lunch. OK?"

"Sounds good."

Silence descends between them again.

"Look, Jake," Kate finally says as they near campus, "I know you want to know what's going on with me …"

"I haven't said a thing," he protests.

"You forget who you're talking to? I know you," she challenges him. He just shrugs.

"I want to tell you, but right now I can't," she says, somewhat exasperated. "I can't because I don't know myself. I'm still trying to sort all this out. Just be patient with me."

"I love you," he says, kissing her hair.

"Back at you," she says, squeezing his hand.

They walk for a few more minutes in silence. "I've got to go this way," Jake says as they reach a split in the sidewalk on campus, his head nodding to the left.

"And I've got to go this way," she responds, nodding to the right.

"See you for lunch."

"See you for lunch."

A brief kiss and they go their separate ways.

CHAPTER 33

Jake is with Samee, Setareh, and Michelle when Kate finds them in the Commons shortly after 1:30 p.m. Samee and Setareh are sitting as close to each other as possible, both on the edge of their chairs, holding on to each other as if each is afraid the other will disappear.

"Hi," Jake says, waving at her as she approaches.

"Hi back at you!" she says, smiling.

The others turn toward her, wave and greet her.

"Samee was just starting to tell us what it's like being in jail," Michelle tells her as Kate pulls up a chair to sit next to Jake.

"Really?" she says, looking at Samee.

"Yes," Samee says, "it was an experience. And not a good one."

"I bet," Kate says.

Samee resumes his tale, about how he was kept in isolation, how he was fed baloney and cheese sandwiches for all three meals, along with water and, in the morning, coffee. He didn't eat the baloney because the guards either wouldn't tell him or didn't know if there was pork in it. And, of course, it wasn't halal. He slept on a cot with one blanket, meaning he was cold at night. He had no TV, no radio, nothing to read, and no one to—the guards weren't interested in conversation with someone they thought of as a terrorist. And how happy he was when he was freed.

"I cannot thank you enough for saving me," he tells Kate. "Without your help, who knows what would have happened to me."

As he talks, Setareh begins to cry softly and hold him tighter. He strokes her hair and kisses her forehead.

"Don't worry about it," Kate tells him. "It's the least I could do."

"We'll never forget you," Setareh says, regaining her composure.

"Thank you," Kate replies in a subdued voice, choking up.

"On the bright side," Samee says, "you are all invited to a celebration tonight at our place. We are going to have a feast—all kinds of Syrian and Persian dishes. We're going home in a bit to start cooking, and we want you to come."

"Of course we will," Jake says.

"And bring your detective uncle," Setareh says. "We want to thank him especially. If it wasn't for his help, I may never have seen Samee again."

"I'll ask him," Kate says skeptically. "Uncle Pete is not one for social events with people he doesn't know well. Believe it or not, he's kind of an introvert."

"Well, ask him, please," Samee says.

"Trust me, I will. But if he doesn't come it's only because he would be embarrassed to be the center of attention. But I'll try."

"Good," Setareh says.

"We have to go," Samee says, unwinding from their mutual grip.

As they collect their stuff, Michelle looks at her watch. "Crap, I'm going to be late for practice," she says. "Bye, guys." She grabs her backpack and heads out at a near run.

"Oh," Samee says, turning back as he and Setareh start to leave, "remember, no alcohol."

Jake just gives him a dismissive wave.

"Alone at last," Jake says lightly as they watch the other three head out.

"Why no alcohol?" Kate asks.

"Setareh is more observant than Samee, and the Koran bans intoxicants."

"I'm hungry," Kate says.

"Of course you are," Jake responds, drawing a smack on the shoulder. "Ouch!"

"Come on, cripple. Let's get some lunch."

"Right," he says, getting up.

When they get back to the table, they unload their trays and start eating in silence. Jake wants to ask her about her parents and how she's doing. Kate starts to say something several times during the meal, but then decides not to. That sets the pattern for the next several days.

That night, they go to the celebration, and even Uncle Pete and his wife make a brief appearance, much to the joy of Samee and Setareh. They leave after about half an hour, laden with Middle Eastern food.

When they're alone, Jake restrains his curiosity. Kate starts to say something a number of times, but then either stops or says something else. Finally, one evening when they are alone in her bedroom, locked away from her roommates, she broaches the topic.

"Sweetheart," she says to Jake, sitting down next to him on the bed, "thank you for giving me room with this thing about my family."

Jake just nods in response.

"I can't tell you," she says, taking his hand and squeezing it. "I'm still trying to figure it out myself. I keep going back and forth: Do I just walk away from them? Do I try to heal the rift? If I do, how do I do it? Daddy is a hard man who is dug in with his beliefs. I can't change him, I can't reason with him, and I won't go back to the way I was. I could pretend when I'm around him. But that would be a lie. And I don't know if I can do that. I don't know if I *want* to do that. And if I do that, how do I build a new kind of relationship with him and Momma? My mind is just running in circles. I just don't know what to do or what I want to do. The whole thing is making me dizzy."

"You know," Jake says, stroking her hair, "I think you have already decided what to do. You just can't bring yourself to face the implications of that."

An extremely unhappy Kate looks at him, and sighs. "I hate you," she says flatly. Jake smiles in response. "What am I going to do?" she pleads.

"*You* are going to live your life. *You* are going to find a way to build a new relationship with your parents. I don't know your dad. I don't know if he'll ever accept you. You may have to live with that. But, you know, I find it hard to believe any father would completely turn his back on his daughter. Just keep trying. Don't give up, but, above all, be who you are and hold onto that."

"You think?" Kate says quietly.

"I think. I also think it's late, we both have stuff to do early tomorrow and I'm sleepy. You are wearing me out."

Kate gives him a light punch in the stomach. "OK, bed it is."

As they undress, Jake stops in the middle of taking off his pants, one leg in and one out. "Can I ask you something?"

"Sure," Kate says.

"What does your father say about you working on a master's in physics?" he asks, resuming undressing.

"Nothing, because he doesn't know," Kate answers, slipping into a nightgown.

"He doesn't know?"

"He thinks I am going to be an elementary school teacher."

"Oh? That's right. That's what you said to Pete," he replies, recalling that bit of the conversation he hadn't paid any real attention to at the time.

"I lied. What can I say?" she says with a shrug. "It's a job he thinks is right for a single woman."

"Oh," is all Jake can manage to respond with.

"He's told me that I can do that until I get married, and then I must stay home to take care of my husband and kids."

"Really?" Jake says, humor creeping into his voice at the thought of anyone telling their daughter that in this day and age.

"Really."

"Well, how do you explain it taking so long for you to graduate?" he asks, wondering how she pulled this off.

"I told him I was going to school and working part-time as a waitress."

"A waitress. Not a lab research assistant." Jake says it as a statement of fact, not a question. "So you are already lying to him," he adds, immediately sorry for having thrown that in her face.

"If I had told him the truth, his head would have exploded," she says, sadness and a sense of fatalism in her voice. "And I would have been kicked out a lot sooner. But no more lies. I'm past that."

"And the husband thing?"

"He thinks I am looking for one. I guess none of it matters anymore. I can tell him the truth about everything," she says with a sigh, sitting on the bed. "Assuming I ever talk to him again."

Jake doesn't respond, letting the conversation end there, and wondering whether Kate has found a candidate for a husband by accident. "Sleep. I need sleep," he finally says. They crawl into the queen-size bed and are quickly asleep.

In the morning, they run the gauntlet of hostile stares and snide remarks from Ashley and Kaitlyn.

Kate and Jake now just ignore those two and spend less and less time at the apartment. Kate no longer keeps much food there, and when they are together, they don't eat there, grabbing something on their way to campus or at the Commons.

The roommates' hostility to Kate's relationship with Jake no longer bothers either one of them. In fact, they now joke about it, finding humor in the mounting frustration those two women apparently are suffering from because of their inability to get a rise out of Kate, or get rid of Jake. They can no longer even get an acknowledgment of their existence from either Kate or Jake, who breeze around the apartment as if they are the only ones there. Several times either Ashley or Kaitlyn would blast music in an attempt to get a response. It didn't work. Kate bought earplugs which, behind the closed bedroom door, worked well enough to make the noise tolerable. Then one night the people who live downstairs called the police about the noise. That official visit marked the end of that stunt.

CHAPTER 34

With Kate having started to confront her family problem, and Samee and Setareh recovering from the terror of his arrest, the six friends fall back into their old routines of class, work, study, and hanging out together.

The only major change is when Karl and Michelle tell the others they are engaged—no wedding date has been set. The announcement launches the three women into extensive discussions about, first, rings, and then, wedding plans. Neither Karl or Michelle has much money, nor do their families. So, the wedding, when it comes, will be simple and inexpensive—"cheap" is the word Karl repeatedly uses, irritating Michelle to no end, who keeps correcting him. "The word is inexpensive," she keeps telling him. Children are not mentioned—but only barely. Karl keeps cutting Michelle off when she starts to bring up the topic. Kate just looks at Jake and raises her eyebrows with a sly grin.

Kate and Jake now spend most of their time at his apartment, sleeping at hers only occasionally and going there to get things she needs. More and more of her stuff is staying at his place, and they talk on and off about her moving in, partly to get away from her roommates and mostly because they are spending most of their time together anyway. The only real roadblock is that Kate's name is on the lease along with the other two, so whether she's there or not, she has to pay her share of the rent.

"Don't worry about that," Jake tells her during one discussion about a move. "I can handle this place right now. And then when your lease is over, you can start paying half here."

"No, if I am going to live here, I have to pay my own way."

"But we're together," Jake protests.

"I know, but I want to be an equal partner."

"You are. The money doesn't matter. If we're together, then we share our problems, and our finances. Look at it this way: When you are paying rent at your place, half of that money is mine, and half of the rent I pay here is yours."

"That's idiotic logic," she snaps back, irritated.

"Yeah, well, but it sounds good," he says with a grin.

"Only to an idiot!" she says, leaning in toward him.

"OK, guilty as charged."

Kate sits back and looks at him quizzically. "I'll think about it."

"You do that."

That's how things stay for a bit more than a month. Ashley and Kaitlyn are continually rude to both of them when they are in Kate's apartment, crowding her out of the bathroom as often as they can and complaining loudly if Jake uses it. The verbal complaints keep getting louder, and when Kate isn't in the room, the two women keep warning Jake "the real Kathy" will emerge someday. And he will discover what a slut she is.

Jake ignores them, not bothering to respond to their slurs and insults, sometimes just smiling at them, which seems to irritate them even more. Kate worries about the abuse he's being subjected to.

"I'm sorry for bringing you here," she says after one particularly unpleasant encounter.

"Ah, don't worry about it," he says. "Those two have nothing on a mad master chief."

"A master chief?"

"Yeah, an E-9, the top enlisted rank in the Navy. I've seen a master chief rip an ensign a new one, and the ensign just shrank from him, like the boot he was. This one master chief could reduce you to a pile of shit without ever raising his voice. He was that good."

"Good?"

"Yeah. It was an amazing thing to watch. It was a horrific thing to experience."

"That happened to you?"

"Oh yeah. And those two," he says, waving his hand back at the apartment as they were leaving, "can't touch a master chief."

"What did you do?"

"Umm, well, that's kind of a long story."

"Give me the short version."

"OK," he says, pausing. "In its briefest form, there was this ensign who wanted to get off our cruiser and onto a carrier, an aircraft carrier. For some reason, which none of us could figure out, he had it in for the ETs, electronic technicians," he explains when he sees the quizzical expression on Kate's face, "and made their lives miserable. So, when his orders finally came through, we convinced him he needed to get a bubonic plague shot ..."

"A what? Why?"

"Yeah, that's what he asked. We gave him a bullshit explanation that, I guess, sounded good to him. Then we gave him the vaccination— and it had the desired effect: He was sick for more than a week. Nothing serious, but enough to make him feel like shit for a while."

"How did you know he'd get sick?"

"The other corpsman on the ship looked up his medical record and found out the shot he got right out of the academy had made him sick."

"Wait a minute. If he already had one, why would he need a second one?" she asks.

Jake grins at her. "Exactly. We told him we got a report that the batch of vaccine his first shot was from was ineffective."

"How did the ... master chief ... find out?"

"As the ensign was getting ready to ship out, he looked like crap, and the master chief commented on it, so he told the chief what had happened."

"And the master chief did what?"

"He didn't tell the ensign; that's for sure. I don't think he liked him either. What he did do was ream the two of us a new one. He never raised his voice, but he just cut us down to nothing."

"And that was it? No punishment?"

"Master chief did tell us never to do that to the ensign again. We told him we wouldn't."

"But the ensign was leaving the ship."

"Exactly."

CHAPTER 35

It's Friday evening. Jake comes into his apartment to find Kate already there, her legs stretched out across the couch, reading a book, and sipping tea. As he walks into the living room something seems off.

"Hi, Sweetie, you're home early," he says, trying to figure out what's different.

"Yes, I got a bit ahead of where I need to be and just decided to give myself the rest of the day off. It's nice to relax, just read a good book for fun. My brain really appreciates it."

"I bet it does," he says, crossing the room and reaching down to give her a kiss. Then it hits him——it's the music. "When did you start listening to my grandparents' music? I thought you didn't like it."

"I don't, well not much of it. But this one," she says, waving at the speaker, "I do."

Jake listens for a moment. "Who is that?"

"Helen Reddy," Kate says without hesitation.

"Why her?"

"I heard one song that has become my anthem."

"Oh yeah? Which one is that?"

Kate picks up her phone and scrolls through the song list. "This one," she says, as she starts to play again.

I am woman, hear me roar
In numbers too big to ignore ...

"Oh, this one. I—" Jake starts to say.

"Shush, listen," Kate orders.

And I know too much to go back an' pretend
'Cause I've heard it all before
And I've been down there on the floor
No one's ever gonna keep me down again
Oh yes, I am wise
But it's wisdom born of pain
Yes, I've paid the price
But look how much I gained
If I have to, I can do anything.

"That's me," Kate says reflectively, a touch of pride in her voice, as the song ends.

"So it would seem," Jake responds, picking up her legs to slide under them as he sits on the couch. "You like her other songs too?"

"Most of them. Some of them."

"But not all." He says it as a statement not a question.

"Of course not," she says. "That just wouldn't be right."

"Why not?"

"Just because," she says, then changes the subject quickly. "I have dinner ready."

"And you managed to wait for me?" he says playfully.

"Ass," she says, kicking him lightly.

"So, what's for dinner?" he says, sniffing the air, but not smelling anything.

"A big salad with all kinds of lettuce, veggies and fruit."

"Oh," he says, a bit let down.

"Listen, meat-and-potatoes man, you need some diversity in your diet. No arguments."

"Can I grumble a bit?"

"Just a bit," she says, swinging her feet to the floor and heading for the kitchen, Jake trailing after her.

Kate dishes up the salad in a couple of bowls while Jake sets the table and gets them beers. As they eat, Jake asks her what she wants to do with the rest of her evening off.

"Dance!" comes the quick, definite reply.

"That salad wasn't half-bad. How about The Garage?"

"Glad you liked it. The Garage is kind of loud and crowded."

"True," he says with a shrug. "Do you know of somewhere else we can dance?"

"There's that place out on the highway," she says after thinking a minute.

"Oh, you're into country line dancing and clogging, are you?" he asks mischievously.

Kate crinkles her nose. "Not really. I guess it's The Garage."

"Well," Jake says, looking at his watch, "it's 7:38. If we clean up and walk over there, it will be at least eight when we get there. It shouldn't be too crowded, at least for a while."

"Then let's go!" Kate says, springing to her feet.

They quickly put things away, stick the dishes and glasses in the dishwasher and are out the door in less than ten minutes. They make the walk in just short of fifteen minutes. Jake's right: The Garage is less than half full this early in the evening, but the music is playing, and there's plenty of room on the dance floor. They spend the rest of the night dancing, drinking beer and flirting with each other. Karl and Michelle come in around 9:30 and join them at their booth. Their arrival turns the evening into a bit of a party as the four friends try to talk over the blasting music and dance, sometimes with their partners, sometimes with the other, and at times all four together. When that happens, they manage to create a space on the crowded floor for themselves.

The four of them close the place down, draining the last beer from the pitcher as the lights go up and the music goes off.

"I guess they want us to get the hell out of here," Karl offers.

"You think?" Jake replies.

"Do I have to?" Michelle rejoins. "I think I'm a bit drunk."

"Honey," Kate says, putting her hand on the other woman's arm, "you're past a bit."

Michelle just nods in response as Karl helps her up and into her jacket. The four of them pour out onto the sidewalk along with the rest of the holdouts. They start walking off together when Kate stops Jake.

"Let's go to my place," she says. "It's closer and I want to sleep. Right now."

"You got it," he says. "See you later," he tells Karl and Michelle as he and Kate head in the opposite direction.

"Night," Kate says.

"Night," Karl says, waving over his back. Michelle mumbles something Jake can't decipher as she leans heavily on Karl.

Jake shakes his head and, taking Kate's hand, starts walking. "I don't think I've ever seen her that drunk."

"Me either, but I think she just wants to celebrate. One of her grandmothers told her she'd buy her wedding dress for her. And the other one is giving them two thousand dollars for the reception. She said Karl's family is kicking in about four thousand."

"That's great. Good for them."

"Yeah," Kate says, snuggling up against Jake. "It's chilly."

"It's that time of year. Look," he says, pointing at the cloud forming from his breath in the cold night air. They walk the rest of the way in silence. When they go into Kate's apartment, Ashley is on the couch necking with her boyfriend. Two other guys are playing a video game. Some noise is coming from Kaitlyn's room. The two playing a game glance at them as they cross the room and go into Kate's bedroom.

"That was easy," Jake observes when they are safely inside.

"Yup," Kate says in a sour tone.

They quickly undress. Jake strips to his boxers, while Kate gets into a nightgown. They are soon in bed and asleep, curled up together.

"What the fuck!" Jake exclaims as he's jerked awake by the pounding on the bedroom door.

"It's 3 a.m.," a drowsy Kate says, picking up the clock on the nightstand next to the bed.

"Hey! Open up!" the male voice on the other side of the door yells. "It's my turn! Open up!"

"Go way!" Kate yells back. "We're sleeping!"

"Open up!" he persists, sounding drunk. "It's my turn! He's been in there long enough! Open up!" The pounding on the door becomes more insistent.

"What the fuck!" Jake says, swinging his legs out of the bed. He's on the side away from the door.

"I'll take care of it!" Kate says.

"He's drunk," Jake says in disgust as he looks for his pants in the dark.

"I said I'll take care of it!" Kate insists. "I can handle this."

"All right," Jake says, putting his pants on, "but I'm here if you can't."

"I will," she says, snapping on the lamp on the nightstand.

"Open up! It's my turn!" the guy yells, still pounding on the door and jiggling the handle to see if it will turn.

Kate yanks the door open. "I said go away!" she yells at the drunk on the other side.

"No way," he says, happy now the door is open, as he pushes her back toward the bed. "It's *my* turn," he announces as he grabs her breasts.

Taken by surprise, Kate retreats, trying to get out of his grasp. Before she can extricate herself, the guy lets out a scream—Jake has grabbed him by his hair and yanked him back as hard as he can, slamming the interloper into the door and then launching him through the doorway. The guy stumbles into the living room, falling facedown. He stretches out his arms, stopping himself from hitting the floor. He turns around and scrambles to his feet. Jake sees Kaitlyn, Ashley, their boyfriends, and the other guy sitting on the couch and chairs watching the show.

Jake defiantly looks at them and begins to turn back into the bedroom.

"Look out!" Kate calls.

Jake pivots with an elbow out, catching the guy in the face, breaking his nose and sending him flying backward.

"You son of a bitch," the guy's friend says, launching himself toward Jake. Before he can reach him, Kate pulls Jake back into the room and slams the door shut, locking it. They hear a body slam into the door. And then silence. They listen intently but only hear voices too low to understand what is being said. But they realize they are trapped for now—outnumbered and the only one way out blocked.

"Now what?" Jake asks as they sit on the bed.

"I guess we better get dressed. We're obviously not going back to sleep."

"Shit."

"You can say that again."

"Shit."

"Really? You had to say it again?"

"You told me to. So, I had to," he says, trying to lighten the mood a bit.

Kate slaps him lightly on the arm. Then they dress and sit back on the bed again, with Kate leaning against him, both becoming drowsy.

About half an hour passes when they hear new voices in the living room, bringing them wide awake, followed by a knock on the door.

"Police. Open up."

Kate and Jake look at each other.

"Shit," he says.

"Don't say it again," she says, getting up and opening the bedroom door. "Hello, officer," she says as sweetly and innocently as she can.

"Come out of the bedroom. Both of you," he orders.

"Yes, sir," she says as Jake follows her into the living room.

Two officers are there, the one who knocked on the door and his female partner. Ashley, Kaitlyn, and the four guys are arrayed around the room on the couch or in chairs. The one Jake hit is holding a bloody towel to his noise and has some swelling around his eyes.

"Did you hit this man?" the male officer asks Jake.

Jake looks at the guy and back at the officer. "Yes, sir. I did."

"He's accusing you of assault and battery, so I'm going to have to take you into custody. Turn around and put your hands behind your back."

Jake looks disgusted but complies, turning his back to the cop. The officer puts handcuffs on him; then, taking Jake's arm, he starts to take him out of the apartment.

"Wait a minute!" Kate says forcefully. "I want him arrested!" She points at the guy with the broken nose.

"You can't do that!" Ashley protests, as she and the other five all stand up, the smirks on their faces disappearing.

"Why?" the female officer asks Kate as her partner stops, stopping Jake along with him.

"He assaulted me! He grabbed my breasts and pushed me back into the bedroom when I answered the door! He was pounding on it, and I wanted him to go away! But he attacked me!"

"Is that true?" the female cop asks the guy with the broken nose.

"No, it's a lie!" Ashley says before the guy has a chance to respond.

The female cop looks at her, then at the guy, then back at Kate.

"That's why Jake hit him," Kate insists. "He was defending me!"

The two officers look at each other. The male cop just raises his eyebrows. The female cop pulls her handcuffs out. "Stand up," she tells the guy with the broken nose. "You're under arrest for sexual assault."

As he reluctantly gets to his feet, the others protest that he can't be arrested.

"Well, he is," the female cop tells them. "And if any of you get in the way, I'll arrest you too."

That makes them all back down.

"But I was told I could!" the guy in cuffs now protests. "She said it was my turn!"

"Who told you that?" the male cop asks.

"Ashley," he says, nodding his head toward her. "She said it was my turn with Kathy and the other guy had to go."

"You what!" Kate says, turning on Ashley, ready to strike.

The female cop steps in front of her. "Stop! Or I'll arrest you."

"Why don't we just arrest the lot of them and sort this out at the station," the male cop says.

"I'll call for backup," the female cop says, reaching for her radio.

"Wait a minute," Jake says. "What if everyone drops the charges? No harm, no foul."

The two cops look at each other. The female cop asks the guy she has the cuffs on, "You want to do that?"

"Yeah. I don't want to go to jail." Turning to Kate, the guy says, "I'm sorry. She told me you wanted to. I didn't know." He's almost crying by the time he's through.

"What about you?" the female cop asks Kate.

"Fine with me," Kate says, glaring at her roommates, disgust in her voice.

"All right then," the male cop says, turning Jake around to take the handcuffs off him. "But if we have to come back, you are all," he says, looking at each in turn, "coming in. Understood?"

They all acknowledge what he's said, and the two officers leave.

The eight are left standing in the living room. Kaitlyn and Ashley are glaring at Kate and Jake. Their boyfriends and the uninjured guy all look like they want to jump Jake. But the cop's warning restrains them.

Kate and Jake look at their antagonists and then retreat into the bedroom.

"Can I move in with you?" she asks. "Right now."

"No problem. Tonight or in the morning?"

"Tonight. We can get everything out of here and into my car."

"Sounds like a plan."

First light is filtering through the sky as they finish carting her belongings to the sidewalk. Kaitlyn and Ashley watch them with hatred. Their boyfriends have fallen asleep on chairs. The guy with the broken nose and his friend have left.

They load Kate's midsize sedan and head for Jake's apartment. When they get there, they decide to unload later. Both are exhausted. They go upstairs, strip and climb into bed. They are asleep as soon as their heads are on the pillows.

CHAPTER 36

Kate and Jake work into the early afternoon to unload her car and get the apartment they now share somewhat organized. Of course, they did sleep late. And they did have a leisurely breakfast at the Chew.

As Vivian gives them their coffee, Kate holds up a hand. "Please give us a minute before we order."

"Sure, honey," Vivian replies and heads off to help other customers.

"What gives?" Jake asks, a bit perplexed.

"You, my love, are having something different for breakfast."

"What? Why? I happen to like eggs over easy," Jake protests.

"There are other things in life than eggs over easy. Diversify. You might like it, but you'll never know if you don't try."

"Hmmm," he says in mock thought, "diversify in everything?"

Kate looks at him for a moment before she realizes where he is going with this. "Everything but girlfriends. You are such an ass."

His reply is to smile broadly. But he does order an omelet, sausage, and whole wheat toast, throwing Vivian into a bit of a spin.

"Happy?" he asks Kate, smiling broadly.

"Ecstatic," she replies with an equally broad smile.

After the drama of the previous night, they are both relaxed and happy to be finally finished with Ashley and Kaitlyn. They take turns shutting the other down when that topic comes up. They both want to put that whole problem in the past—and forget it. But it still is fresh in their minds.

"You know," Jake says at one point during breakfast, "I'm sort of glad that happened last night …"

"Shut up!" Kate orders him. "How do you like your breakfast?"

"It's good. You were right about diversifying, at least for breakfast," he hurriedly adds.

As they are finishing eating, Kate says, "I don't think I'll ever understand what drives people like Kaitlyn and—"

"Do you like baseball?" Jake interrupts her. "I like baseball. Watching a game in a stadium is just a pleasant way to spend an afternoon or evening. I don't particularly care to watch it on TV. You can't see how the players are moving around for each batter. Want to drive over and catch a game this summer?"

Kate just looks at him. "We need to make a grocery list. What you have in your apartment is an embarrassment."

"Oh, it's not *that* bad," Jake protests.

"Yes, it is," she insists. "Come on, let's go."

Kate surveys the food stocks, commenting continuously on what's missing and throwing out some items that are well past their use-by date to Jake's protest that they're still good. She plans a menu for the week, with Jake's input, and they make a grocery list. After their trip to the grocery store, they get down to their respective studies. They keep so busy that neither one thinks about the previous night.

Life falls into a pleasant pattern of work and study, and hanging out with friends. Kate introduces Jake to her fellow physics research assistants, while Jake brings her into his circle of historians. He has absolutely no idea about 90 percent of what her conversations with her fellow physicists are about. And while she can understand what Jake and his fellow graduate history students are talking about, she just can't get vested in the subject to the extent they are. But those things matter little to both of them. They just enjoy being with each other, so each tolerates the other's obsession. Each encourages the other to keep on going.

And, of course, there is their core group of friends. The glow of their engagement has worn off enough that Karl and Michelle no longer talk about the wedding all the time. She just brings it up now and again, mostly now, and again and again.

Samee and Setareh have recovered enough from the trauma of his arrest that they no longer start worrying when the other isn't around for ten minutes; the two graduate students do have their separate classes to attend and to teach. But Setareh compulsively texts Samee every half hour and begins to worry if he doesn't respond immediately.

Kate is still dealing with the fallout of her daddy's decision to cut off all ties to her. She is able to talk to her momma when he isn't around, but sometimes her momma will just say she can't talk now and hangs up. Or she will go into the backyard. When her daddy asks who's on the phone, Kate has heard her momma say it's just a girlfriend or one of her sisters.

Jake can see the pain is still there, but he also can see Kate is handling it better as time goes on—gaining strength and resolve to keep building her life.

He also senses she is changing. He can't put his finger on it, but she seems to be becoming distant from him in some ways. He finds it worrying, and frightening. She likes being with him, seeking him out in the library or the Commons when she is finished work or class. She wants him to go with her to see her fellow students and willingly goes with him to see his. She is as intimate with him as always, holding his hand or cuddling up to him as they walk, touching him when they are sitting together, smacking him lightly when he says something she objects to. And she initiates sex about as often as he does.

But something about her is changing. He has seen her gazing at him with a small smile on her face. At other times she is staring out into the distance, looking contemplative. He has tried to ask her about what is going on several times, but she always puts him off.

One afternoon in January, they are working at the table in their apartment when Jake looks up to find Kate staring blankly out the window. From the distracted expression on her face, he doesn't think she is really looking at anything. He decides to try again.

"Hey," he says quietly, "what are you thinking about?"

He waits a few seconds for a response, which he doesn't get.

"Sweetie," he says a little louder, "what are you thinking about?"

After a few seconds, Kate comes back, sort of. She focuses on him, a look of mild confusion on her face. "I'm sorry. What did you say?"

"I asked," he says, laughing a bit, "what are you thinking about?"

"Oh."

"And?"

"And what?" she replies, still not back in the here and now.

"What were you thinking?"

"Just about stuff."

"What stuff?"

Kate sighs. Her eyes scan around the room without focusing on anything. Then she settles her gaze on Jake. "Just stuff."

"You know," he says as gently as he can through his exasperation, "you seem to be off in Never Never Land a lot lately. What's going on?"

Kate sighs. She looks at her hands in her lap. "Just stuff."

Jake keeps his mouth shut, wanting badly to know what *stuff* but not willing to ask, not willing to push her where she doesn't want to go.

"I was thinking," she finally says, "about my past. About my future. About my present."

"About us?" Jake couldn't keep from asking.

"Only in a good way," she says, reaching across the table for his hand, which he gives her. "I am still sorting things out. I love you."

"I love you, too," he says, returning the light squeeze of her hand.

"Let's get back to work," she says, pulling her hand back, obviously not wanting to continue the discussion.

"Good enough," Jake says.

CHAPTER 37

Life is good.

The spring semester's over, and Jake decides to take some time off from his thesis to give his brain a rest. Besides, his teaching assistant position is over until the fall semester, so he's stocking shelves at the grocery store he and Kate routinely go to. All the reading he does is just for pleasure; it's still mostly history, but has nothing to do with his thesis.

Kate is finishing a research project she's been working on for one of her professors after successfully defending her thesis, which comes as no surprise, and receiving her master's hood during the university's graduation ceremonies two days ago. They spent the rest of that day celebrating with their friends. Uncle Pete and his wife, Mary, came to the graduation ceremony, then took Kate and Jake to dinner at the fanciest restaurant in town. First Mary and then Pete encouraged Kate not to let her father stop her studies or keep her from fulfilling her dream of becoming a research physicist. Jake watched as their advice hit home, Kate sitting up straighter and brightening.

Kate and Jake spent the rest of the night dancing at The Garage.

They stay in bed most of the next day, dozing, making love, dozing again, making love again. The cycle is only broken when they get up for a quick bite. Then they're back under the covers. Finally, that evening, they shower and dress, then go out for dinner. They wander around the campus in the cool evening air. Few faculty and almost no students are left. The Commons has closed for its post-semester cleaning. The dorms are mostly empty.

Kate chooses the route they take, stopping at a variety of places. It seems to Jake that she's saying goodbye to them. She hasn't said anything to him about her doctorate. He knows she's been accepted at the university, but she hasn't said whether that's what she'll do. In the back of his mind, he worries she will go somewhere else. There is a lot of competition for a doctoral candidate with her qualifications. Then again, she may decide to take some time off before pursuing her doctorate. She could keep working as a research assistant at the university, only as the holder of a master's degree. That would mean more responsibility, and more money.

But Kate hasn't said anything to him about her plans. Jake has hinted about wanting to know, but she ignores the hints. The one time he asks her point-blank, she tells him she hasn't decided—and will let him know when she has.

Jake pushes troubling thoughts out of his mind. He concentrates on the happiness he's found and the happiness he tries to bring to Kate.

Life is good.

Kate finishes her work in the lab, spending the next few days sleeping in. She occupies her time reading light literature, watching movies, and listening to music. When Jake gets home from work, she keeps touching and hugging him, almost as if she's making sure he's there. But she rarely looks directly at him. Their conversations are light, filled with laughter and fun. When they are not talking, Jake catches her looking melancholy. When he asks her about it, she shakes her head and says it's nothing, just post-graduation letdown.

He lets it go.

For life is good.

Chapter 38

A Monday morning in late June. The sun is streaming into the living room from windows with the shades drawn all the way up. Jake is off today. He sits on one end of the couch, his back against the arm, his legs stretched out over the cushions, intertwined with Kate's legs, who is sitting the same way at the other end.

Jake looks up from the biography of Thomas Jefferson he's reading to find Kate gazing out the window, her book resting open in her lap.

"You OK?" he asks, sensing her sadness.

"Yes," she responds, not shifting her gaze. Then after a brief pause, "No."

Jake sits up, closing his book but not saying anything, just being attentive to her.

Kate looks at him, then down at the floor, then back at him. "We have to talk," she finally says.

"I guess we do." The worry obvious in his voice.

Kate sighs heavily, her eyes filling with tears.

"I'm leaving," she says, almost in a whisper.

Jake is still silent, trying to digest what she just said, too terrified to say anything.

Kate shifts so she is sitting in the middle of the couch. She reaches out and takes his hands, kissing them. "I'm going to UM."

"Why?" Jake finally manages to get out, his voice hoarse and shaky.

"They're giving me a lead research assistantship on their premier project, and all tuition, fees, and books will be paid for, and I'll get a living stipend." She looks down at his chest and then back at his face, the tears starting to roll down her checks.

"Oh," he manages to choke out. "Why not here? I thought you were offered pretty much the same deal? Why don't you want to stay together?"

Kate stretches out so that she is lying across his lap with her head on his chest. He can feel her sobs as her tears dampen his shirt.

"I have to go," she finally manages to say.

"Why? It's more than six hundred miles away. We'll never see each other." He reaches down and gently kisses the top of her head. "When do you leave?"

"In the morning."

"What!" Jake jumps up, pushing her away. "You're just telling me now? How long have you known? It's got to be a couple of months at least, probably January."

"December," Kate whispers, looking at the floor as she sits on the couch.

"December? And you're just telling me now? What the hell!"

"Please don't be angry," she begs him.

"Angry? Damn right I'm angry!" he says, beginning to pace about the room, avoiding looking at her. "You've known for six months and you're just now telling me, the day before you leave?"

"I'm sorry," Kate responds quietly.

"Why? Don't you trust me? Do you think I'm going to turn violent? Throw you out?"

"No," comes the meek reply.

"Then what?" he demands.

She looks up at him tearfully. "I didn't want to hurt you."

Jake stops in midstride. He just stares at her for a bit. "You what?" he finally blurts out. "What do you think you just did!"

"I'm sorry," she says, getting up. She wraps her arms around his middle, hugging him. He stands with his arms at his side for a bit, before sighing and wrapping his arms around her. They stand that way for a time, just holding onto each other.

Finally, Kate looks up at him. "Let me explain," she says, taking a deep breath and moving back a few inches, but still holding onto him.

"OK," he says, his voice choked with emotion.

"Just don't say anything until I'm finished."

Jake just nods.

"I love you," she starts.

"I love you ..." he starts to say.

"Shh," she says, holding a finger across his lips. "This is hard for me, so don't talk."

Jake just nods.

Kate sighs and starts again. "I love you, but I don't know if I'm in love with you. And I know you love me, but you can't know if you're in love with me."

"Now wait a—"

"You're talking!" she says sharply.

"Sorry," he says meekly.

"Look," she says, "we've become dependent on each other. You are the support system I needed to change my life, to stop being"—Kate swallows hard—"to stop being the way I was, to be able to stand on my own feet."

Jake opens his mouth to say something but shuts it sharply at a look from Kate.

"And you have told me that being with me healed you. You stopped drinking. Stopped having that horrible dream. All that is why I love you. But that is not enough to build a life on. We both need to find out if our love is more than that, if we are in love with each other. I love being with you, and I think you love being with me. We have fun together. We support each other. We are comfortable with each other. We are the best of friends." She pauses. "But are we in love with each other? Neither one of us can really answer that question right now. I have to leave so I can find the answer to that question."

She looks up at Jake, brushes her lips against his, then puts a finger across his lips to keep him from talking.

"There is another reason," she goes on. "I have to finish growing. I'm an embryo, as the song says. I can't finish growing if I stay here, if I stay with you."

"So, you're breaking up with me? This is it?"

"No!" she says forcefully, stepping back from him.

"Then what?" he says, confused about where she's going with this.

Kate sighs. "We both need distance to figure out how we really feel about each other. For the next year, we won't see each other, we won't talk. If after that, we still feel the same way as we do now, then we can make a life together. We will know we're truly in love."

"And if we don't?"

"Then we don't. At least we'll know."

Jake walks over to the dining table, sitting heavily in a chair, staring down at his hands.

Kate walks over, sitting in the chair next to him, taking his hands in hers. "I promise you that I will not date anyone for the next year. I will be celibate. All I'm going to do is work and study."

Jake looks up at her, nods, and looks away.

"I couldn't tell you before," she says, "because it hurt too much for me to talk about it. Talking about it makes it real, and I couldn't face it. I'm so sorry to drop this on you this way."

"And now?" he asks.

"And now, I have no choice because I have to leave in the morning."

"Why now?"

"I start in the lab on Monday."

Jake nods. "Do you have a place to stay?"

"Yes. I'm going to room with another physics doctoral candidate," she says, hurriedly adding, "a female doctoral candidate."

Jake gives her a weak smile.

"Her name is Amy. She has a two-bedroom house and just lost her roommate to graduation. And," she hurries on to reassure him about being celibate, "she's engaged to an Army officer who is deployed for the next nine months, so there won't be any men coming through the place."

"You don't think I trust your word?" Jake asks.

"I know you do. I just wanted to let you know … because of my history."

"That's in the past."

"I know. I just wanted to say it."

Jake sits back in the chair, staring out the windows. "Want help packing?" dejection and sorrow in his voice.

"Are you trying to get rid of me?" Kate says, trying to lighten the mood.

Jake just gives her a sorrowful look.

"Sorry. Bad timing. Yes, I would like help."

They spend the rest of the evening packing. Jake runs down to his store for boxes they use for her books and papers. He also gives her a suitcase when she runs out of room in her three. They break for pizza.

"Are you going to be able to get all this in your car?" he asks as they finish.

"It will be tight," Kate says, surveying the pile of suitcases and boxes, "but since I will be the only one in the car, I can use the front, too."

"Good thing you have side mirrors," Jake opines.

"What?" she responds, a bit confused.

"You're going to have to stack stuff so high in the back seat, you won't be able to see out of the rearview mirror. So be careful."

"I will," she says, reaching out to take his hand. "We can load the car in the morning."

"OK."

"Let's go to bed," she says, leading him to the bedroom. He follows without a word.

CHAPTER 39

$\mathcal{O}$n the morning, Kate turns down his offer to go to The Delightful Chew for breakfast. "It's more than a twelve-hour drive. I have to start as soon as possible."

While she is taking a shower, Jake makes a pancake, bacon, and scrambled egg breakfast, wondering whether it will be the last time they will ever eat together.

When Kate comes out of the bedroom, buttoning her blouse, her hair still damp, she smiles at him, while surveying the set table. "I thought I smelled something good."

"Can't have you leave on an empty stomach," he tells her, pulling a chair back for her.

"Why thank you, sir," she says, sitting down.

They eat in silence, occasionally glancing at each other. When they are finished, Kate starts to take her plate into the kitchen.

"Don't," Jake says softly, putting a hand on her arm. "I'll clean up later. You need to get on the road. You have a long drive."

Kate nods and puts the plate down. An hour later, her car is so loaded there is barely room left for her.

"We did it," she announces as they survey their work.

"I'll be celibate, too, for the next year," Jake says, not taking his eyes off the car. Kate squeezes his hand in response. "You better get going. You have a long drive."

Kate wraps her arms around his neck, giving him a long, passionate kiss.

"Drive safely," he says as they disentangle.

"I will," she assures him.

"I know," he says as she starts to leave, "you don't want to talk for the next year. But will you text me when you get there? Let me know you're safe."

"I will. I love you. You take care of yourself. This year will be over before you know it."

Jake just nods. "I love you, too," is all he is able to say. He watches her get in her car; she glances back at him as she starts the engine and drives off. He watches her car until she is out of sight.

Back in the apartment, he stares at the dishes on the table for a long minute. He doesn't feel like cleaning up right now, so he leaves them on the table and goes into the bedroom to get ready for work. At the store, he plunges into work to keep his mind off Kate.

On his way home that evening, he starts to pass a liquor store. Glancing in the window, he stops, staring into the store. Finally, he goes inside and buys a 750-mililiter bottle of bourbon.

When he gets home, he sits at the dinner table, putting the brown paper bag with the whiskey on the table. He stares at it for a few moments. Then pulls the bottle out of the bag, setting it on the table. He stares at it for a few more moments.

Finally, he gets up, goes into the kitchen, returning with a glass. He puts that on the table, staring again at the whiskey. A resigned sigh is followed by Jake uncorking the bottle and pouring himself a stiff drink. Recorking the bottle, he stares at the glass for a couple of minutes. Reaching out, he picks it up and takes a sip, feeling the warm burning liquid cross his tongue and flow down his throat. He closes his eyes as he takes another sip.

Before he can swallow, someone knocks on the apartment door. He holds the booze in his mouth as puts the glass down, wondering if he really heard a knock. Another knock. He swallows the bourbon.

'Maybe whoever it is will go away,' he thinks.

Another knock. Followed quickly by another, then another, then another. The persistent knocking gets louder.

Jake just wants to be left alone, but whoever is at the door obviously is not going to let that happen. He shoves back from the table and strides quickly to the door, swearing under his breath. He grabs the door handle, throwing the door open.

"What!" His anger boils out of him. But the sight that greets him freezes him as if he was a statue.

"I was wrong," a tearful Kate says. "I don't want to leave."

Jake just stands there, staring at her in wonder.

"Say something!" she says. "Please! Forgive me!"

More silence. Jake's jaw is moving but nothing comes out. All he can do is reach out and pull her to him, wrapping his arms around her as they exchange a passionate kiss.

"I got about a hundred miles," she says as they go into the apartment. "I realized the mistake I had made. I am in love with you. I don't need a year to figure it out, so I came home."

Jake helps her out of her coat but is still not able to say anything.

"Please, say something!" she implores him.

"I love you," is all he can say.

At that, she flies into his arms. Their passionate kissing ends with them in the bedroom, shedding their clothes and ending in each other's arms, which is how they make love, and how they fall asleep.

Jake sleeps deeply and late into the morning. As he begins to wake up, he decides he will call in sick today. This is a day for celebration.

He is lying on his back, his left arm stretched across the bed where he had been holding Kate. He doesn't feel anything. He pats around the bed but does not feel her. He opens his eyes but shuts them almost immediately as the sunlight streaming into the bedroom hurts his eyes. He uses his ears to try to find her. No sound is coming from the bathroom. He doesn't hear anything from the kitchen. He sniffs the air, detecting no odor of cooking.

"Kate!" he calls.

No response.

He forces his eyes open, squinting against the pain.

"Kate!" Now he's worried. Why would she have left the apartment? Maybe she went to get stuff out of her car. After all, she is moving back in.

Jack forces himself to swing into a sitting position on the side of the bed. As he sits up, his head starts to ache. He's not sure why he seems to have a hangover. He had two little drinks. *'Maybe I'm drunk on love,'* he thinks, laughing. Pushing himself off the bed, he finds he's a bit wobbly. And he finds he has his clothes on. That confuses him.

He shrugs it off and walks tentatively into the living room. Kate's not there. Her coat is not on the chair where they left it last night. Squinting out the window against the intense glare of the sun, he doesn't see her car.

'I wonder where she went?' he asks himself. He decides to call her, to make sure she's all right. When he opens the screen on his phone, he sees he has a message. Thinking she texted him, Jake opens it up.

And freezes.

He stares at the screen in disbelief, trying to understand the message in context with what happened last night.

"Arrived safe. Take care of yourself. C u in a year. Luv u." It is from Kate. She sent it at 10:46 last night.

Jake slumps into a dining table chair, still staring at the phone. Long minutes pass before he can put it down. That's when he notices the bourbon bottle: two-thirds of the whiskey is gone. He stares at in confusion. *'I barely had two drinks. And we didn't drink anymore when she got here ... got here.'*

Slowly Jake's mind grasps what happened: Kate didn't come back. And he had a lot more than two drinks. He got roaring drunk. And he just had a vivid dream after he stumbled to bed—so vivid he woke this morning convinced it was real.

"Shit!" he barks, immediately regretting doing that as pain shoots through his head. He sits back in the chair, staring at the bottle.

"She's really gone," he says softly. He realizes two other things—he had a drunken dream that made him happy instead of devastating him, and he couldn't live that way anymore. Kate told him that he had to learn to live independently of her; he has to ween himself from his dependence on her.

"I can do it. I have to do it." He picks up the bottle, goes to the sink and pours what's left down the drain. He puts the now empty bottle in recycling. He looks around the apartment, trying to decide what to do.

Making up his mind, he goes into the bathroom, finds the aspirin. He swallows four tablets with a water chaser. He goes into the bedroom, closes the blinds, undresses, and climbs into bed. He plugs his phone in, then sets the alarm for 2 p.m., an hour before he has to be at work.

He lies down, then immediately picks up his phone again. Going to his music library, he connects it to his Bluetooth speaker. Scrolling through the artists, he stops at B.B. King. Blues, he decides, is the right music for now. The song he starts with is "Is You Is Or Is You Ain't My Baby?"

Lying back in bed, he closes his eyes, letting the rich sound of the music flow over him while the aspirin fights his hangover.

"Well," he says to the cosmos, "I guess I'll know in a year if she is."

CHAPTER 40

*E*arly December sunlight filters through the partially closed blinds, crossing Jake's eyes. He fights waking up, holding onto the dream of Kate back with him. He can smell breakfast cooking as they start their day together.

Finally, he gives in. Opening his eyes, he stares at the patterns of light on the bedroom ceiling. *'Funny,'* he thinks, *'my eyes are open, but I can still smell breakfast. I must be having a dream within a dream.'* He reaches across the bed where his dream had Kate curled up next to him.

It's empty. The bed is cold.

As he expected.

He shakes his head. The smell won't go away. Bacon and coffee are the dominant odors.

'I'm going crazy,' he thinks, swinging his feet onto the floor. Puzzled, and a bit worried about his mental state, he wanders out into the living room, wearing nothing but his pajama bottoms.

And freezes.

Kate is in the kitchen cooking. The coffee pot is full. She is shoveling eggs onto plates. As she turns, she sees him, her glance quickly going to other things.

"Oh, good, you're awake." Her voice is quiet. Her eyes avoid his. "I didn't know what you would want for breakfast, so I sort of made everything: bacon, eggs, toast, pancakes. I would have made an omelet, but you don't have the ingredients. You don't like cheese anymore? And you have almost no butter or cooking oil." She glances quickly at him and then away.

"I haven't been to the store in a bit," Jake finally says. Questions are racing through his mind, but that is all he can say at the moment.

"I see," Kate replies quietly. "I guess it doesn't matter. There is plenty here to eat. Come, sit down and have breakfast."

"How? Why? When?" is all Jake can stutter out.

Kate finally looks at him. "Because I miss you," she says. "I realized I'm in love with you." As their eyes lock, tears well up in her eyes. She takes a step toward him.

"Wait a minute," Jake says, stopping her in her tracks.

"You don't want me here?" The fear is palpable in her voice.

"No," he says, shaking his head, "not that. It's just that I've had this dream before. Several times. And it always ends up the same way. You're not here, and I feel lonelier than I did before."

"I'm here now," Kate says through her tears. She slowly walks up to him and wraps her arms around his neck. Reaching up, she kisses him.

It takes Jake a few moments to respond, to realize this isn't a dream. When that dawns on him, he returns the kiss with passion.

"This better not be a dream," he says when they finally disentangle. "Ouch! What was that for?"

"I had to pinch you so you know you're awake," Kate says, feeling welcome now for the first time. "And I may be a dream but only when you're awake."

"OK, but next time could you find a less painful way to tell me I'm awake? I forgot how hard you pinch."

"Next time?"

"Right," Jake says, looking for a good exit. "Let's eat. I'm hungry."

"Me, too. That's a long drive."

"When did you get here?" he asks as they sit down.

"About an hour ago. Good thing I stopped at the supermarket first," she says as she puts eggs, bacon and toast on her plate. "You are out of everything."

"Yeah, well, I had other things on my mind," he replies, sliding some pancakes and bacon onto his, then adding an egg for good measure. "At least I still have syrup."

"If it doesn't kill us. Did you see the use-by date?"

"Syrup never goes bad."

"Tell that to the doc when I take you to the ER."

"You made pancakes so I would kill myself?" Jake asks, enjoying the banter they are falling back into.

"Die and I'll kick your ass."

"Dead and I won't feel it."

"How would you like to wear your breakfast?"

"No, I think I'll just eat it," he says, then decides his best course is to change the subject. "How did you get in?"

"I still have a key."

"I guess it's a good thing I didn't move," he quips.

Kate sits up with a jolt. "Move?"

"Yeah, well, what would have happened if some other guy was living here when you decided to make an unannounced visit? And cook breakfast?"

Kate just stares at him, a look of horror on her face.

Jake can't keep a straight face when he sees her expression. "Don't worry, Sweetheart, I never thought of moving. I always hoped, dreamed, that you would come back. Announced or unannounced."

"You bastard!"

Jake just grins at her, then reaches over to kiss her. She pulls back a bit, slaps him on the arm, and then kisses him. "Don't you *ever* do that again!"

"OK," he says, sitting back. They fall into idle chatter about their lives over the last semester, their work. They avoid the topic that preoccupies both of them: What's next?

After they clean up from breakfast, Kate suggests they go for a walk. "I want to see what's changed."

"You've only been gone a semester. So, nothing."

"Is the Chew still there?"

"Of course. We can have breakfast there tomorrow if you are still here."

"I don't have to go back until tomorrow afternoon. I don't teach until Monday afternoon and my seminar is after that."

"Great," Jake says as they stroll toward campus.

"Are any of our friends still here?"

"Yes, all of them. You didn't keep in touch with them?"

"No," she says, then pauses. "I was afraid they would remind me of you, and I would lose my resolve not to contact you for a year."

"And how did that work out of you?"

"Ass," she says, smiling. "So tell me about them? Or do I beat it out of you?"

"Please," Jake says in mock fear, "anything but that." He kisses her and then quickly goes on. "Karl graduated, but he's waiting for Michelle to finish next semester."

"What's he doing?"

"He," Jake says with a laugh, "became a cop."

"I thought he swore never to do that again."

"Yup. But he says he has a right to change his mind. He's working for the city police department as a patrolman."

Kate just shakes her head. "Why doesn't that surprise me? Are they still planning to get married this spring?"

"Yup," Jake responds. "Samee and Setareh both graduated. She's teaching at the university, and he got a programing job with a research corporation off campus. And they're pregnant, about two months along."

"That was fast."

"Yup. Right after they got married, they got knocked up. I wish you had been there. I'd never been to a Moslem wedding before. It was interesting. And the humor came from Setareh's father, who kept mumbling about this being the Land of Crusaders."

Kate gives a short laugh, then says, "We'll have to get together with all of them." They fall into silence as they walk around campus for the next several hours, recalling events and other people they knew. The cold feels good against their exposed skin as they keep up a fast pace.

"Here," Kate says, "let's go in here." She leads the way into a coffee shop just off campus. They get their coffee, picking a table by the front window where they can see the people passing by.

"Soooo, you finish your master's this semester," Kate says.

"Finished. Past tense. I defended my thesis last month. The only thing I have left is to finish is teaching my classes."

"Oh. Then what?"

"I'm going after a doctorate."

"Oh. Here?"

"No, I took your advice to heart not to get all my degrees at one place."

"I gave you that advice?"

"Indirectly. You said it about yourself. I figured that would apply to me as well."

"Oh. So where did you apply?"

Jake runs off a list of five universities. None of them are UM.

Kate looks down at the table, then out the window. Her face a mask of sadness.

"And UM," Jake finally says. Kate looks hard at him, then kicks him under the table.

"Ow! You're getting violent!"

"You ba—"

"Don't say it!" he says, holding up a hand.

She glares at him for a moment. "Did you get accepted?"

"I start next semester. They gave me a partial scholarship and a teaching assistantship. With that and the insurance settlement, I should have enough to pay the bills. I haven't spent any of that insurance money I got after the ..." Jake says, leaving the rest unsaid. "And UM has an excellent history department."

"I don't know whether to kiss you or kick you again!" Kate responds, avoiding the subject that is still painful for Jake.

"Let's stick with the kiss. I don't know if my shins can handle any more abuse," he says, the amusement obvious in his voice as he regains his composure.

Kate reaches across the table and kisses him.

"I have to ask you one question," she says, staring into his eyes.

"Shoot."

"Do you still love Charley?" she asks, worried about whether she has to share him with a memory.

Jake stares out the window for a long minute. Then he looks at her, taking her hand across the table. "I will always love Charley in a way. But," he says, "she's gone and I am deeply, completely in love with you. Charley's my past. You, my love, are my future."

"When can you move?" Kate asks in response.

"As soon as I turn in the final grades. Say, about two weeks. Are we going to be living together?"

"Are you joking?" she asks incredulously.

"I just want to be sure we are on the same page."

"Yes, we'll be living together, if you want to," she responds.

"I wouldn't have it any other way."

"Good," Kate says, pausing for a moment. "Wasn't it a bit presumptuous of you to apply to UM without knowing if we would be together?"

"As I said, they have an excellent history department. Besides," he says, looking out the window at the people walking by, "I was holding onto hope that we would be back together."

"I love you."

"I love you." The conversation pauses. Then Jake asks, "Are you going to find a place for us?"

"What? Oh, that. How do you feel about living with two women?"

"Didn't we try that already?" Jake asks skeptically. "As I recall, that didn't work out too well."

"This is completely different. By two women, I mean my housemate and me. We have a two-story house with three bedrooms, with the smallest bedroom serving as an office. Amy has the master bedroom, but our bedroom is really big, and we will have the hall bathroom to ourselves, so you'll only have to put up with my bras."

"I'm glad to hear that," he says, laughing a bit. "She cool about me moving in?"

"Yes, she is. I've told her all about you."

"And she's still good with that?" he asks, raising his eyebrows.

"Yes, silly. More than good. There's a frat house a few houses down. Those guys won't quit hitting on us. Having you around will help quiet that down."

"Maybe I'll move tomorrow."

"Don't be an ass. We can take care of ourselves."

"I have no doubt of that," he says, smiling.

"Having you around will just reduce that hassle factor some."

"Nice to know I'm wanted." The comment prompts a light kick under the table.

"Besides," Kate says, "since meeting you, I don't like sleeping alone anymore."

Jake looks at her across the table, a small smile on his face. "I think we should do something about that."

"Yes. Right now."

Printed in the United States
by Baker & Taylor Publisher Services